STEPHANIE, SWEET STEPHANIE

Here Stephanie had lived, making this apartment her arena of adultery in the afternoons, and a chamber of insane horror for her husband at night.

Here Stephanie's murdered body had been found, and had taken her monstrous secret with it to the grave.

Here Stephanie remained to haunt Paula from the moment she crossed the threshold as Stephanie's successor . . . and step by step took Stephanie's place in a living hell. . . .

THE INTRUDER

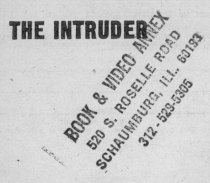

Big Bestsellers from SIGNET

The
INTRUDER

By
Brooke Leimas

A SIGNET BOOK
NEW AMERICAN LIBRARY
TIMES MIRROR

PUBLISHER'S NOTE

This novel is a work of fiction. Names, characters, places and incidents are either the product of the author's imagination or are used fictitiously, and any resemblance to actual persons, living or dead, events, or locales is entirely coincidental.

COPYRIGHT © 1980 BY BROOKE LEIMAS

 SIGNET TRADEMARK REG. U.S. PAT. OFF. AND FOREIGN COUNTRIES
REGISTERED TRADEMARK—MARCA REGISTRADA
HECHO EN CHICAGO, U.S.A.

SIGNET, SIGNET CLASSICS, MENTOR, PLUME, MERIDIAN AND NAL BOOKS are published by The New American Library, Inc., 1633 Broadway, New York, New York 10019

FIRST PRINTING, DECEMBER, 1980

3 4 5 6 7 8 9

PRINTED IN THE UNITED STATES OF AMERICA

The
INTRUDER

Prologue

Each time she tells the story it changes slightly. She tries to be accurate and precise but still it changes, as if it were happening over and over again with minor variations. There are three of them with her in the room. One of them is sitting behind the desk, and the other two have placed their chairs on either side of her. She feels trapped. They keep offering her coffee, which she accepts, though it's invariably bad. She's grateful for its warmth. Their politeness is chilling.

"Start from the beginning," the man behind the desk says to her softly.

She wants to comply, but the beginning seems to change each time. She's reminded of those brightly painted Russian dolls that open up to reveal another one inside. Was there a beginning and an end? They listen to her attentively. They're not taking notes, but she's sure that there's a tape recorder somewhere in the room. She doesn't mind that, though she does mind the way they stare at her, as if she were an object under the microscope of their cold, watchful eyes.

"I've already told you the whole story," she says.

The man behind the desk shakes his head with patience. He smiles at her. He has thin graying hair, a narrow foxlike face, and flat lidless eyes that never seem to change. His vast patience is more ominous than a burst of anger.

"Please bear with us, Mrs. Girard," he says. "And this time try to give us all the details."

She's been married for over five months, but she's still not used to being called Mrs. Girard, and is surprised when people address her by her married name. She thinks of herself as Paula Kirkpatrick, born and raised in Vermont. If she went home to Rutland, her mother would start fixing her favorite dinner and her father would reach out his immense

1

hands to swing her up in the air as if she were a child. Her father looks like an aging football player, but he's a veterinarian. The best in Vermont.

The man behind the desk watches her patiently.

"Please give us all the details," he repeats. "You say you moved to New York over two years ago?"

"I've told you that. Yes."

"And yet you maintain you never met your husband's first wife."

She shivers and tries to control it. They mustn't sense her fear.

"I never met her. No. She'd been dead for a year before I even met Nick."

"I see. Just for the record, exactly what did your husband tell you about his first wife's murder?"

Murder. He uses the word with a calm brutality calculated to shock. He's still treating her politely, but she can sense the claws of steel beneath the velvet gloves. She places the empty coffee container on his desk and looks at him for a minute before answering.

"He told me she'd been killed during an attempted burglary one night in their co-op. He was out of town on a business trip when it happened. He always blamed himself, I think. He felt it wouldn't have happened if he'd been there."

"I see. Let me make sure I have it straight. You met Mr. Nicholas Girard a year or so after Stephanie Girard's death, and six months later you were married and moved into his apartment. The apartment where his first wife was killed. Tell me, Mrs. Girard, didn't it bother you living in a place where someone had been killed?"

He's inviting her to confide in him, to expose her innermost thoughts to his analytical inspection. He doesn't want to know just the facts, he wants to hear about all her feelings and experiences, invading her privacy until she's totally vulnerable to his interrogation. Like a form of mental rape, she thinks.

Anger gives her composure.

"I knew that there are any number of burglaries in New York," she says, shrugging lightly. "Any number of killings. I thought the police had pretty well closed their books on the case."

2

The man behind the desk smiles at her again, and this time his flat gray eyes light up with a peculiar glow.

"The police never close their books on murder, Mrs. Girard," he tells her softly.

He reaches into a drawer and pulls out a notebook, a notebook she knows well. His thin mobile hands caress the leather binding while he watches the slow, terrified widening of her eyes. He leans across the desk and stares at her intently.

"You didn't tell us everything, Mrs. Girard, did you?" he says. "Please start again. From the beginning. And this time don't omit any important details."

She's back in the middle of the nightmare once again. A thin spiral of horror rises up within her like a faint scream she knows they can sense. They're competent men, experienced at their job. As she starts to tell the story once again they all shift a little closer, like hunters surrounding a frightened stag at bay.

1

It was one of those rainy, gusty days that drench New York with monotonous regularity each April. Garbage cans rattled in the wind. Great puddles accumulated in the streets to form a traffic hazard for both cars and pedestrians. Water streamed down from awnings and extended porches.

Paula Girard ran up the steps of Dover House and shook the dripping hood of her raincoat off her hair. The doorman held the door open for her.

" 'Afternoon," he said, shrugging his uniformed shoulders by way of greeting. "Terrible weather, isn't it?"

"Terrible," Paula agreed.

The first time she had visited Dover House she'd been taken aback by the vast lobby with its marble floors and faded mirrors in their ancient frames. It was like walking back into the nineteenth century, she'd thought. But now she'd been living in the building for over a month and was already used to it. She hardly gave the lobby a second glance except to notice that rubber runners had been laid down to protect the fading Oriental rugs and the pristine sheen of the marble floors. She was headed for the elevators when the hallman stopped her.

"Magazines for you, Mrs. Girard," he said, handing them to her. "Terrible weather, isn't it?"

"Terrible," Paula said obediently.

She had no sooner stepped into the elevator than the elevator man started to clear his throat in preparation to making his own weather commentary. But this time Paula beat him to it.

"I'm glad it's finally raining, aren't you?" she said perversely. "It's been a dry month."

He peered at her with surprise. The tenants of Dover

5

House could usually be trusted to hold conservative views about the weather.

"Ach," he said dubiously. "I suppose it's all right for them that likes it."

"It's good for the crops," Paula said firmly.

"The crops?" he said, as if he'd never heard of the word. "It's a long time since my missus and I were out in the country," he confided. "Not since the kids have grown. And, to tell the truth, I always did think it was overrated. Nothing to see but a lot of fields."

He smiled the wide, crooked smile he reserved for his favorite tenants, and Paula smiled back. He liked a bit of a chat, she thought as she let herself into the apartment. So much for the myth of unfriendly New Yorkers. She put down her bag of groceries and took off her boots and raincoat before walking across the wide hallway to the living room and one of the tall windows facing the park. The rain was easing off and a misty fog was beginning to swirl in, giving the park the mystic quality of a surrealist watercolor. The muted sounds of traffic reached her through the closed windows.

God, how she loved the city! She could still remember that time, two years ago, when she had first seen that incredible skyline etched against the sunset. It had been love at first sight. Oh, sure, she knew that the streets were dirty, the subways at rush hour a disaster, and many of the neighborhoods unsafe. None of it could spoil the city's magic for her. She could sense its vitality like that of a powerful heartbeat.

The large grandfather clock in the hallway struck the half hour, and Paula looked at her watch. It was four-thirty. She had no business staring out of the window like a moonstruck tourist. Nick would be home by six, and Cindy Michaels and Charlie Nabokov would be coming soon after that. They would all have dinner together before going upstairs to Countess Marcovaldi's party.

The party. If only she weren't feeling so uptight about the party. Fortunately dinner was almost ready. She had made the eggplant casserole last night, and Nick had volunteered to pick up the appetizers on the way home. The table in the dining room was already set. All that she had to do was wash the spinach and mushrooms for the salad, and get herself ready for the party.

The salad could wait, she decided. She would take a bath first. A hot leisurely bath would be just the thing. That and a cup of tea, her mother's childhood remedies for everything ranging from a cold to jittery nerves before an important date.

She went into the bedroom and got undressed before walking barefoot into the adjoining bathroom. The tub was old and massive, large enough for two people, as she and Nick had discovered. She turned on both taps until the water gushed out in a full stream, and then added some of the expensive bath salts Cindy had given her for her birthday. There, she thought, as the perfumed steam reached her nostrils. The first step to glamour.

While the water was running, she went into the bedroom and took the dress she planned on wearing out of the closet and laid it down across the bed. It was the most expensive dress she'd ever owned, a short cloud of gray chiffon, muted and elegant, that should be just the thing for tonight's party. It was important that she look her best, because tonight she would be meeting their fellow tenants for the first time, and they had all known Nick for years and would be curious to meet his new wife.

She mustn't let him down. At twenty-nine Nick had already become a vice-president of a small but well-respected firm on Wall Street. He knew dozens of people and seemed totally at home wherever he went. Whereas she still felt disconcerted by anything more formal than a buffet dinner. Well, she'd just have to try, that's all. She'd learn to belong.

Like his first wife, said a small unwanted voice at the back of her mind. Like Stephanie.

Stephanie had been tall with shining blond hair and legs a mile long. Paula had seen a number of pictures of her and had thought she must have looked exactly like what she was: a wealthy ex-debutante who had attended the very best of schools and had belonged to some of the most exclusive organizations in the city. She had been everything Paula could never be, not if she lived to be a hundred.

The tub was getting full. She turned off the taps and went over to inspect herself in the mirror. Dark eyes, eyebrows shaped like birds' wings, dark hair that flared up around her face as it always did from the humidity. She had her grandmother's dark Welsh looks, her mother had once told her.

7

Her grandmother had been considered a beauty in her day. Maybe so, but fashions change with time, and today's great beauties were either willowy and blond or else had the elegant look of Queen Nefertiti. You have to learn to make do with what you have, she thought.

She lifted a strand of hair off her forehead and leaned closer to the mirror. The scar above her right temple was fading, and should hardly be noticeable in another few months. She'd been lucky the accident hadn't been much worse. Such a stupid accident at that. Four months ago, after she and Nick became engaged, she'd been driving to Vermont to visit her parents, and in swerving to avoid a dog running across the highway, she had rammed the rented car squarely into a tree. The only results—other than the rental agency's rage— were the eight stitches taken in her forehead and, invisible but more serious, the slight internal contusion she had suffered. There had been headaches and small lapses of memory. She wasn't to go back to work for at least six months, the doctors had told her, and her boss had cooperated by giving her a leave of absence. But at least she'd completely healed in time for the wedding. That was the important thing.

Much more important than her looks or that small scar on her forehead. She didn't usually worry about these things, and she wouldn't now if she weren't so anxious for Nick's friends to accept her. And why shouldn't they? She and Nick loved each other. They made each other happy. That was what counted.

She started humming to herself and walked over to the tub. She had just dipped a tentative toe into the water and decided it was much too hot when the phone started to ring. Why did the phone always ring when she was in the bathroom? She grabbed a towel and ran to pick up the extension in the bedroom.

"Hello?" she said.

"Hello, darling," said her mother, and Paula smiled and held the receiver an inch away from her ear. The telephone connection between Rutland and New York was perfectly satisfactory, but her mother's voice always rose by a decibel to compensate for the long-distance factor.

"Your father and I called to congratulate you on your

one-month anniversary," her mother was saying. "Are you going out to celebrate tonight?"

"That was last week," said Paula.

"What? What was last week?" her mother shouted across the intervening miles.

"Our wedding anniversary, Mom. We were married one month ago last week."

She heard her father's deprecating cough, and could imagine him sitting at the extension in his study, his massive shoulders hunched over his old desk.

"Hello, Paula," he said. His voice was mild. "How are you, sweetheart? So the anniversary was last week, was it? I'm afraid your mother got the dates mixed up for once." His wife's absentmindedness was legendary in the family. His wife, however, ignored his gentle teasing.

"I distinctly remember," she said, "that Paula and Nick were married two weeks after my pottery show. I had to work night and day to get the house back in shape for the wedding."

"One week," said Paula's father. "It was one week after your pottery show. That's why you had to work night and day to get the house back in shape."

Paula pressed the receiver more closely to her ear. She felt a rush of homesickness no less intense for being momentary.

"How is everybody?" she asked, keeping her voice casual.

"Pretty much the same," her father told her. "And how are you, sweetheart? No more headaches, no more of those forgetful spells?"

"I told you that all cleared up months ago," said Paula. "The doctors say I'm perfectly all right. I'll be going back to work in another two months."

He was still concerned about the aftereffects of that accident. Why did parents insist on asking the same questions over and over again? Next her mother would ask her whether they'd been looking for another apartment.

"Have you been looking for other apartments in the meantime?" her mother asked on cue.

Paula sighed. "No, we haven't," she said. "If we give up this apartment, we'd have a hard time finding another one as nice. And we'd have to sell this one first, to raise the money for another co-op. Where would we live in the meantime?"

"I'm sure you'd find something," her mother said briskly. "You know I've never liked the idea of your living in that place."

That was an understatement, to put it mildly. Her mother knew that Nick's first wife had been shot in the apartment during an attempted burglary, and—proceeding on the theory that lightning always strikes twice in the same place—had objected strenuously to the idea of Paula moving into Dover House after her marriage.

"It's as safe as Fort Knox," Paula told her patiently. "They've added an elevator man since . . . since it happened. And there are two locks on the door, *and* a bolt. Please stop worrying, Mom."

"It's not just the safety," her mother said stubbornly. "I would think the associations would be unpleasant for you, to say the least."

She had hit a vulnerable spot, and Paula was silent. That was the odd thing about her mother. She was the most absentminded of women, but she had the uncanny ability to know what her children were thinking or feeling at any given time, even when they were hundreds of miles apart.

Her father's calm voice broke the silence.

"Is Nick home?" he asked. "We'd like to say hello."

"No, he's not home yet. He stopped to pick up some wine and appetizers. We're having a couple of friends up to dinner. Cindy Michaels and Charlie Nabokov. Do you remember them from the wedding?"

"Of course I remember them," said her mother. Cindy had been Paula's roommate before she married Nick, and Charlie was Nick's best man. "I didn't know they were going together."

"They're not," said Paula. She saw no need to tell them that Cindy was involved with a married man that she and Nick had never met. "They're just coming up to dinner, and then we're all going to a party someone is having in this building. A real countess, no less. Countess Bibi Marcovaldi. A good friend of Nick's."

"A countess?" said her mother, as if there were something faintly disreputable implied in the title. "A good friend of Nick's?"

The question was loaded with meaning she didn't attempt

to disguise. There was a silence amplified by the electronic miles that separated them, and Paula sighed again.

"Mom. She's supposed to be sixty-five if she's a day. She sounded very nice over the phone when she called to invite us. She said it would give me a chance to meet all my new neighbors."

Her mother started to say something, but her father interrupted before she had a chance.

"Have a good time, sweetheart," he said firmly. "It sounds like you're busy right now, so we won't keep you. Give our best to Nick."

"We'll call you over the weekend," said her mother.

"Yes."

"The rates are half price over the weekend."

"Yes, Mom. I know."

"We'll talk to you later, then. Take care of yourself."

"And you too. We'll be talking to you later."

The apartment seemed oddly quiet after she hung up. She thought she felt a draft blowing in from the living room, but when she went to check, all the windows were closed. It was getting dark outside, and a gentle rain continued to beat against the windowpanes. She walked around and systematically turned on all the lights, but it didn't seem to help. The brightly lit room still seemed alien, cold. It's power of suggestion, thought Paula. I must ask Mother to stop referring to Stephanie's death. It happened more than two years ago, after all. If everyone refused to live in a house where someone else had died there'd be few houses left. She couldn't afford to indulge her mother's superstitions.

By the time she walked back into the bathroom the bathwater was lukewarm, and she let in more hot water before getting in. She wished Nick were home. It was always more fun taking a bath with Nick.

2

"Last call for wine," said Nick Girard. "Unless anyone would like a touch of brandy with their coffee? Or something to smoke? We're not due at Bibi's for another hour."

"Spare us," said Charlie Nabokov, leaning back in his chair. He was tall, lanky, and prematurely balding. The flickering candlelight accentuated the hollows etched beneath his eyes. "It's not a good idea to get stoned before visiting the haunts of the very rich," he drawled.

"Don't complain to me about the very rich," Nick told him dryly. "You forget I helped you with your income tax earlier this year."

They had finished dinner a while back, and were sitting around the table as though to prolong the pleasure of the evening. And yet there was an underlying tension in the room. Charlie Nabokov was being his most sardonic and morose, while Cindy Michaels, on the other hand, seemed possessed by a nervous excitement she was finding it difficult to control. She was looking lovelier than ever, Paula thought without a trace of jealousy. Her cheeks were flushed, her short blond hair shone like a halo of light around her face. But her eyes seemed too bright, her soft laughter startling in its intensity.

It was quite obvious that her excitement was tinged by an undertone of fear. Something to do with the man she was seeing, no doubt, thought Paula with concern mixed with that irritation we feel when unable to help our closest friends. Why on earth did Cindy, who could have her pick of half a dozen men at any one time, insist on eating her heart out over a married man? She had stopped dating anyone else, as far as Paula knew. Certainly she'd made no attempt to respond to Charlie's earlier interest.

Charlie Nabokov was one of Nick's oldest friends, a free-

12

lance writer whose main source of income was the sizable trust fund left him by his maternal grandmother. He'd been living at Dover House for years, and it was largely through him that Nick had made arrangements to buy his own apartment. He was the same age as Nick, and yet he looked at least ten years older, tired and worn out, as if something were eating at him from inside, corroding his personality like a dose of acid. And yet there was an undeniable sex appeal in those sardonic features and that seductive, educated voice.

"Hey, funny face," said Nick. "A penny for your thoughts."

Paula looked up, startled, and smiled at him from across the table. Their eyes met and held, and Paula felt a slow flush rise to her cheeks. After a month of marriage there were still times, like now, when she felt the impact of his dark good looks as a deep ache inside her.

"A penny for your thoughts," he repeated lightly.

"I wouldn't accept the offer," Charlie advised her. "Not when you consider today's inflationary rates."

"Shut up," Nick told him amiably. "How about it, Paula?"

"I was just thinking," said Paula, "that I still can't believe all this is real." She made a small gesture that included the room.

"Give it a year," said Charlie, "and you'll not only be taking it for granted, you'll be after Nick for bigger and better things."

"And you're a writer?" Cindy told him mockingly before Paula could answer. "I thought writers were supposed to be good at judging people. This is the original girl with stars in her eyes. She knows exactly what she wants, and furthermore, she has an uncanny ability for knowing if it's going to happen. Do you remember your first month in New York?" she said, turning to Paula.

Paula nodded, half angry at Charlie's sarcastic comment, half amused by Cindy's prompt response.

"Paula was staying at some women's hotel over on the East Side," Cindy continued, "when I suggested that we share my apartment in the Village. The following week she came lugging this immense suitcase chock-full of clothes I told her she couldn't possibly wear. She'd have to wear them until she got a job, she pointed out, and I warned her that jobs weren't easy to get. And so what happened? Within a month she was working at one of the best public-relations agencies in the city. Within a year she'd met Nick. But the odd thing is, I felt that she knew all along that it was going to happen. Didn't you, Paula?"

Paula shrugged lightly. Had she been that transparent? It was true that she'd felt a vivid sense of promise that the things she'd hoped for would finally happen, that this was the time and the place for her. And now, because that feeling of remembered magic seemed still far too real, she was reluctant to discuss it.

"It's true. And tonight we're actually going to a party given by an honest-to-goodness countess," she said, changing the subject. "Is she a widow, by the way? Or are she and her husband divorced?"

"They're not divorced, and he's very much alive," Nick told her.

"But they don't get along?"

"They get along very well," said Charlie. "They have a very successful marriage, international style. When his appointment to the U.N. expired, he went back home to Rome and she stayed here. They visit each other twice a year. At Christmastime and in the autumn, I believe."

"I don't understand. Why don't they simply get a divorce?"

"Isn't that the ideal marriage situation?" Charlie asked caustically.

But Nick intervened.

"A divorce would be out of the question in their case," he explained. "He's a papal knight, belongs to the Knights of Malta, the whole ancient European thing. They can't get a divorce, and they can't maintain separate residences in Rome because that would cause a scandal neither one of them wants. He's said to have a friend, a young actress from whom he's supposed to be inseparable."

He stopped abruptly. He'd suddenly remembered that Cindy herself was involved with a married man, and was afraid he was treading on delicate ground. But Cindy's expression remained unchanged. She was obviously intrigued by Bibi Marcovaldi.

"It all sounds like something from a period novel," she remarked.

14

"It does," Nick agreed. "But when you meet Bibi, don't be fooled by those turn-of-the-century manners of hers. She has a mind as precise as a finely tuned clock. She's discussed her investments with me once or twice. She knows exactly what she's doing. The money is hers, I believe, but she supports her husband and his mistress in the manner to which they've grown accustomed."

"It's easy to be generous when you're born with a silver spoon in your mouth," Charlie remarked.

"Oh, I don't think she's always had it easy. There were difficult times, I understand. A man I know, an old professor of mine at Columbia, told me she saved his brother's life during the Second World War. She was strongly antifascist, and her villa was a safe house of sorts. He said that at any one time there'd be a number of British or Jewish refugees hidden in her basements while she entertained the cream of the Gestapo up in her drawing room."

"She sounds like a remarkable woman," Paula said thoughtfully.

Nick smiled at her.

"She is, but you'll never get her to take credit for the things she did. I asked her about it at one time, and she merely shrugged if off. 'But one had to do something,' she told me. 'You have no idea what those people were like. So dreadfully common.' "

"You're very fond of her, aren't you?" said Cindy.

"She's been a good friend," he said simply, and for a minute his mobile face looked closed in and expressionless.

He must have needed friends badly after Stephanie's death, thought Paula, and something dark and painful stirred inside her. She only hoped that they would be her friends too. It would be important to Nick to maintain his old relationships.

"If someone will clear the coffee cups, I'm going to change," she said.

She walked over to Nick and kissed him lightly on the lips before walking into the bedroom. She slipped out of her shirt and jeans and stood shivering in her bikini pants and bra. It seemed colder here than in the dining room. A touch more lip gloss and some blusher for her cheeks were called for, she decided, looking at herself critically in the mirror. There. She was glad they had asked Cindy and Charlie to have dinner with them before the party, not only because she enjoyed their company, but also because thinking about them and their problems had helped to take her mind off some of her own anxieties. What did she have to worry about as long as she and Nick had each other? We're so lucky, she thought, and felt the slow glow of her happiness spreading inside her.

She started humming gently to herself, sprayed a touch of perfume on her wrists and in the cleavage between her breasts, and walked over to the bed to slip into the dress she had placed there earlier. The hum died abruptly in her throat.

"Oh, no," she whispered, staring down at the dress.

The delicate chiffon was torn right down the middle of the bodice to down below the waistline. She touched the tear with unsteady hands. Why hadn't she noticed it earlier? She must have torn it the last time she wore it, but if so . . . why hadn't she remembered? She'd been so sure that she was totally well again, that the small lapses of memory she'd suffered for a few weeks after the accident were a thing of the past. Obviously she'd been wrong. Would they recur again and again, making a normal life next to impossible?

"You're a natural-born fighter," one of the doctors had told her while she was still in the hospital. "I'm convinced there's a strong link between personality and the rate of recovery. You'll get well soon because you're determined to get well." Yes. But how could you fight something over which you had no control? One thing for sure: Nick mustn't know or even suspect. He'd be sick with worry if he knew. This was one thing she'd have to cope with on her own. And it was just one small incident, after all. It didn't necessarily mean that she was having a relapse. Why should it? She had never felt better in her whole life.

She picked up the torn dress and hung it up before looking at the other things hanging in her closet. She finally selected a camel-colored wool dress with a white trim at the neck and sleeves. It wasn't as elegant as the gray chiffon but it would have to do.

When she joined the others in the living room, Cindy nodded her approval and the fellows whistled with appreciation. Paula smiled at them, but her earlier excitement was gone. She no longer wanted to go to the party, she had no wish to meet any of her neighbors. Not just now. She wanted to be alone with Nick, safe in the shelter of his arms. None of this showed on her face as she thanked them for their comments.

At exactly nine o'clock they took the elevator and went up to Bibi Marcovaldi's penthouse apartment.

3

Countess Beatrice Maria Marcovaldi had never once been bored by her own company. It was paradoxical, therefore, that all her life she had been surrounded by a host of admirers, lovers, and acquaintances who were more than ready to put up with her caustic wit for the sake of her unique, incandescent charm.

Now she was surrounded by a small group of people who were listening to her with interest and amusement. Her own face was deadpan, but there was humor lurking at the corners of her mouth, and her immense blue eyes stared up at them with well-feigned surprise, as if she couldn't quite understand the reason for their laughter. Her thick white hair accentuated her deep suntan, and her body was thin and wiry—the body of a tomboy, Paula thought. An aging tomboy.

When she finished her anecdote, the group around her broke into a fresh burst of laughter, and she smiled at them, well pleased. And then, as though feeling the tug of Nick's and Paula's gaze, she turned around and looked directly at them. She waved a slender, eloquent hand in their direction and started walking toward them.

She walked haltingly, leaning upon her cane. She had a pronounced limp that, oddly enough, reinforced the illusion of a tomboy. She might have just had a bad tumble on the ski slopes rather than be suffering from arthritis she'd had for many years.

When she reached Paula and Nick, she smiled at them, and her face seemed swallowed by those immense blue eyes.

"So you finally came," she said to Nick, offering him her cheek. "And you've brought Paula."

She took Paula's hand and held it in her own.

"I'm so very glad you came, my dear. I've been looking

18

forward to meeting you, and it was very naughty of Nick not to bring you before. And isn't that Charlie Nabokov standing next to the fireplace? With that lovely blond girl. *Such* an improvement on his last girlfriend, I must say. The one with the false eyelashes and that peculiar shade of lipstick."

Nick shook his head and grinned down at her. "You're hopeless, Bibi," he told her. "And that isn't Charlie's girlfriend; that's Cindy Michaels, Paula's former roommate. She had dinner with us earlier. You don't mind that we brought her along?"

"My dear, I'm delighted. I love having beautiful young people at my parties," she said, still holding on to Paula's hand. "It's quite a good party, don't you think? Quite civilized. I mean there's been no violence of any kind. So far."

The room was filled with well-dressed people chattering away in low-pitched, well-bred voices. Paula tried to imagine them indulging in a violent brawl and failed totally. Her doubts were reflected in her smile.

"You don't believe me," said Bibi Marcovaldi. She appealed to Nick. "Tell Paula what it's like," she urged him, and went on before he had a chance to speak. "Why, at one time," she said, "when we were trying to decide on new wallpaper for the lobby, everyone got so upset they wouldn't talk to each other for months. It was rather peaceful, actually. We started the co-op association some two years ago," she explained to Paula. "There are times when I feel it was a terrible mistake."

Two years ago, thought Paula. Around the time of Stephanie's death. They must have felt the need to draw together after that, to make plans for additional protection. Certainly the lobby couldn't be safer now. Outsiders would stand small chance of getting in.

"I'm sure the association serves a good cause," she said diplomatically.

Bibi Marcovaldi, whose family had dwelt in diplomatic circles for a number of generations, felt no need for diplomacy.

"A good cause?" she said, sounding alarmed. "Oh, I do hope not. Good causes always tend to bring out the very worst in people. I've never quite understood why," she added reflectively.

"No need to worry," Nick reassured her. "I'm sure we're all motivated by the most selfish reasons."

A flash of amusement lit the wide blue eyes. Her charm was winning, and Paula started to understand why Nick had enjoyed the many hours he'd spent in her company.

"Your husband is a sensible man," Bibi told her now, "and sensible men are very hard to find. But right now I'd like to talk with you. You don't mind if I steal Paula away for a short while?" she said, turning to Nick.

She stared at him as though waiting, not for a reply to her question, but a different, more subtle response. She was leaning heavily on her cane. The hand holding the cane shook ever so slightly, but she managed to hold herself up very straight.

"As long as it's only for a short time," Nick told her. "I can't spare Paula for very long."

They exchanged a glance that Paula couldn't quite understand, and then Bibi turned around to lead the way toward two straight-backed chairs around a small table. Paula followed her, casting a tentative look back at Nick, who smiled at her encouragingly.

"Well, here we are," said Bibi Marcovaldi as she settled herself in one of the straight-backed chairs. "I've been wanting to meet you for weeks, you know, but I thought I'd give you and Nick a chance to settle down before asking you for dinner. I saw you in the lobby a couple of weeks ago and knew right away you were Nick's wife."

"You did? How did you know?" said Paula, overwhelmed as much by Bibi's presence as by her rush of words.

The brilliant smile lit up the old face with barely suppressed mischief.

"Well, actually I knew because the hallman told me. But I would have known anyway. Nick had told me you were from out of town, and I didn't think you looked like a New Yorker."

"Oh, dear," said Paula. "And I've tried so hard."

"I meant that as a compliment, my dear. There was something about the way you smiled at the hallman and the way you held yourself. And the way you walk, of course. You've lived in the country, haven't you?"

20

"I was born and raised in Vermont. My parents own a few acres just outside of Rutland."

"I too was born in the country," said Bibi Marcovaldi, and didn't mention the size of her family's estates. "We spent most of our summers there. I had a horse and a pet pig named Caligula. Did you have any special pets?"

"We had two dogs. And my father was always bringing wild animals home for my two brothers and me to take care of. He's a veterinarian, you see, and animals are his love as well as his profession."

"I knew it. There's something special about growing up on the land, something you never lose. It gives us a type of kinship, don't you think? I'll tell you a secret. When I saw you in the lobby that day, you reminded me of someone, and it took me a while to realize that you reminded me of myself when I was young."

Oh, wow, thought Paula. She examined the older woman's face for signs of mockery, but the look that met hers was as direct and guileless as that of a child.

"It was your smile, I think," Bibi continued. "Something so expectant about your smile. Suddenly I was reminded of the way I felt when I left school . . . one expects so much when one is young. But I'm afraid I'm rambling. I wanted to tell you how glad I am that we finally met. You know I'm very fond of Nick?"

"He told me you were good friends."

"We've managed to help each other once or twice. I hope that you and I will also become friends. I'm glad you came tonight. Tell me. Do you like large parties?"

"They terrify me," Paula heard herself admitting, much to her own surprise.

"Do they?" said Bibi. "They terrify me too. All those new names to be remembered, and all those people so eager to pounce on one with their latest gossip. I'm always intimidated by large parties."

Paula couldn't imagine her being intimidated by anything or anyone. She told her so, and watched as a shadow dimmed the older woman's eyes.

"I have been intimidated many times," she said. She paused as though remembering. "Does that surprise you? It shouldn't, you know. We all have our fears, our special shadows that follow on our footsteps. But you don't have to worry about the people here tonight. I predict two things: they'll all be eager to meet you, and all the women will be jealous of you."

"Jealous of *me?*"

"But of course. They'll be madly jealous because you're in love and it shows all over you. That's the true secret of beauty, I've always thought, much more effective than creams or massages. Though also more expensive, I'm afraid. There's no such thing as free love. Being in love can be the costliest thing of all."

She grinned at Paula, and the fine tracery of lines across her face deepened into wrinkles. There was something about that ancient gamine face that reminded Paula of a girlfriend she'd once had in grade school. They used to be best friends and would exchange confidences over ice cream and popcorn. She was almost tempted to tell Bibi about how nervous she'd been about meeting Nick's friends. It would have been easy to confide in her. But it was a long time since grade school, and she was no longer given to exchanging confidences.

"I'm glad we met," she said instead. "It will be nice to have a friend here in the building. May I come up to see you from time to time?"

An unfamiliar diffidence crossed Bibi Marcovaldi's face, and her thin fingers strayed to the strand of pearls around her neck.

"I was wondering . . ." she said. "Nick told me you wouldn't be going to work for another month or two, and he's afraid you'll be bored staying in the apartment by yourself. If that's true—and please tell me if it isn't—I thought we might be able to help each other out. I'm on the board of a number of museums, you see. And half a dozen charities. There are all sorts of meetings to go to and letters to be answered. I used to handle it all by myself, once, but now . . ."

She extended her slender hands across the table, and Paula noticed for the first time that the joints were swollen with arthritis, the skin above them stretched out and inflamed.

"There are things I can no longer do," Bibi said simply. "I had an assistant until last month, but she left for the West Coast when her fiancé got his law degree. I thought that if you had a few extra hours each week . . . We could talk

22

about the money later, and I fully realize you wouldn't do it just for the money. But you might find it amusing for a while. And you might meet some interesting people."

Paula flushed with pleasure. "I'd love to do it," she said impulsively. "As many hours as you need."

She couldn't believe her own good luck. So much for her anxieties about fitting in. She knew just enough about public relations to be aware of the opportunities that working for Bibi would open up for her. There was no doubt that Bibi could have her choice of assistants, and that she'd made the offer primarily for Nick's sake, but that didn't matter. She would repay her by doing a good job.

Providing she didn't have any further lapses, she thought as she remembered the torn chiffon dress, the dress she hadn't remembered tearing the last time she wore it. She pushed the unpleasant thought to one side, excited by the prospect of working once again. She hadn't realized until now how much she'd missed her job.

"That's settled then," said Bibi. "We'll start whenever you're ready."

"Tomorrow afternoon?"

Bibi laughed. "There's no hurry, child. But tomorrow afternoon would be just fine."

After that, the evening seemed to fly. Nick stayed by her side and introduced her to at least two dozen people who were all friendly and welcoming and charming, and they all drank wine and it got so late that they asked Cindy to spend the night with them in the guest room instead of going back to her apartment in the Village. Paula relaxed amid the conversation and the laughter, and wondered how she could have possibly been nervous about coming up.

There was only one unpleasant incident during the whole evening, and that was so minor that it hardly mattered. As they were getting ready to leave, Paula glanced into the ancient mirror above the fireplace and thought how well she and Nick looked side by side. Behind them people were moving around in the slow shuffle of leave-taking, and she leaned more closely against Nick's shoulder. And then she stiffened. The group behind them had parted, to reveal a woman's face staring intently at her. Their eyes met in the mirror. There was such malevolence in the woman's face that Paula caught her breath.

"What's the matter?" said Nick.

"Who's that woman?"

"Which woman?"

Paula took his hand and pulled him with her around the people who were now blocking their view, but the woman, whoever she was, had already slipped out. It didn't matter, not really. Hadn't Bibi warned her that there might be women who would be jealous of her?

While they were waiting for the elevator to go back down to their apartment, Nick squeezed her hand and she returned the pressure.

"Guess what?" she said. "I'm no longer a member of the unemployed."

"What do you mean?"

"Bibi asked me if I'd work with her part-time."

"Hey, that's great. Now you can support me in the style to which I'd like to become accustomed."

She grinned at him, and was rewarded by seeing her pleasure reflected in his eyes.

4

Nick sat up against the pillows and waited impatiently while Paula got undressed. She hung up her dress in the closet, unhooked her bra, and stepped out of her bikini. She noticed that her nipples were hard and erect, but didn't know if it was from excitement or the cold. Normally she slipped on her white terry-cloth robe before brushing out her hair, but tonight she was naked when she sat down at the dressing table. The shyness she'd felt during the first few weeks was beginning to fade. Why, I really feel we're married, she thought with surprise.

She sat down at the dressing table and started to brush her hair. One hundred strokes each night, her grandmother had said, a tradition her mother had followed and passed down to her. Her naked breasts quivered with each movement of her arm.

"Come to bed," Nick said urgently.

She laughed. "Don't be in such a hurry," she told him.

They'd come a long way, she thought. They could play games with each other now, games that both heightened and prolonged their pleasure in each other. The sex always seemed to reflect their mood. There were times when they were violent with each other, clinging together like two wrestlers unwilling to loose the fight. There were times when their mood was fragile, incredibly tender. And there were times, like tonight, when they felt playful and inventive.

"If you don't come to bed," said Nick, "I'm coming over to get you. I'm warning you, that's all."

"And then what will you do?"

He told her in some detail what he planned to do. The effect of his predictions was somewhat ruined when they both started giggling.

"Shh. We'll wake up Cindy," said Paula, pointing to the next room.

"In that case," Nick told her, "I'll just go to sleep."

"Oh no you won't," said Paula. They'd made love every night during the past five weeks. "Besides, if you do go to sleep, I'll find a way to wake you."

"Do you want to bet?"

"Yes. Do you?"

"No," he said, and opened his arms wide as she got up and slipped in with him under the covers.

Afterward they rolled into their usual sleeping position, his arm cradling her against him, his mouth against her hair. In a few minutes his even breathing told her he was asleep.

She lay awake, totally content and floating on her glow of inner excitement. They had come a long way. She could still remember their first time together, the desperation of their first touch and the way it had turned into joy as they'd made love over and over again before finally giving in to exhaustion and to sleep. They had awakened with the winter sun streaming like molten gold across the bed, and he had made love to her again, still rigid with that all overpowering need. Afterward she had opened her eyes and looked at his face just inches from her own, and the sun had refracted her tears into a million prisms. It was then that she'd known she'd finally come home.

Would it last? she wondered. It had to. She thought of the man she'd lived with for three years after college, and remembered the night he had come home and told her it was over. "We should start seeing other people," he'd said, and she'd looked at him blankly, too shocked to understand the meaning of his words. He had changed his mind soon after that and asked her to marry him, but by that time it had been too late. She had left for Rutland soon after that, but it had been no better at home. One desolate night had followed the other. The quiet of the countryside had pressed against her like a massive weight. Finally she'd packed her things and moved to New York.

Never again, she promised herself. She'd never run home again like a frightened child, and she'd never again give up without putting up a fight for what she wanted. Never again.

It must have been even harder for Nick. He never talked

about Stephanie, though she had tried to bring up the subject on more than one occasion. And yet, in the long run, she could understand his silence. He must have loved her very deeply, he must have felt bereft by the suddenness of her violent death. He'd seen a number of women after that, she knew. His expressive face and dark good looks would be attractive to women. But he'd never found anyone to fill his needs until he'd met her.

I'll never let anything get between us, she promised him silently. Her thoughts were becoming vague. She was almost asleep when she heard the soft opening and closing of their bedroom door.

"Cindy?" she whispered sleepily. "Is that you?"

There was no answer. Paula slipped out of bed and walked barefoot into the living room. The lights were out and Cindy's door was closed. Paula hesitated, wondered whether to knock, and then changed her mind. Whatever Cindy had wanted, she must have decided it could wait until the next day. She walked back to the bedroom and closed her own door, but it still seemed drafty in the room, as chilly as it had been earlier in the day. Maybe they should consider storm windows, she thought as she slipped back into bed and snuggled up next to Nick for warmth. In less than five minutes she was asleep.

"But why don't you just stop seeing him if he's making you so miserable?" said Paula the next morning.

She was curled up on the bed in the guest room sipping her coffee while Cindy applied her makeup at the dressing table. She had showered and had breakfast with Nick, and had come in to chat with Cindy as soon as Nick left for work.

"We've been through all this before," said Cindy irritably, and continued to apply her eyeliner. She looked tired this morning. Her eyes were slightly puffy and her cheeks pale without any makeup. The hand holding the eyeliner shook ever so slightly.

It was so unfair, thought Paula, that Cindy of all people should get hooked in that trap. When she'd first moved to New York, it was Cindy who had shown her the ropes and introduced her to a number of men who'd proved both

pleasant and amusing. It was through Cindy, in fact, that
she'd first met Nick. It was Cindy who had steered her away
from the crowd of would-be-swingers who were too insecure
in their pursuit of pleasure to indulge in anything other than
one-night stands. Twentieth-century castrati, Cindy had called
them. And now Cindy, so generous and sensible at the same
time, was caught up in this disastrous affair with a married
man, helpless to escape the trap of her emotions.

"I know we've been through it before," said Paula, trying
to keep the pity out of her voice. "But nothing has changed,
has it? And last night, when you came to our room, I thought
you needed to talk, to discuss it further . . ."

She stopped in midsentence. Cindy's expression was one of
sheer surprise.

"Last night? But I didn't come into your room last night.
Believe it or not, I fell asleep the minute my head touched
the pillow."

Paula stared at her. She distinctly remembered the door
opening and closing during the night. *Someone* had walked
into the bedroom, and since Cindy was the only other person
in the apartment, it had obviously been her. Why was she lying about it now? To conceal the extent of her unhappiness,
perhaps, her inability to sleep.

"But if you really want to talk about it, why not?" Cindy
was saying. "Not that there's anything new to discuss. I
haven't seen him in over a week. We were supposed to have
dinner at the apartment three nights ago, as it happens—it
was our six-month anniversary—and I'd left work early to fix
a special dinner. A duck with all the trimmings, champagne,
the whole bit. Only he didn't show up. He called at the last
minute to say that his boss had asked him to entertain some
clients from out of town. There was no way he could get out
of it."

That's probably one of the stories he told his wife the
nights when he felt like playing around, thought Paula, but
she suspected that Cindy had already guessed as much. And
to add insult to injury she'd been left with a splendid dinner
of which she'd probably been unable to eat a single bite.
Damn. Double damn, thought Paula.

"Why don't you kick him out?" she said, and could have
kicked herself the minute she said it. This was the wrong ap-

proach, and Cindy was bound to snap at her and tell her to mind her own business. But then, surprisingly, Cindy smiled and reached for a cigarette before turning around to face her.

"Give me credit for having some sense left," she said. "I know it can't go on like this—I can't cope with it much longer. I told him the other night he'd have to make a choice. Either his wife or me. They have no children, so it isn't as if there were really a family involved."

"And what did he say?"

"He said he'd talk to his wife about a divorce."

So that explained Cindy's tension last night, that fey excitement tinged by an undertone of fear. She'd done what she could, and now all there was left was the terrible waiting and the hope. She probably jumped each time the phone rang in the silence of her apartment.

"Don't you think his wife already knows about you?" Paula asked softly.

Cindy shrugged and turned back to the mirror. She looked more relaxed now, as if the conversation had eased some of her pressures. She picked up a small brush and started to apply an earth-toned blusher across her lovely cheekbones.

"Does his wife know?" she said. "Probably. I'm sure he hasn't told her, but I don't see how you could help but know if your husband were having an affair. She's probably just waiting for it to blow over. Playing it cool. That makes her sound very cold-blooded, I know, and yet the funny thing is I have a feeling I'd like her if I met her."

"I don't think I could ever keep silent if I thought Nick was having an affair," said Paula, and her stomach knotted painfully at the thought.

"Oh yes you would," Cindy told her. "You would if you wanted to keep him. It's the jealous wives who loose their husbands, the ones who make scenes. By the way, did you know that Stephanie was the jealous type? Charlie told me last night. 'Obsessively jealous,' was the way he put it. She must have made Nick miserable, he said. Did Nick ever mention it?"

"Nick never talks to me about Stephanie," said Paula.

No one ever talked to her about Stephanie. It was as if her death had erased everyone's memories of her previous existence, or else locked them away in some small secret room to which there was no access. It was because she'd died by violence, Paula had thought, but maybe there were other reasons she didn't know about. Such as Stephanie's jealousy. Why had she been jealous? Paula brushed the thought impatiently out of her mind. Now was no time to start speculating about something that was all over and done with. Right now it was Cindy who needed her full attention.

"Do you think he will?" she said. "Talk to his wife about a divorce, I mean."

"He said he would," said Cindy. She shrugged with assumed indifference, but the small break in her voice gave her away, and her face looked vulnerable, filled with an almost desperate hope. She looked down at her hands and played nervously with her hairbrush.

"I think he really loves me, you know," she said very softly. "We're good together—not just in bed, but in other ways too. We laugh together, we save up things to tell each other when we meet. Do you know what I mean? I never knew what it could be like until I met him. And it's the same for him. He and his wife went through a trial separation two years ago, he said, and things just haven't worked out since they got back together."

"Well, in that case she shouldn't object to a divorce."

"I hope so," said Cindy, so softly that Paula sensed rather than heard her words.

No one should care so much and be so uncertain of the outcome, thought Paula, looking at her friend's still and intent face. She shivered, and felt a chill spreading from her spine out to her arms and legs. Her fingers tingled. What was it her grandmother used to say? "By the prickling of my thumbs, something evil this way comes." What a silly superstition, she thought, but she was unable to shake the feeling of unease that gripped her like a premonition. Something was going to happen.

"What's the matter?" said Cindy, staring at her oddly.

"Nothing's the matter. Why?"

"You looked so strange right now, as if you were miles away somewhere. Do you know something you're not telling me?"

"Don't be an idiot," said Paula, getting up.

She made breakfast for Cindy and tried to distract her by

chattering away about the party and the work she'd agreed to do for Bibi Marcovaldi. They compared notes about people they'd met, and by the time Cindy left for work she looked her usual self: exquisite, smiling, her short blond hair brushed like a defiant halo around her head.

Well, that's that, thought Paula as she went back into the kitchen to do the dishes. She hoped things would turn out the way Cindy wanted, though it was odd to think of love as a game of musical chairs, with one odd man out. Supposing she had met Nick while he was still married . . . would she still have fallen for him as quickly as she had? It was idle speculation at best, she decided. Nick was not the type of man to indulge in a secretive affair. But in that case, why had Stephanie been jealous? "Obsessively jealous," Cindy had said.

Paula sighed and went out to the hallway closet to get the vacuum cleaner. Nick had never told her much about Stephanie except for the bare facts of her background and her death, and she in turn had been reluctant to question him, believing everyone was entitled to a degree of privacy. And yet now she was beginning to find it important to know more about her.

Why, I'm becoming jealous of a dead woman, she thought, angry at her own introspection. She looked out the open living-room window. The sun was bright, the air smelled newly washed. As soon as she was done cleaning the apartment, she'd go out for a walk, do some grocery shopping, and take her gray chiffon dress to the cleaner's. Maybe they could mend it and she'd be able to wear it again. If only she could remember when and how she'd torn it.

It was good that she was going back to work, she decided. She was beginning to fret about too many things simply because time was beginning to weigh heavily on her hands. And they were such silly, unimportant things. The details of Nick's first marriage. A woman she'd never met looking at her with dislike as she was leaving the party. A dress with a tear she'd forgotten about. It could happen to anybody.

Talking to Cindy made her realize how lucky she really was. Cindy, who sat at home nights waiting for the telephone to ring; Cindy, who had nothing to rely on except a vague promise that most likely wouldn't be kept. Whereas she had Nick and the lovely home they shared, and now the bonus of

31

work with Bibi Marcovaldi until she was ready to go back to her old job. She had everything she'd ever wanted, she told herself firmly and wondered why she was still unable to shake that small chill of unease. "By the prickling of my thumbs . . ."

Damn superstition, she thought, putting the vacuum away. Before going out she would change into her tailored slacks and her best sweater, the cashmere sweater Nick had given her as a surprise gift. She liked wearing the things he had given her. It was almost like having a part of him around.

5

She was taken aback by the sheer quantity of mail Bibi Marcovaldi received on any one day. Lengthy petitions from a wide range of charities, warm personal notes from museum directors and theatrical impresarios, detailed and, to Paula, incomprehensible statements from a Wall Street broker, not to mention the innumerable invitations to cocktail parties, private art showings, and political dinners. And then there were the letters postmarked from a number of countries scattered throughout the world.

"I will read the personal mail and the statements from the stockbroker," Bibi Marcovaldi told Paula. "Old loves and new investments, those are things one must see to oneself. Is that not so? The other things we will work on together."

She picked up a letter and scanned it briefly before looking up at Paula. "I see that Stanley is trying to raise money for another play. I must say this for him: he has perseverance. Did you hear about Stanley's last show?" And she started to tell Paula an amusing and faintly scandalous story about a well-known theatrical producer.

Much to her own surprise, Paula found that within a few short days she had the hang of it. She learned that Bibi turned down most invitations almost automatically, found out how she liked to have her correspondence handled. She spent a good deal of time on the phone and talked to people whose names she had seen in the newspaper; two afternoons in a row she accompanied Bibi to an art gallery; and one day, when Bibi's arthritis was worse than usual, she represented her at a meeting of the board of directors of a large art museum.

Her worries about recurring lapses of memory affecting her performance proved to be unfounded. Indeed, she had sel-

33

dom worked more efficiently or enjoyed a job more, partially because of its novelty, partially because Bibi's amusing commentaries added a special zest to much of what she did.

She would have thought herself totally cured had it not been for the small bouts of absentmindedness she still had at home. They were small and quite unimportant, but they bothered her because they meant that she was still suffering from some of the aftereffects of the accident. But why did they affect her only when she was at home?

There was the time, for instance, when she spent most of the morning cleaning up the apartment and came down from Bibi's to find the newspapers scattered all over the dining-room table. And yet she was sure she'd straightened them. And then there was the time, more disturbing, when she found a lipstick-stained glass on the kitchen sink. It was half filled with a pale-amber liquid, and she picked it up and held it up to her nostrils. Scotch? But she never drank in the daytime. Could she have had a drink before going up to Bibi's and forgotten about it? It bothered her, as did the dirty ashtrays she'd thought she had washed, or the books she was sure she had put back in the bookcase.

She found herself getting nervous and restless when she was in the apartment by herself, but the nervousness disappeared the minute Nick came home. She loved their evenings together. She would look at the clock and wait for the sound of his key in the door.

One night he walked in after work bearing a huge armful of daffodils.

"The first ones of the season," he announced, handing them to her.

She laughed. "You must have bought out a flower stall," she said.

"Practically. The vendor told me I must have a lovely lady. I assured him he was right."

He mixed them a drink and watched her while she arranged the flowers. It took three different vases to hold them all. There was a curious expression on his face as he sipped at his drink.

"For years," he said, "I used to be one of the last ones to leave the office."

34

"Yes?" she said, trying to keep her voice casual. She wanted him to go on. He hardly ever talked about the past.

But he merely shook his head and laughed. "And now," he said, "I can't wait to come home."

"Because of me?"

"Who else?" he said. "You realize, of course, that I'm probably going to get demoted at this rate."

She went over to him and sat down next to him on the couch. There wasn't much chance of his being demoted, she knew. On the contrary, he was being considered for a promotion. They clicked their glasses together in a silent cheer, and then she curled her feet up under her and leaned against him. Part of them always touched when they sat or walked together, as if their physical intimacy expressed a need that no words could fulfill. Would it always be like this, she wondered, or would they eventually grow apart like so many couples she knew? No, she thought fiercely. Not everybody grew apart when the novelty wore off. She had a sudden vision of her parents sitting hand in hand while they watched television.

Nick leaned over to kiss her lightly on the lips and she snuggled closer to him with a sigh of contentment. The fire crackled in the grate, and the great masses of daffodils gleamed golden in the firelight. At that moment there was absolutely nothing else she wanted in the whole world. She had it all, right here.

But the next morning, after Nick left for work, Paula's feeling of restlessness returned. The apartment seemed alien without him, the rooms too large and cold, the furniture as impersonal as that in a motel. She had opened the windows to let in the cool spring air, and when the bedroom door slammed shut in the strong breeze, she was as startled as if she'd heard a shot. What's wrong with me? she wondered. It was probably power of suggestion, she decided. Her mother's concern must have subconsciously communicated itself to her. Next thing she knew she'd probably be looking under the beds for hidden robbers, she thought with disgust.

And yet she wasn't consciously afraid. For one thing, she was convinced that the chances of anyone else breaking into the apartment were minimal, if not nonexistent: security in the lobby had been reinforced since Stephanie's death, and

she had none of the jewelry or furs Stephanie had owned—
there'd be little inducement for a burglar. For another thing,
she had never experienced physical fear. She had grown up
with two older brothers, who had taken her training well in
hand—she had gone hunting and fishing with them, and gone
climbing up mountains that professional climbers regarded
with respect. She had never been afraid of the dark, or of the
sound of footsteps down a desolate street, or of the silence of
a shadowed subway platform. Her brothers had taught her
how to take care of herself.

And yet her feeling of unease about the apartment persisted like a nagging toothache. She wasn't surprised that Bibi
Marcovaldi was the first to sense it.

"You may think me impertinent," Bibi told her one day, as
a way of broaching the subject. They had finished their allot-
ted quota of letters and phone calls for the day, and Teresa,
Bibi's maid, had brought them a tray of tea and small delicate pastries, as she always did at that time of the afternoon.
After only two weeks they had already established precedents
and routines.

"You may think me impertinent," Bibi repeated. Her quest-
ing eyes looked almost aquamarine in the late-afternoon
light. "And yet . . . I hope you will not be offended if I ask
if something is wrong."

"Wrong? I don't understand," said Paula, stalling for time.

"You've seemed tense lately. I hope the work isn't too
much for you."

"Oh no," Paula said quickly. "I love working with you. It's
like stepping into a world I never knew existed. I hope you're
not sorry you asked me to work with you?" she added. "I
realize that it was a spur-of-the-minute thing."

"My dear child," said Bibi. She was holding the delicate
china cup in both her hands. The joints of her fingers looked
angry and inflamed. Her arthritis was getting worse. "Of
course it was a spur-of-the-minute thing," she said. "I knew
we would get along the minute we met. Let me tell you
something. When I was very young I always trusted first impressions. And then, as I got older, I thought, No, that's
wrong. First impressions can often prove misleading. It was
only when I got older still that I realized I had been right in

36

the first place. I've learned to trust my instinct. Do you believe in instinct?"

"Of course," said Paula. "My father says that instinct is nothing more than a collage of data collected by the subconscious. My mother, on the other hand, maintains that it's much more than that—that it's a telepathic ability that most of us could develop further if we choose."

"They're both right, I daresay. I only know that it was instinct that saved me on more than one occasion, that made me recognize potential danger. Not necessarily my own, you understand."

That shadow that Paula had noticed once before clouded the wide blue eyes. She seemed to be looking backward into a past that must often seem more haunting than the present. And then she shrugged her thin elegant shoulders and smiled gently at Paula.

"And so I hope you won't think me impertinent if I say you seem troubled," she said. "Or ask the reason why."

"I don't know," Paula answered slowly. "I *have* been jumpy lately, but I really don't know why."

"I don't have to ask you if everything is all right between you and Nick. One only needs to see the two of you together to know that. So it must be something else. Could it be the unpleasant associations in the apartment?"

It was almost exactly what her mother had said, Paula remembered. She hesitated. How far should she confide in Bibi? Would she be betraying Nick by telling her something she hadn't discussed with him?

"I don't know what it is," she answered truthfully. "There are times when I think I haven't fully recovered from the accident, and that I should go back to talk to the doctor—if only I didn't hate seeing doctors so much. And then there are other times when I feel that moving into this building was a mistake. Not because of what happened to Stephanie, but because she and Nick lived here together for three years. There are dozens of people in the building who must have been fond of her, who must think of me as little better than an intruder."

It was Bibi's turn to hesitate. She put her cup down and leaned across toward Paula.

"There might have been people who were fond of Steph-

anie," she said. "I myself never was. I disliked her, in fact.
I know there's a convention that one should never speak ill of
the dead. *De mortuis*, et cetera. Like most conventions it's a
silly one. I thought her vain, superficial, totally selfish. And
totally wrong for Nick. That doesn't mean I wasn't shocked
by the details of her death."

"I never heard any of the details," Paula admitted.

"Nick never told you?"

"It can't be a pleasant subject for him to discuss. He told
me that she was shot during an attempted burglary. And that
he was out of town at the time it happened."

"Yes. I do believe that he blamed himself for that, that he
felt he could have prevented it had he been here. And yet,
who knows? He might have been killed as well. As for the
details, they were simple enough, from what I could gather. It
seems the electricity had gone out in their apartment. The
co-ops are expensive, as you know, but the building is old
and the condition of the plumbing and electrical circuits
leaves much to be desired, to say the least. At any rate, I understand that around ten o'clock Stephanie called the doorman on the intercom to complain about the electrical failure,
and asked him to have the fuses checked by the maintenance
crew. No one knows for sure what happened after that. Did
the burglar manage to force her lock, or did she let him in
thinking it was the superintendent? I don't expect we'll ever
know. At any rate, she did make an attempt to defend herself. She was found with a large kitchen knife in her hand.
The knife and her arms were covered with blood, so she did
manage to injure whoever it was before she was shot."

"A knife?" whispered Paula. She had a vision of Stephanie
attempting to ward off her attacker, trying to stave him off.
She was filled with pity. The vision seemed too frightening
and real.

"I didn't know she had a knife," she said.

"But yes. That is what cleared Nick of all suspicion. You
know how the police are, ready to believe the worst of anyone. The husband is the first to be suspected. A realistic ori-
entation, I must admit. But at any rate the laboratory tests
proved conclusively that the blood on the knife was not
Nick's. Neither was it Stephanie's. They never did find her

killer, as you know, and now it seems unlikely that they ever will."

"Probably not, not after two years," said Paula, trying to keep her voice at a normal pitch.

Two years ago was a long time, she thought, though Bibi's calm, practical voice made it seem as though it had happened only yesterday. She found herself wondering if it had been totally dark in the apartment, or if Stephanie had lit candles and confronted her attacker by their flickering light. It was odd that Stephanie's attempt at self-defense made her death seem both more terrible and more real. Perhaps because it made Stephanie herself seem more real? She had been superficial and selfish, Bibi had said, but she must also have been brave. Once again Paula felt that deep twist of pity deep down inside her.

"It happened a long time ago," Bibi was saying, "and we've taken measures to ensure that it won't happen again. Still . . . the associations remain, do they not? I love having you and Nick here in this building, and yet I've wondered at times whether it wouldn't be better for you both to find another place. I mentioned it to Nick when I first heard you were getting married, and he said he'd talk it over with you."

"He did ask me how I felt about it," Paula said slowly. "He also pointed out that another co-op would be hard to find in today's market."

"Ah yes, the businessman's instinct. It becomes overpowering at times, does it not? He's right, of course. Apartments are difficult to find. But I'm sure we can arrange something if you decide to move."

She noticed the quizzical look on Paula's face.

"I would help you, of course," she said almost brusquely. "We are friends, are we not? We must all help each other."

Paula hugged her impulsively and left with mixed emotions. She had known little about Stephanie or about her death, and now Bibi Marcovaldi had started to unlock that secret door. She hadn't realized how much the secrecy had bothered her until now, when she felt an immense feeling of relief. Yes. And yet she was bothered at the same time. Did she really want to fling that door wide open and see what lay behind it?

Both her mother and Bibi Marcovaldi seemed to feel that she and Nick were making a mistake by staying on in the apartment. She had dismissed her mother's reaction as a parent's natural concern, but it was more difficult to dismiss Bibi Marcovaldi's opinion. She was the most sophisticated woman Paula had ever met, and yet she had that curious quality that made it easy to accept her as a contemporary.

And there was something else. If, in spite of her logical reaction, she had been affected by her mother's power of suggestion, how would Bibi's hesitant opinion affect her now?

Later, after it was all over, Paula would wonder whether that conversation hadn't in fact sensitized her in some way, helped to set the stage for what would happen. Her restlessness had reached a peak, and she was beginning to feel the exploring tendrils of that same feeling of premonition she'd experienced the morning she had talked with Cindy. When she took the elevator to go down to her own floor, she barely acknowledged the elevator man's friendly comments and failed to see the look of concern he gave her as she stepped out.

She unlocked the door of the apartment and was chilled by the wind blowing through the open windows. Funny, she'd thought she'd left the windows closed. It would take hours to reheat the place. She put her notebooks down on the hallway table and looked into the living room. And then she stood stock-still.

"Easy," she told herself, the way she'd once talked to a skittish mare they'd owned when she was a child. "Just take it easy."

She felt the blood draining from her face and sensed the erratic drum of her pulse beat deep in her throat. "Easy," she repeated, and took a number of deep steadying breaths before walking across the room to close the windows.

40

6

———◆◆◆———

The living room looked as if it had been hit by a cyclone. Ashtrays lay smashed on the floor surrounded by the debris of cigarette butts and ashes. The shreds of torn newspapers littered the couch and the Oriental rug. And the vases of daffodils were shattered, the delicate pieces of china lying in shards in the midst of large puddles of water spreading across the floor.

The daffodils. Her heart pounded as she saw the daffodils. Someone—and there could be no doubt that it had been someone, and not just the wind—had systematically torn the delicate heads off the slim green stalks before scattering the golden petals around the room as though performing some ancient ceremony. A ceremony of malice.

Paula picked up one of the severed flowers and held it in her palm before letting it drop down to the floor again. She cleared the litter off one of the chairs and sat down to survey the damage. She didn't know how long she sat there. She felt light-headed, and had learned enough from her father to realize she was probably suffering from shock. When she felt steadier, she went into the kitchen and made herself a cup of tea strongly laced with honey. Natural sugar was the best remedy of all for shock, if she remembered correctly. She must have been right, because by the time she finished sipping her tea, she was functioning rationally once more.

She was surprised to find that her first reaction was one of relief. What she had believed to be her small lapses of forgetfulness had convinced her the accident had left her with a permanent damage that might prevent her from ever functioning again as a totally healthy human being. Now she knew she needn't have worried. It was just barely possible that she might have forgotten whether or not she'd

41

straightened up the apartment. It was even possible, though less likely, that she'd forgotten having an early-morning drink. But she knew with absolute certainty that she could never have caused the destruction that lay in front of her. The torn newspapers. The shattered ashtrays. The torn daffodils. Most of all, the daffodils.

I'm all right, she thought with so much gratitude and relief that she almost cried out loud: *I'm all right*.

Someone had been here, someone who had gone through the room in an excess of rage. She could sense the rage—that and the cold that had nothing to do with the chill spring temperature outside. Someone had been here. Someone who hated her, who resented her presence, who considered her an intruder.

She was seized by an answering sweep of anger. This was her home, hers and Nick's, and someone had managed to get in. She knew of other people whose houses had been broken into, whose things had been stolen. They had felt both outraged and defiled. And yet this was worse, because it had been such a senseless and malicious thing to do. An evil thing. Her rush of anger cleared her head more effectively than a whiff of pure oxygen.

She started to pick up the broken vases and ashtrays, and put the pieces in a plastic garbage bag. When she was done, she took a number of large sponges from the kitchen and wiped up the spilled water as best she could. While she was sweeping up the crushed flowers into a dustpan, her anger flared anew. She took a few steadying breaths before taking out the vacuum cleaner to go over the rug. When she was done, she put the vacuum cleaner away and examined the living room. She'd done a good job. Except for the large damp patches on the rug, all traces of the malicious vandalism were gone. The apartment was back to normal.

What should she do next?

As always when in doubt, she wondered what her parents or her older brothers would have done under the circumstances. They would have called the police, of course. Yes. But things were somewhat different in her case. This was New York, not Vermont. The cops in New York had better things to worry about than a few bunches of flowers torn off their stalks. Particularly when nothing had been taken. Partic-

42

ularly when the locks were virtually burglarproof, and no one could have gotten in unless they had a key.

Good grief, yes. Why hadn't she realized that right away? Whoever had come in must have had a key, and since the locks had been changed after Stephanie's death, there's only one way they could have gotten one: from Nick himself. Of course. She knew him well enough to realize he hadn't been celibate for the months before he met her. He had obviously given the key to his apartment to some former girlfriend and forgotten to get it back when they broke off. And she, whoever she was, had let herself in and torn up the living room in a jealous rage.

And if she had let herself in once, wasn't it possible, even likely, that she had been here before? She must have been the one who had left that glass and bottle of Scotch on the kitchen sink. The dirty ashtrays and newspapers littered in the living room.

There was one major problem with that explanation, thought Paula. She couldn't quite imagine any woman who would coolly let herself into a married man's apartment and risk being caught by his wife. Unless she wanted a direct confrontation.

Paula shivered. She suddenly realized how little she really knew about people's behavior. The most normal people sometimes did the craziest things, as witnessed by various accounts in the news; but it was one thing to read about something in the newspaper or see it on television, and another thing entirely to experience it in real life. How on earth would she tell Nick that one of his former girlfriends was irrational, perhaps even insane? For the first time in years she felt very young. But it still didn't occur to her to be afraid. Not then.

By the time Nick got home she had dinner ready and the table set. He threw his coat and briefcase on a chair and gave her a brief hug. He seemed exuberant.

"Guess what?" he said. His dark eyes were glowing, his face was ruddy from walking in the wind. "I think I'm about to pick up a new account. A big one. If it works out, the commission will more than pay for that vacation we've been planning. Europe? India? Israel and Egypt? You just name the place."

He turned around to hang his coat up in the closet.

"And how about you?" he said. "Did you have a good day, or is Bibi turning out to be a slave driver?"

She hesitated, and was glad his back was turned to her, so that he couldn't see her face. Now would be the time to tell him, and yet she couldn't bring herself to do it. Not just yet. She didn't want to dampen his deep glow of pleasure.

They chatted over dinner, but hard as she tried, she realized she wasn't acting like her usual self, so that it was inevitable that he should notice something was on her mind.

"Something is bothering you, isn't it?" he said after she had poured their coffee. He leaned back and lit a cigarette. "Out with it. Does it have anything to do with Cindy?"

She shook her head. She could put it off no longer, though it was a pity to spoil his joyous mood. She'd have to tell him now.

"Nick, have you ever had a mistress?"

"A mistress?" he echoed. He grinned at her. "Do people still have mistresses these days?"

"You know what I mean. Did you ever have a girlfriend who had a key to this apartment?"

"Why do you ask?"

"Because," she told him, "someone was here today."

She was looking directly at him as she said it, and was startled by his expression. His face tightened, and the look in his eyes became impersonal, objective.

"Are you accusing me of having another woman here in this apartment?" he said so softly that she realized she had made him angry. He was one of those men whose voice dropped to a whisper when he was furious.

"I think it must have been a woman," she said, holding her ground. "A man would have had no reason to—"

He didn't let her finish.

"I don't think I can go through all of this again," he said, and this time there was something else in his voice beside anger, a deep undertone of weariness, as if they were rehashing an argument they'd had time and time again. But this is our first argument, she thought. If it is an argument.

"I never mentioned it before," she said, bewildered.

He shook his head as though to clear it of unwelcome memories.

"Of course you haven't. I'm sorry," he said, but she could

44

tell that he was still annoyed. "You want to know if there were women in my life before I met you? Of course there were. I stopped seeing them after you and I got together."

"That isn't what I meant. Was there anyone you particularly liked?"

"I don't believe in sleeping with women I don't like."

"Please, Nick. I'm not asking just out of curiosity. I have to know if there's someone with a key to this place, someone who has a reason or thinks she has a reason to be jealous of me. To resent me. You see, when I came down from Bibi's today, the windows were wide open and the place was a mess. Newspapers and ashtrays flung all over the room. The flower vases shattered. And the daffodils you gave me were scattered all over the rug and the furniture."

Now his expression softened, and his face was once again the familiar one she knew. He reached for her hand.

"My poor baby," he said. "And you cleaned it up all by yourself. You should have waited until I came home to help you. The windows were open? It was very windy today. And I suspect this block is right in the middle of a wind tunnel."

"But it wasn't just the wind. And I did close the windows before going up to Bibi's."

"You just thought you closed them, love. Anyone could forget."

She had handled it all wrong, she realized dully. She should have left everything exactly as it was, and then he would have known someone *had* been here. He would have seen for himself that it wasn't the wind that had torn the heads of the daffodils off their stalks. He would have seen the cold, systematic malice. How would she ever get him to believe her now?

She tried once again.

"It wasn't the first time," she told him. "There were other times when I left the place as neat as a pin and came back to find it messy. Times when I put the newspapers and magazines away only to find them scattered all over. Someone has been coming here," she added almost desperately.

He was leaning toward her now, her hand in both of his. She saw love and concern in his eyes.

"When did all this start?"

She tried to think back, confused by his odd series of reactions.

"I think it was after we went to Bibi Marcovaldi's party," she said. "The night I first met Bibi."

"Right after you started working for her, in other words. I thought it might be good for you, keep you from getting bored, but perhaps it was too much for you."

"What does my job with Bibi have to do with it?"

"The doctors told you that you should take it easy for a few months. Give yourself a chance to recover. You've been overdoing things, that's all. You must rest," he added, trying to keep the concern out of his voice. "Perhaps you should make an appointment to see your doctor sometime this week."

She stared at him, appalled. During the past few weeks she had found herself wondering if she were still suffering from the aftereffects of the contusion she'd incurred in the accident, but this afternoon's incident had convinced her that all the odd little discrepancies that had bothered her until now were not the product of either forgetfulness or imagination. They were real. Nick, on the other hand, had the opposite reaction. And if Nick didn't believe her, no one else would either, she suddenly realized.

"Perhaps you should stop working with Bibi for the time being," Nick was saying.

"And why should I do that?" she asked him. Her eyes had widened with anger and her first tinge of fear. Her darkened pupils gave her hazel irises a bright golden glow. The look she gave him was direct and even.

"Because," he said patiently, "I want you to get well."

"But I *am* well," she said. How on earth did you convince people that your mind was functioning? You didn't. It was something you expected them to take on faith. "I'm positive that I'm perfectly well. And I'm equally positive someone's been here in this apartment."

He lit another cigarette and returned her even look. They could have been adversaries arguing a point of business across a conference table.

"Very well," he said. "Let's consider it logically. You claim that today's incident wasn't the first. I won't ask you why you never told me about the previous ones because I think I understand the reason, but let me ask you this. How often have you noticed signs of some—what shall I call it—disturbance in the apartment?"

"I'm not really sure. They were almost too small to notice just at first. Perhaps seven, eight times?"

"I see. So what you're saying is that someone, a woman, has been coming here— What makes you think it's a woman, by the way?"

"Because once there were traces of lipstick on a glass."

"That would make it a woman, I suppose. A woman or a transvestite, and I expect we can safely eliminate the latter. Very well. So, during the last three weeks, this mysterious woman has been letting herself in to use our apartment as a sort of public lounge, totally unmindful or uncaring of the fact you'd most likely call the police if you found her here. A peaceful visitor, for all that. Until today, that is, when she got out of the wrong side of bed and decided to vent her feelings by creating havoc in our living room."

"It sounds ridiculous when you put it like that."

"It sounds absurd when I put it like that. But if it will make you feel better to get the locks changed, by all means go ahead. You'll find the names of a couple of good locksmiths in the address book on the hall table."

Paula got up to do the dishes, and for once Nick didn't offer to help. They spent the evening in unaccustomed silence, glancing at each other occasionally as if thinking of ways to mend the breach. It had been their first argument, and neither of them was quite sure how to deal with it, unwilling to concede a point and at the same time miserable in the loneliness of their isolation from each other.

They were straightening up the living room before going to bed when Nick said, almost offhandedly, "There weren't that many women, you know. And only one to whom I gave a key. We were good friends—better friends than lovers, in fact. She returned my key when she met someone who really mattered to her."

He was picking up the morning and afternoon newspapers and Paula couldn't see his face.

"We were both lonely at the time, in need of someone. We just helped each other out for a short while, that's all," he added, and she heard the echo of pain and half-forgotten wounds in his voice.

He fell asleep the minute his head touched the pillow. She sat at the dressing table and watched him for a minute, his dark hair tousled and still damp from the shower, his lean face relaxed and younger-looking in sleep. It was the first time since they'd been married that he had gone to sleep before her, without making love. Her sense of loneliness grew in the silence of the room, though she tried to ignore it. She would have to be careful of what she discussed with him. Stephanie's death and its aftermath must have been a difficult time for him to go through, and she would have to be careful not to reopen old wounds. She didn't doubt for a minute that he'd been telling her the truth about his friend. "We just helped each other out for a short while, that's all." She was glad for him that there had been someone. It didn't sound like a passionate affair, but at least there'd been friendship and a degree of warmth.

But in that case, why had he overreacted when she'd asked him if someone else had the key to their apartment?

For she certainly hadn't imagined that bleak look in his eyes, the barely repressed anger of someone who's weary of going over the same subject again and again. And yet it was the first time she'd brought it up. Suddenly she remembered that Cindy had told her Stephanie used to be obsessively jealous. Had her questions brought back unwelcome memories? It seemed likely. That, combined with his concern for her health. She knew how often concern could be converted into anger.

And supposing he's right, she thought. Supposing that she had been overdoing things and that her ever-vivid imagination were further inflamed by her anxieties of the last few weeks. She might have well forgotten to close the windows, the wind might well have torn through the living room and wreaked the damage she'd found when she'd come in. It was certainly a more likely explanation than her belief in some anonymous, vengeful intruder.

She must get a better grip on things, she decided. She turned toward the mirror and looked critically at herself. Her eyes looked immense in the half-lit room, her face pale and dreamlike in its frame of thick, tangled dark hair. Why did

48

people always look different at night than they did during the daytime? Maybe because they feel more vulnerable when the sun goes down. Maybe the atavistic fear of the dark had persisted through the millennia to give the nights their excitement and that special haunting, bittersweet quality born from forgotten fear.

She picked up her hairbrush, and as she glanced down at it, she grew very still. There were a number of long golden hairs twisted among the bristles. They hadn't been there when she'd brushed her hair that morning. She stared at them for what seemed like a long time and then picked one out with tentative fingers. Its long length glimmered with the sheen of evil.

But that's silly, she thought, conscious of the fact that the late hour and her argument with Nick had combined to alter her awareness. There had to be a logical explanation. Cindy was blond. Had Cindy borrowed her hairbrush? But Cindy hadn't been here for three weeks, and besides her hair was short, layered in wavy strands around her head. But if not Cindy, who? Who could have used her hairbrush?

The woman who'd been here earlier today, of course. She knew it with a cold, fatalistic certainty. It hadn't been her imagination after all. She replaced the hairbrush in the top drawer of the dressing table and went into the bathroom to wash her hands.

She was very tired. She slipped into bed and snuggled against Nick for warmth. He stirred and put his arm around her, and almost before she knew it, she was asleep. Against all odds and expectations she slept well, the dreamless sleep of oblivion.

But it was that night that first blunted the fine edge of certainty that she'd always had. It was that night that first taught her you couldn't be sure of anything, not even your own senses. Because, had she been called to take an oath, she would have sworn that the door never opened that night, that no one entered the room. Further, she would have sworn that Nick never got out of bed. She had already discovered that some acute sense of affinity that bound them together woke her the minute he was awake, so that they seemed to function almost as one entity. She would have sworn he never left her side that night.

And yet, when she opened the drawer the next morning to show him the hairbrush with its entwined strands of hair, it was no longer where she'd placed it the evening before. She didn't use much makeup and the drawer was half empty. Nevertheless she had removed most of its contents before she realized that it was a waste of time. The hairbrush was gone.

7

The vast complex of New York Hospital sprawls in a number of buildings on the Upper East Side of the city, facing the river. It numbers among its staff some of the best medical brains in the country, and is reputed to offer unusually sophisticated, up-to-date care. In all other respects it's much like any other large city hospital. Its long corridors, redolent of the pungent smell of cleansers and a number of other less easily defined odors, sprawl endlessly past closed doors bearing mysterious technical names designed to strike fear in those unwary enough to ponder their meaning. Its gift shops are filled with those large odorless flowers and small trivia that visitors can buy as an offering to hospitalized relatives and friends before making their escape. The elevators are crowded by visitors and out-patients as well as members of the hospital staff, doctors, interns, nurses, and technicians.

It is quite easy to recognize the former from the latter. The visitors and out-patients have an uneasy air of claustrophobics about to be trapped in an encircling maze. They tread the corridors as nervously as cats in foreign territory. The hospital staff, on the other hand, tends to cluster about in small chattering groups, or to consult undecipherable notes on their inevitable clipboards, or to walk to their specific destinations with an urgency no less alarming for all that it's controlled.

Dr. Schneider's private office was located in the neurology section. An effort had been made to disguise its function as a medical office, and the results had been relatively successful. The bright rug softened the look of the functional furniture. The shelves behind the desk did not contain the usual tomes of medical literature, but had been filled by someone—Mrs. Schneider?—with an interesting collection of American Indian artifacts, and, paradoxically, a collection of books that seemed to include Homer as well as Shakespeare. Two well-used pipes were propped up on a large clean ashtray on the desk top. The wide uncurtained windows overlooked the river.

Dr. Schneider picked up one of the pipes and fingered its bowl.

"I never smoke during working hours," he explained, "but I like to have them around." He smiled at Paula. "A psychologist friend of mine said I use them as a security blanket," he added.

She smiled back at him. She found him remarkably easy to talk to, and wondered why she'd been so nervous about seeing him when she knew the anticipation was always worse than the actual experience.

"Well?" she said. "What do you think?"

He'd just finished checking her over in one of the examining rooms. She was well used to the procedure by now: the small bright light flashed into her eyes, the check of her reactions and reflexes. She was used to it, but she hated it still.

"What do you think?" she repeated.

"I think you're a perfectly healthy young woman," he said. "And I'm wondering why you came to see me now—two weeks before your scheduled appointment."

"Nick wanted me to," she answered simply. "I've been doing some work for one of our neighbors. He's afraid that it might be too much for me."

"Is there a special reason for his concern?" He noticed her hesitation and added gently, "You must tell me if something is bothering you. Didn't you know that's how we usually reach a diagnosis? We let the patient tell us exactly what's wrong with him."

"And then translate it into medical terms?"

He returned her smile. "Precisely," he said.

"I seem to have been absentminded recently," Paula told him, that slight note of hesitation still in her voice. "Nick is afraid I might be regressing, having a recurrence of those lapses of memory I had after the accident."

"I see. And do you share his concern?"

"No," she said with conviction. "That is, I did for a while, but I don't anymore. There's something else I wanted to ask

52

you, however. Is there anything about the injury I sustained that would cause me to hallucinate? To imagine something that isn't there?"

He put his pipe back into the ashtray and looked at her intently. His clear gray eyes looked almost translucent in the sunlight. His gaze was as direct and straightforward as hers.

"Would you tell me exactly what you think you imagined?"

"I'd rather not," she said.

"Very well," he said, not the least disconcerted. "We won't go into details until and unless you want to. But would you say that this thing or occurrence you might have imagined was extraordinary, beyond the realm of logic? Let me put it this way. Have you been seeing little green men from Mars or hearing voices come from the refrigerator?"

She shook her head, grateful for his faculty of expressing himself without falling into medical jargon.

"Nothing like that," she said. She thought of her torn dress, the mass of flower petals torn off their stalks, the golden hairs threaded through her hairbrush. The brush that wasn't there when she looked for it the next morning.

"Nothing like that," she repeated. "The things that happened are almost too insignificant to mention—except that it's hard to understand how or why they happened. Unless someone is making them happen, someone who dislikes me very much. That's paranoia, isn't it—imagining enemies lurking in each corner. Is there anything about my injury that could have induced paranoia?"

He smiled with genuine amusement, and she found his amusement more reassuring than anything he could have said or done.

"Paula, listen to me. As you know, we ran a battery of intelligence and psychological tests on you over two months ago. They show the profile of a very stable, intelligent young woman—a young woman with highly acute perceptions, I might add. There were no traces of any emotional trauma induced by your injury. As far as I was concerned, you'd made a full recovery, an opinion seconded by other members of our staff."

"And yet you didn't want me to go back to work for six months."

"True. We wanted you to have a chance to heal at your own pace. I'm sure I'm not telling you something you don't already know when I say that, while we've made tremendous advances during the last few years, we still know comparatively little about the functions of the brain and its reaction to trauma as well as to various stimuli. We do know that quite often the psychological effects of the trauma persist long after the patient has made a full physiological recovery. I wouldn't have been particularly surprised or concerned if you'd had small recurrences of your spells of amnesia. If you'd had trouble remembering the sequence of certain numbers, for instance, or been forgetful about names and dates. But as for absentmindedness . . ."

He noticed with pleasure that she seemed more relaxed now, those disconcertingly direct eyes of hers fixed on his with attention and an objective interest.

"Some of our most brilliant minds are noted for their absentmindedness," he said. "There was a professor in my college whose fits of absentmindedness were legendary. It was rumored that whenever he drove himself to campus, his wife used to pin a note to his jacket. 'Don't drive my husband home,' it said. 'He has his own car.' And he was considered one of the most brilliant men in the field. So I wouldn't worry about being absentminded on occasion. We all are. If you enjoy working for your neighbor, by all means continue to do so. As for your imagining something that isn't there—hallucinating, as you choose to call it—I would consider that highly unlikely. Unless you've been taking hallucinogenic drugs. Mescaline? Acid?"

"Good grief, no," said Paula, truly taken aback.

"Good girl. Mind you, they have a sound medical potential, but it's a potential that has yet to be explored. They're not toys to be played with. But as I said, every test we've taken would indicate that hallucinations are highly unlikely in your case. I don't want you to fall into the trap that so many people do: that of blaming everything that happens on a healed injury. If we experience something we don't understand, it's usually because we don't know the explanation, not because there is none. Take an extreme example. A man from the previous century would be certain he was hallucinating if he saw a jet sailing across the sky, wouldn't he?"

"Not to mention computers and penicillin and our flights to the moon."

"Just so. Take another example. Some of my more sedate colleagues like to attribute all sightings of unknown flying objects to what was once known as hysteria. I, on the other hand, prefer to think that, in some instances at least, what has been sighted are the results of secret scientific tests."

"Ours or another country's?"

"We can't be sure, can we? Wouldn't you like to tell me exactly what has troubled you?"

"Not now," said Paula. "But thank you. You've been very kind. And very helpful indeed."

She stood up and picked up her coat and shoulder bag. They shook hands. His handshake was firm and brief, yet personal at the same time. His straight brown hair had fallen across his forehead. Why, he's not much older than I am, she thought with surprise. She was at the door when he called to her.

"Paula?"

"Yes?"

"If you need to talk to me for any reason—any reason at all—just call, won't you? If I'm not here, just leave a message and I'll call back that same afternoon or evening."

His tone was casual, almost offhand, but it was offset by the earnest look in his eyes. Once again she was struck by his relative youth. She had met a number of physicians at her parents' house and had often been offended by their spurious platitudes, by their harsh cynicism combined with their almost unbearable pretensions. They had talked of their patients as of so many mechanical parts coming down the assembly line. But this man really seemed to care about people, and hadn't as yet bothered to protect himself with the impenetrable armor of brisk cynicism. He really cared. It was written all over that thin ascetic face and those clear, concerned eyes. And yet he dealt with some of the most frightening aspects of trauma. She wondered how he coped.

"Thank you," she said, feeling the words inadequate. She smiled at him briefly before leaving the room.

She felt almost light-headed as she walked to the elevator. She had needed reassurance and he had given it to her. He had, in effect, given her a clean bill of health, and at this particular time it was the best gift of all, Christmas and birthdays and anniversaries all rolled into one. *She was all right.* The incidents of the last few weeks paled into insignificance by comparison. She could handle them now. She had no doubt that someone had been playing malicious games intended to frighten her, but she felt certain that she'd be able to find out just who, and what, lay behind it.

Now that the question of her health was settled, the thing that bothered her most of all was not the identity of the malicious jokester as much as Nick's reaction to her questions. She was sure it was somehow tied in to his marriage to Stephanie, and the two days that had passed had only served to reinforce her conviction. She was treading on delicate ground, she realized. He was edgy about the subject. Overly so. She couldn't question him further without risking a reopening of the breach that still stood, barely healed, between them.

Whom could she talk to? Bibi Marcovaldi? Charlie Nabokov? Cindy?

She realized with a swift pang of guilt that she hadn't talked to Cindy for two weeks. When she reached the lobby, she glanced at her watch. Eleven o'clock. She was done much earlier than she had expected. She had told Bibi that she would be late coming in this afternoon, and though she could easily be there by one o'clock, she suddenly felt reluctant to go back to Dover House. She needed some time to herself. Some breathing room.

On an impulse she walked into the public phone booth and searched in her purse for a dime. Cindy answered on the second ring. She seemed delighted to hear Paula's voice. Yes, she was free to have lunch, she said. Yes, she could leave early. Would the Magic Pan be all right? It was always crowded at lunchtime, but the crepes were well worth it. She sounded happy and exuberant.

"I've been trying to reach you all morning," she told Paula. "I've got something to tell you."

They made an appointment for eleven-thirty. Paula checked her watch once again. It was five after eleven. She could walk to the Magic Pan easily, and she could use the exercise. When she walked out of the building, the spring sun felt warm against her face.

8

Paula turned west on Sixty-eighth Street and walked down Third Avenue toward the Magic Pan. With her mind still buoyed by Dr. Schneider's quiet, unobtrusive reassurance, she found keen pleasure in glancing at the windows of the antique shops and boutiques while she threaded her way through the well-dressed crowds. Even after two years in New York she was still amazed by the vast profusion of stores and the wares they offered, and the variety of people still went to her head.

She knew the city well enough by now to realize that there were vast areas that couldn't differ more from the opulent elegance of the Upper East Side, vast overcrowded areas where the question of life left the realm of metaphysics to enter the stark world of day-to-day survival. But these contrasts were the very essence of the fascination the city held for her. She had driven through parts of Harlem and the South Bronx and been appalled by the devastated streets, the desolate, abandoned buildings taken over by junkies and young, vicious street gangs, but she had also seen neighborhoods laboriously and lovingly rebuilt block by slow block, like fruitful gardens trained to grow in the wilderness.

When she had first moved to New York, a number of her friends in Vermont had been appalled, as if she were moving to a strange land well outside the boundaries of the nation. And yet it was this city, more than any other, that represented the principles the country claimed to stand for, the principles that her relatives swore to uphold while sheltering inside their neatly painted houses with their manicured lawns. It was this, more than any other city, that was the boiling caldron of democracy.

When she reached the Magic Pan, it was still half empty.

Paula was not surprised, as eleven-thirty is definitely not considered lunchtime in New York. She was surprised, however, to see Cindy waving to her vigorously from among the mirrors and potted plants surrounding her tiny table. Being on time for an appointment was not one of Cindy's many virtues.

"There you are," said Cindy. "And about time, too, or I would be in danger of becoming a solitary drinker. I'm on my second glass of wine."

She looked radiant. Her cheeks were deeply flushed, her hair glowed in the dimly lit room. Paula felt the deep sense of pleasure that Cindy's company invariably brought her. She threw her coat across the back of her chair and sat down.

"What's this about a second glass of wine?" she said. "I can tell by looking at you that you're not drinking to drown your sorrows."

Cindy cocked an eyebrow. She seemed her old self—amused, composed, totally in charge of herself and the situation. But what thread of excitement glowed through her like an exposed wire.

"Drinking to drown my sorrows? On the contrary. We're celebrating. This lunch is on me. Bill has finally asked his wife for a divorce."

"Has he really? And what did she say?"

"She agreed to it. And why wouldn't she? They've been at odds for a long time. Now all they have to do is decide how to divide the property. Toss a coin for the custody of the dog. That type of thing."

"Hey, that's really great," said Paula. "So it's all working out the way you wanted it to. Now that it's all settled you'll have to bring him over to dinner, the sooner the better. We're both dying to meet him, of course."

Cindy laughed and shrugged delicate shoulders.

"Not so fast," she said. "I don't know if it's superstition or something equally inane, but I don't want to bring him over until he's finally moved out of the house. Do you know we've never met any of each other's friends? I wonder if you'll like him."

"You sound nervous about it."

"I am. Isn't that ridiculous?"

"Is it? I don't think so. Don't you remember how nervous I

58

was about meeting Nick's friends? Not to mention how I felt about introducing him to my parents."

"You really had nothing to worry about. Not with Nick. He's the type of man who gets along with almost everyone. It's different with Bill."

"In what way?"

"He's introverted. Almost unfriendly at times," said Cindy. She picked up her wineglass and lifted it as if to shield herself from Paula's intent gaze. "He turns me on more than any other man I've known," she confided. Her voice dropped. "And yet . . . do you know he's never satisfied me in bed? It's odd, isn't it? Maybe it's because we've never had enough time together. There's only so much we can do in one hour. Or less. It will be different when we have the whole night to spend together," she added, but this time there was a lack of assurance in her voice, as if her confidence were ebbing in the course of the discussion.

Paula was taken aback and tried not to show it. She remembered her first night with Nick as clearly as if it had just happened. She'd never had any doubts after that night. Now, as she looked at Cindy, she realized the extent to which their roles had been reversed. Until now it had been Cindy who, warm and generous by nature, had used her sophistication to steer Paula away from the more obvious dangers of a single life in the city. Loneliness can drive people to do crazy things, Cindy used to say. But now she had fallen into the very trap she'd warned Paula against. Could she actually be considering spending a whole lifetime with a man who didn't satisfy her?

"Do you want to talk about it?" Paula suggested.

But Cindy was already regretting the impulse that had prompted her admission.

"There's no point in talking about it," she said, almost defiantly. "Not until we're living together. Until he moves out of his house. Until he leaves New Jersey. Can you imagine me in love with a hidebound suburbanite from New Jersey?" she added with a flash of sardonic amusement.

The waiter came to take their orders and they were silent for a while after he left. Paula was tempted to beg Cindy to reconsider, to think twice about the step she was taking. There were far too many women who had been convinced that their men would change after marriage only to let themselves in for a rude awakening. But if Bill had already asked his wife for a divorce. it was too late to say anything, Paula decided. She sat back in her chair and looked around the room.

The tables were beginning to fill up and the low murmur of conversation was punctuated by the higher notes of occasional laughter. The pungent aroma of spices mingled with the rich effluvia of perfumes and the acrid smell of cigarettes. A small candle flickered on each table. From the appearance of the room it would have been difficult to guess whether it was morning, afternoon, or night.

She looked across the table at Cindy and was aware of the silence stretching out between them. And that, too, was odd, because they had developed the gift of sitting together without speaking while remaining at ease, so that this sudden awareness of their silence was as shocking as a sudden confrontation with a stranger. She had meant to talk to Cindy about the things that had bothered her during the last few weeks, and yet now that they sat across the table from each other, she found it impossible to introduce the subject.

"Charlie Nabokov has been asking about you," she said instead.

"Has he indeed? He called to ask me for a date, you know."

"Did he? He didn't mention it."

"He wouldn't. He's such an odd duck. Not that he doesn't have his own appeal, there's something subtly sensual underneath that sardonic manner of his. And then there's his money, of course—or rather, not the money itself as much as the self-confidence and arrogance it seems to shed on those who have it—have you ever noticed? Yet he's an odd duck nevertheless. I suspect that cynicism he affects is just a poor disguise for an all too real bitterness. Though I don't see what on earth he's got to be bitter about. He and Nick have known each other for a long time, haven't they?"

"Since high school. I think that Charlie considers Nick to be his best friend. He must drop by at least twice a week."

"Does he?" Cindy asked. "And yet, when he speaks of Nick, it's almost with resentment, as if he envied him—and not without some reason, when it comes right down to it.

When they were in school, it was Nick who was the star of the tennis team and one of the leading lights of the Debating Club. It was Nick who had his choice of all the prettiest girls. And later on, in college, it was Nick who graduated *summa cum laude*. He was very popular, it seems, while Charlie, on the other hand, was always hovering somewhere in the background, just barely scraping by. He did get on the college paper, but only because he was willing to do all the monotonous work that no one else wanted to touch with a ten-foot pole."

"Did Charlie tell you all this?"

"He did, in some detail. I ran into him when I left the office last week, and we stopped for a couple of drinks before I went home. Come to think of it, I'm not sure the encounter was totally accidental. He knows where I work and what time I leave."

"It docs sound like he was on the lookout for you."

"It does, doesn't it? Anyway, he seemed to take an almost masochistic pleasure in running himself down while recounting Nick's virtues, but in such a way that he managed to make them sound like so many vices. You know, damning him with faint praise. And yet you say he drops by all the time. How do you feel about it?"

Paula hesitated. Her feelings about Charlie Nabokov were ambivalent, and she wasn't willing to explore them at this point.

"I'm not sure," she admitted. "He can be amusing when he wants to be, yet there are times when his unexpected visits *are* annoying. I don't get to spend that much time alone with Nick as it is, and it's disconcerting to have Charlie ringing the doorbell just when we'd planned on a quiet evening at home."

"You'd better watch it or you'll fall into the same relationship Charlie had with Nick and Stephanie while she was still alive. The three of them went everywhere together, from what he said. He made them sound like the Three Musketeers. And yet his comments about Stephanie were negative, if not downright malicious. I told you he said she was obsessively jealous. He also referred to her as a neurotic refugee from a plastic ghetto and a would-be prima donna. Odd, isn't it? They were supposed to be friends, after all."

Paula laid down her fork and looked up at Cindy. All her senses had sprung wide awake, as if she had suddenly heard the unexpected knell of an alarm.

"Wait a minute," she said. "What exactly did he mean when he said she was obsessively jealous? I've been wondering about that. Did he bother to explain?"

Cindy brushed a strand of gleaming hair off an elegant cheekbone.

"Oh, I don't know," she said dismissively. "Some ridiculous nonsense. She was convinced, for instance, that Nick was bringing one of his girlfriends up to the apartment. She claimed she saw her on at least one occasion, and that she was always finding her clothes strewn all over the room. She was neurotic, obviously. What married man in his right mind would bring his girlfriend home? No way. Take it from me, I've become an expert on these matters."

She broke off, looked at Paula, and frowned.

"What's the matter?" she said. "You look as white as a sheet. Does it bother you that much to hear about Stephanie?"

Paula shook her head. She seldom if ever smoked, but now she reached for Cindy's pack of cigarettes, shook one out, and lit it. She inhaled the fumes deeply into her lungs. She said, "Supposing I told you that I too have seen signs of another woman in the apartment?"

"I'd say you were joking, of course."

"I assure you I've never been more serious in my whole life."

Cindy started to say something, thought better of it, and stared at Paula as if she'd never seen her before. And why not? thought Paula. She knew how improbable and farfetched it sounded, how unlikely it was that anyone would believe her. Hadn't she herself doubted the evidence of her own senses to the extent of running off to the doctor's for a checkup?

"Just exactly what did you see?" said Cindy, torn between curiosity and disbelief.

"Nothing I can prove," Paula said shortly. "I won't go into all the details now, but I'll tell you something that happened two days ago. Someone used my hairbrush. I found her hair woven through the bristles."

THE INTRUDER

"Is that all?" said Cindy, who had obviously been expecting something more sensational.

"Not quite," said Paula. "I put the brush away in a drawer, but next morning, when I looked for it, it was gone."

"For heaven's sake," said Cindy. "You probably forgot where you put it. As for someone else using it, why, someone is always asking me if they can borrow my hairbrush or comb. One of your visitors must have used it. It's that simple. There, we've solved that mystery. What next, Dr. Watson?"

"It's not quite that simple. You see, it's been a busy time for Nick and me, and we've had no company since you were there last. Except for Charlie Nabokov, and he hardly counts. What hair he has left is light brown, not blond."

"In that case, if I was your last visitor, then I must have been the one to use the brush. What difference does it make, anyway?"

"It wasn't your hair. I know that for a fact, because I wash the brush at least once a week, and besides, it was much longer than yours. And it's important because someone—a woman—must have been in the apartment while I was out."

"Aren't you basing a lot on some slender evidence indeed? I'm sure there's a perfectly logical explanation if we could only think of it. What does Nick say about it?"

"I didn't tell him," Paula admitted.

"Good Lord, why not?"

"Because I wanted to show him the brush when I told him. But, as I said, by the time I looked for it, it was gone."

Some of her tension must have communicated itself to Cindy, who suddenly looked uncertain.

"It'll probably turn up as you're cleaning house," she said.

"Maybe," said Paula. "At any rate I had the locks changed yesterday, so if anyone was there they'll have a hard time getting back in."

She wished she could feel as secure as she sounded. The locksmith had assured her that the new locks were the best on the market. Burglarproof, he'd said, and judging by their cost, they should be good enough to keep out a crowd armed with battering rams. And yet Paula had the irrational feeling that, sooner or later, whoever had been there would be back. And would find a way of getting in, new locks or not.

9

Once, when out tramping through the woods with her brothers, she had become separated from them and had gotten lost. She was about nine or ten at that time, she remembered, and she had followed the stream that ran through the woods to rush into a ravine deep in the valley. She had walked along happily, watching the cold spring water tumbling over the rocks, humming tunelessly to herself while she picked wild flowers that grew along the bank. The cool air smelled of fir and pungent pine, the late-afternoon sun felt warm against her back. She lay down at the edge of the stream to gaze down into the water. She slept.

When she woke up, night had fallen and the afternoon breeze had changed to a brisk wind. She looked up and saw the dark clouds flying across the face of the moon as the waving branches of the trees around her twisted and bent into fantastic shapes—as menacing as prehistoric monsters reaching wild limbs up to an ancient sky. For one short moment she had felt sheer horror.

Where were her brothers? They must have looked for her and, failing to find her, must have gone home to pick up some flashlights before coming back. She knew she could easily find her way home by following the stream, but she also knew that it would be a treacherous process at night. The sides of the ravine had been eroding for years and the ground beside it was marshy, the land pitted with potholes through which one could hear water gurgling deep below.

Besides, if she tried to go that way, she would miss her brothers, who were bound to come back looking for her. To meet up with them she'd have to find the narrow but well-worn path they had used to come up here in the first place, she thought, edging away from the ravine. The trees looming around her screened out the light of the gibbous moon, and it was so dark on the ground below that she couldn't make out the bushes and thorny brambles that tore at her clothes and hair. It took her half an hour to realize she was lost. The wind howled around her. For the first time in her life she felt the thin edge of that sensation older civilizations had defined as panic: the feeling of alien eyes peering at her from behind each tree, the inward pressure of the forest closing around her like a cage from which there'd be no escape.

Run, something inside her said, *run*, and the command was so strong that she almost gave way to the urge to rush, unseeing, through the windswept night.

But something hardy and tenacious in her had prevailed. If she went running around in circles, her brothers would think her foolish, a dumb, silly girl, and—worse yet—would probably refuse to take her along on future jaunts. Always hold your own, they had told her. She couldn't, she wouldn't let them down. And so she sat in the relative shelter of a massive tree, waiting, and when her father and her brothers found her, she looked at them with immense eyes blinded by their flashlights, like a deer riveted by the lights of a car. But she hadn't cried. When her father swung her up in his powerful arms, she wound her own arms around his neck as if she would never let go, but that had been all right. She had sensed their approval as they made their way back home.

Now she wondered what had made her think of that incident after all these years. Perhaps it was because she was facing another crisis, a different one from that one in childhood, to be sure—more subtle and insidious at the same time, but no less frightening for being much less tangible. She wondered if she still had the tenacity she'd had as a child. For, in spite of all the do-gooders who were forever deploring the fearsome matters depicted on television and the comic books, children thrived on the frisson of danger, and always had. Mother Goose was just one example of one of the bloodiest collection of tales in Western civilization.

No, it was only after one grew up that one realized the full potential of danger. Knowledge and experience both combined to bring a full realization of human vulnerability.

She was sitting in Bibi Marcovaldi's cozy little study, opening letters with the slender knife Bibi used as a letter opener.

The handle was delicately carved and inlaid with a number of amber-colored stones. It was the type of knife that in detective novels was found embedded in the body, cunningly inserted to penetrate the heart, as if the murderer had taken extensive studies in anatomy. What nonsense, thought Paula. Stephanie had used a knife on her attacker, and a large knife at that, but it had done little to help her. She had been shot twice, Bibi had said. A knife was of very little use against a gun.

She shook herself impatiently. She was allowing herself to become morbid, and it would never do. She would have to remain calm and pragmatic if she were to deal competently with her own fear.

Fear? Yes, she was afraid, she finally admitted to herself. Afraid of going back to her own apartment and finding traces of someone else's presence. As Stephanie once had. It was curious that Stephanie's experience, whether real or imagined, had evidently paralleled hers. She, too, had noticed an intruder—had seen her, in fact, if Charlie Nabokov could be believed—and had immediately jumped to the simplest explanation: accusing Nick of having his girlfriend over. Ridiculous, of course. But if that wasn't the explanation, what was it?

Paula continued to sort the mail, so absorbed in her own thoughts that she didn't hear the door opening behind her or Teresa's surprisingly soft footsteps entering the room. She looked up, startled, to see Teresa's massive bulk looming at her elbow.

"Would you like a cup of tea, Miss Paula?" Teresa asked her brusquely. "Or a cup of hot chocolate?" Her heavy features were as impassive as ever, but there was warmth in the deeply set dark eyes. She had developed a soft spot for Paula.

"No, thanks, Teresa," Paula said. "I'm almost done for today. I'll be leaving soon."

How old was Teresa? she wondered. She must be at least Bibi's age if not older, and yet she looked as sturdy and persevering as a rock. She would easily survive Bibi—she would, in fact, consider it her duty to do so.

"The countess is still lying down. She's feeling tired today, I am afraid. She wondered if you would stop to see her before leaving?"

"Of course, Teresa. And thanks."

And then Teresa did a surprising thing. One of her heavy, work-worn hands reached out, hovered briefly in the air, and came down to rest on Paula's shoulder. The contact was so brief it might have been imagined. As though embarrassed by her gesture of affection, Teresa turned abruptly on her heel and quickly left the room. Paula stared after her. What had that been all about? Were her anxieties so transparent to prompt Teresa to pet her like a small child?

She looked at her watch. It was five o'clock. She put the letter opener down and placed the sorted mail in its respective folders. She would tackle it tomorrow. She went into the bathroom to wash her hands and brush her hair before going to Bibi's room.

Bibi was sitting up in the middle of her vast bed, her back propped up with pillows, an open book by her side.

"You must forgive my self-indulgence, my dear," she said the minute Paula came in. "I missed having tea together with you, but I did feel the need for some rest."

"Teresa said you felt tired," said Paula, careful to keep all traces of sympathy or concern out of her voice. Bibi was not the woman to appreciate either sympathy or concern about her health.

"Teresa fusses so," Bibi said, and smiled. "Actually, I'm resting up for events to come. I had a call from the Italian embassy this afternoon. There are some people coming over tomorrow, people who plan to lobby for more liberal automobile import laws, and the ambassador thought I might want to be there to greet them. Which was his subtle way of saying that, since my family owns controlling interest in one of the Italian sports-car corporations, the least I can do is to be on hand and give them whatever assistance I can. So I'll be flying to Washington, D.C., in the morning."

"How long will you be gone?" asked Paula.

She was taken aback by her sensation of loss. She had become fonder of this strange old woman than she had realized until now.

"No longer than a week. Will you carry on while I'm gone? I'll leave you a number where I can be reached if anything urgent should come up. Incidentally, you know that new art gallery on Park, the one that Bergstein just opened.

67

He's having a private showing there this weekend. I wonder if you'd like to go in my place. I should be interested in your reaction."

"But I don't know anything about art," Paula protested.

"Neither do ninety percent of the people who go to these things, and yet they are the ones who make or break an artist. If you should go, be sure to give Nat Bergstein my best regards. I want him to know that he can rely on my support."

They chatted idly for a few minutes before Paula turned around to leave. She was almost at the door when Bibi called to her.

"Paula."

"Yes?"

"You'll be sure to call me if you need me for anything, won't you?"

"Of course," said Paula.

When she went down to her own apartment, the keys turned easily in the new locks. She opened the door and went inside. The sun was beginning to set and the living room was dim in that crepuscular light that precedes nightfall. With total disregard for their next electric bill she walked around the apartment and turned on all the lights.

Each room looked exactly the way that she had left it. Of course. What else had she expected. The locksmith had vouched for the locks. No one but a ghost could get in through a locked door, and in spite of all the eerie stories her grandmother had been so fond of telling, Paula had never believed in ghosts.

Her grandmother, on the other hand, had not only believed in them, she had seen them and heard them time and time again. She had talked to her husband until the day of her death, which was disconcerting, to say the least, as he had preceded her to the grave by some twenty years. Her mother, for that matter, must share some of the same superstitions, or else why would she be so upset about Paula living in a place where someone had been murdered? It was almost as though she expected Stephanie to rise up out of her bloody grave to seek revenge.

Poor mother, thought Paula. It's just as well she didn't know the full story of what had been happening, or she'd be down as quick as a wink—or as quickly as a bus could bring her from Rutland—and Paula would have to explain that she was perfectly safe, point out that there were new locks on the door, a hallman downstairs to screen all visitors, an intercom connected to the lobby that she could use whenever she needed to summon one of the staff. The *staff*. She stood stock-still. That was it, of course. There was the explanation staring her right in the face. She'd been an idiot not to have seen it before.

There were more than a dozen people on the staff of Dover House, from the ancient doorman and elevator man down to the younger crew that took care of the general maintenance. Any one of them would have access to the keys that hung on a pegboard in the superintendent's office. The office was kept locked as a rule, but how difficult would it be to slip a couple of keys off the hook when his back was turned, and return them after making a duplicate set?

Not for any nefarious purpose, to be sure. Nothing had been taken, after all. Not for the purposes of burglary or theft, but merely to use as a hideout when the tenants were gone. A place to sit and read the paper, a place to have a drink or smoke a quick joint away from the superintendent's stern and suspicious eyes. *A place to bring a girl to*. It would be risky. But whoever it was had minimized the risk by checking the habits of the tenants before taking the chance.

It explained everything. The dirty ashtrays, the lipstick on the glass, the disarranged newspapers. Even the torn flowers. There must have been an argument, of course. How long could they have had to spend together? One hour, two at the most. She could imagine that unknown girl flying into a sudden rage, wreaking her destruction before she and the man stared at each other, appalled, realizing that there would be no time to clean up the mess, opening the windows in hope that it would be blamed on the strong eastern wind.

She was stirred by a rush of pity for the unknown girl who was quite probably close to her in age, and had no place to meet her lover except in the clandestine anonymity of other people's apartments. And then her pity for the girl faded to be replaced by an intense feeling of relief.

So that was that, she thought, heading for the bathroom. She wouldn't tell the superintendent that she'd had new keys made, and if anyone tried to let themselves in with the old ones, they'd be in for a surprise. She let herself soak in the tub until the water turned lukewarm before drying herself briskly and then going over to her closet to deliberate on what to wear tonight. It had to be something special, something just for Nick. And then she would take the shrimp out of the freezer and fix it the way he liked, and after dinner they would linger at the table to talk the way they used to. As if the last few days had never happened.

She changed into a long skirt and a tight, high-necked sweater before going into the dining room to set the table. Candles, flowers, wineglasses. Tonight would be a good night to sample that white wine chilling in the refrigerator.

She was in the kitchen making the salad when she heard the harsh shrill of the bell. She paused. It wasn't Nick, she knew. He never rang the bell. Damn. She didn't want any company right now. The harsh peal was repeated. We'll have to get a new doorbell, she thought, walking to the front door.

"Who is it?" she said.

"It's me, princess," Charlie Nabokov's voice sang from outside. "May I come in? It's lonely out here."

She sighed. And then she unlocked the door and stepped aside to let him in.

10

Charlie Nabokov must have come in from outside without first stopping at his own apartment, because he was still wearing an overcoat that he hugged around himself when he stepped into the room, as though bravely enduring the fury of the elements. His coat seemed much too large for him, and so did most of his other clothes for that matter, as though he had bought them off the rack without first bothering to try them on. It was a deceptive impression. His tailor was one of the best ones in town, and it was the way he carried himself that made everything he wore seem to hang baggily around his thin frame. His wiry shoulders were stooped, his neck angled forward, his head had a nervous mannerism of turning from side to side as though he were constantly on the watch for what was happening around him.

"Shall I take your coat?" Paula suggested, and waited for his reply. He might have just stopped by to give her a message for Nick. If he gave her his coat, on the other hand, it meant he planned on staying, and she could forget the quiet romantic evening she had planned.

He looked at her dubiously before leaning forward to kiss her on the cheek.

"Really? I expect it's warm in here, but I'm absolutely chilled. I manage to get through the winters without a problem, but I *always* get chilled in the spring. Do you suppose it's something in the genes? My mother was thin-blooded."

He unbuttoned his coat and gave it to her with a play of reluctance, as though he were parting with his security blanket. Well, that took care of the evening. And why did he always affect concern for his health? For all his slightly dissipated air he was as healthy if not healthier than most. He went jogging with Nick three or four times a week and they

71

ran at least five miles at a stretch. Not bad for a man with his pretensions to delicacy.

"I don't know why I continue living in New York," he said, his thin shoulders twitching. "The air is polluted, the weather foul, the prices impossible. It's getting difficult to get the barest of amenities."

"Have you ever considered living someplace else? You're a free-lance writer. You're not tied down to a specific job. You could live anywhere—someplace better for your health, perhaps."

Either he missed her irony or he chose to ignore it.

"Darling Paula, always so considerate and sweet. Of course I've thought of living someplace else. But *where else* is there?"

He wandered nervously around the living room before stopping at the bar to pour himself a glass of Scotch. He took it without ice, in the English style.

"Will you join me?" he asked, as if he were the host and she the visitor.

"Not right now," she said, repressing her annoyance. "I'm in the middle of fixing dinner. Do you want to join me in the kitchen?"

She went back to the sink and he sat down at the kitchen table, his long legs stretched out like forgotten stilts. Her back was turned to him, but she was aware that he was studying her intently.

"You've lost weight, haven't you?" he said unexpectedly. "It's most becoming, you know. Six months ago, when I first met you, you looked very pretty, very fresh, like a girl straight out from the country." He made it sound as though there were something vaguely deplorable about fresh country prettiness. "But now there's a new tension in your face. It highlights your features, gives them definition."

There was something both questioning and seductive in his tone. For all his peculiarities he was a successful ladies' man, Nick had told her, and she thought she could understand the reason for his success. There was a feminine streak in him that would help him relate to women and see them the way that they saw themselves—a powerful asset for any man to have.

Paula didn't answer him. Her initial ambivalence about

him resurged so that, mixed with her irritation and dislike, she also felt aware of his appeal, knew that if she turned around to face him she would be met by his sardonic, intent gaze, a look of intimacy she would find disconcerting. She continued shredding the lettuce. The silence between them grew until it became redolent with uneasy undertones. He was the first to break it.

"I see you're dressed for the evening," he said. "Do you and Nick have special plans for tonight?"

We do, she wanted to tell him. I want to spend an undisturbed evening with my husband, to have a quiet dinner and sit chatting around the fireplace. Alone.

"Not really," she said. "I expect we'll have dinner and watch some television. Nick has been working hard these last few weeks," she explained.

"That's great," said Charlie. "Because I have a surprise for you and Nick."

"A surprise? Really."

"Yes. I managed to get tickets for the middleweight championships. I had to scour the town for them, you have absolutely no idea how difficult it is to get tickets at the last minute. Impossible, in fact, unless you know the right people. But here I am, tickets in hand. You know how crazy Nick is about boxing."

Paula hadn't known. There was probably a lot she still didn't know about Nick. They'd met less than a year ago, after all, while Charlie had known him since they were in prep school. It was Charlie who knew Nick inside out. The realization put her at a disadvantage.

"I'm sure Nick will be delighted to go with you," she said.

"Nick? But I got tickets for all three of us. Surely you didn't think I planned to leave you at home?"

She turned to look at him, taken aback by the implied arrogance of his statement. He hadn't planned to leave her at home, he'd said with all the self-assurance of a puppet master. He was smiling at her easily, but she didn't miss the glint of something conspiratorial in his eyes, the man-to-woman look with which he was examining her. He was used to going out with Nick and Stephanie, she remembered suddenly. The Three Musketeers, Cindy had called them. Well, she wouldn't become part of such a threesome. She suspected that once the precedent was set, it would be hard to break.

"Count me out," she said shortly. "I don't feel like going out this evening." And then, because she was too young and inexperienced to be rude without feeling guilty about it, she found herself asking him to stay for dinner.

As Charlie had predicted, Nick was exuberant at the prospect of going to the match. He also felt badly about leaving Paula at home by herself and said so.

"Come on, give it a try," he said, linking his arms loosely around her. "Don't you like boxing?"

"I've never been to a boxing match," she admitted.

"All the more reason to see this one. Besides, you don't want that third ticket to go to waste, do you?"

"You can ask one of the fellows in the building to go along with you."

"Hmm," he said, and kissed her. "So we could. But I'd much rather have you."

She was beginning to think she might go after all and was about to tell him that she'd changed her mind when she looked up and caught Charlie's half-mocking glance over Nick's shoulder. She shook her head and moved away from Nick's encircling arms.

"Not tonight," she told him. "I did a fair amount of running around today and I thought I'd just spend the evening curled up with a book."

Since it was already getting late, they didn't have their usual glass of wine before dinner but sat right down at the table, and within half an hour the men had their coats on and were ready to leave. Nick kissed her good-bye.

"Perhaps the next time?" Charlie asked her softly.

"Perhaps," she said.

And then they were gone and she locked the door behind them. She washed the dishes and put them in the drain to dry and then walked to the living room. It was a while since she'd spent the evening by herself and the apartment seemed very quiet. Too quiet, in fact.

It had been foolish of her not to go with Nick and Charlie merely to prove a point, to establish the measure of privacy she wanted in her marriage. Charlie was far from unique, she knew. There were any number of single men and women who attached themselves to a married couple in a symbiotic relationship that, once formed, was difficult to break. Was it unfair of her to exclude Charlie from the companionship he so obviously needed? Nonsense, she thought rebelliously. She had married Nick, not his friends.

She picked up the newspaper and had just turned to the television listings when the bedroom door slammed shut. The sudden noise made her jump. She waited for a minute before getting up to check, surprised at her own reluctance. The wind had picked up and the window curtains were blowing into the room like pale wavering ghosts in a high-school play. She closed the windows, gave the room a quick look, and closed the bedroom door before going back to the living room.

Her earlier sense of relief was ebbing fast. The explanation that had seemed so plausible before dinner seemed unlikely now, if not downright farfetched. Would one of the porters or another member of the staff really bring his girl up to the apartment, sit around, have a few drinks, quarrel, and make love? Once, perhaps, if they were desperate enough. But not again and again. The stress would be too great. And now she thought of it, she knew there was another reason why it couldn't have been any of the building staff, a reason she couldn't quite put her finger on, though it was hovering at the edge of her subconscious. What was it? Never mind, it would come to her sooner or later.

She was determined to have a pleasant evening, to prove to herself that she was still able to enjoy her own company. She knelt by the grate to build a fire and then sat back on her heels, watching the crackling flames with satisfaction. When she was sure the fire had taken, she went into the kitchen to reheat some coffee, and took the steaming mug out into the living room.

There was nothing she cared to watch on television, but there certainly was no lack of reading matter in the apartment. It had been a while since she'd had the almost sensuous pleasure of totally losing herself in a book, of becoming involved in the characters and the plot so that the dimensions of her own life were expanded to include theirs.

She went over to the bookcase lining one wall. Her own books were still in Vermont, but Nick's reading tastes were nothing if not catholic and the collection was considerable. Ponderous-looking books on history and economics were crowded cheek to jowl with both light and serious fiction, classics and reference material. Science-fiction and detective novels stood unabashed next to staid tomes of Standard and Poor's. One of these days she'd organize the shelves into some type of order, she decided.

She browsed contentedly for what seemed like a long time, pulling books out and putting them back, trying to find something that would suit her mood. She had selected two novels and was looking for a third one when she found the notebook. She almost didn't notice it at first. Its imitation-leather binding and stenciled gold edging made it inconspicuous among some volumes of Dickens', and the only thing that attracted her attention was the lack of any title on the cover.

She opened it curiously. It was a notebook of the type commonly sold in stationary stores, and approximately one-third of the pages had been filled with a fine, slightly faded writing. Some of the entries were haphazardly dated, others bore neither preface nor date.

She looked at the first page. She read:

Monday. Had my hair done this morning. Liked the new rinse, but the new girl is all thumbs and I complained to D. while he was brushing out my hair. Later on I ran into Buddy and he actually blushed. It's all turning out too terribly amusing.

Paula closed the notebook and stood very still. A million thoughts whirled through her head like autumn leaves gone haywire, but one was foremost in her mind, as stark and concrete as a denuded tree. It was quite obvious the notebook was a diary. And she had no doubt that it had belonged to Stephanie.

11

Later, after it was all over, Paula would wonder whether it would all have turned out differently had she destroyed the diary unread, instead of going through it like a modern-day Pandora impelled by curiosity to explore a new, dangerous toy. She was realistic enough to doubt it. Whatever evils were contained in that old notebook had already been unleashed, and were even now working their slow damage with the viciousness of a virus eating away at the very tissue of their lives.

Besides, if hunger is the strongest human motivation and love the next, then curiosity must play a close third. She went over to the couch and curled up in her favorite position, the diary in her hands. No argument in the world would have been convincing enough to make her replace the diary at that point. And yet she held it uneasily, as if it might explode at any minute.

Finally she opened it again. The next entry read:

> Dinner for six tonight. Beastly nuisance. I really must convince Nick that we need a maid. Or else have Daddy talk to him. I really can't see spending all my afternoons in the kitchen like some little suburban housewife.

The next few pages told of cocktail parties, dinners, luncheon dates, a recital, interspersed with lively, sardonic comments about her companions of the previous day. A picture of Stephanie started to emerge, and Paula could imagine her, laughing and golden, as she rushed from one appointment to the other or spent long hours gossiping on the phone.

Laughing and golden and more than slightly spoiled,

thought Paula. But then she had little basis for comparison. After all, what did she know of the world of the very rich? Suddenly her eyes caught another reference to Nick.

Had another row with Nick last night, if you can call it a row. He's so drearily self-contained I could scream. Should I tell him about Buddy? That would wipe that concerned, understanding look off his face. Once and for all. At least L. had some life in him.

Who was L.? Paula wondered. And who was Buddy, for that matter? It sounded as though he'd been more than a casual friend. She skimmed past a lengthy and somewhat incoherent account of another fight with the hairdresser and found Buddy mentioned again on the next page.

Nick told me we might be able to afford a maid after all and I told him I no longer wanted one. He looked surprised. Poor Nick. For an intelligent man, he's so stupid at times. But I don't need a maid snooping around at this point, not when things are becoming amusing. Called Buddy just now and made an appointment for this afternoon. He sounded almost too pleased. Hope he doesn't turn out to be a bore after all.

So it sounded as though Stephanie and Buddy *had* been having an affair, though the next day's entry made no mention of the encounter, because it had either too little or too much significance. Had Nick ever known? Paula hoped that he hadn't, for his sake. He wouldn't learn from her, that was for sure. It was weird, this business of reading a dead woman's secrets—secrets that should never have been written down in the first place. Why on earth did people insist on keeping diaries?

The fire was dying down and it seemed chilly in the room. Paula put two more logs in the grate and then went to the closet to fetch a blanket. She sat down on the floor next to the fireplace and wrapped the blanket around herself, Indian fashion, before picking up the diary once again. She was no

longer curious about it. On the contrary, it filled her with re-
pugnance, which she forced herself to ignore. According to
Cindy, Stephanie's experiences had paralleled hers, and if an
answer were to be found at all, it might be here.

Oddly enough, the next entries in the diary seemed to reflect her mood. The writing, which had until now been casual
and offhand, seemed to pick up a darker, somber tone. She
imagined Stephanie sitting cross-legged on the other side of
the fireplace, staring into the flames while she talked on, a
suddenly familiar confidante.

> Had lunch with Mummy earlier. I don't know why.
> She was full of questions and dumb advice, as
> usual. And yet she knows me—I'm afraid I'm my
> mother's daughter in more ways than one. God,
> how I hate the thought.

Paula skimmed the pages, anxious to be done with it and
eager to rid herself of the image of the dead woman who—
without invitation or welcome—seemed to be pervading the
room. The notebook had been used as an engagement book
as much as a diary, and the terse entries seemed to go on and
on, evoking a world she had little wish to know. And then
she read a passage that riveted her attention. She read it
through twice, and then once again.

> Odd thing happened last night. Woke up feeling ab-
> solutely parched—must have been the ham we had
> for dinner—and went into the kitchen for a glass of
> water. The whole kitchen looked different—gave
> me the willies—the glasses neatly arranged by size
> like some damned store display. Must have been
> dreaming on my feet, though, because this morning
> the cabinets looked the same as ever. Messy, to say
> the least.

Odd, Stephanie had written. Odd indeed, thought Paula,
reading that slightly faded handwriting two years later. This
was the first mention Stephanie had made of a subtle change
in the apartment, but in her case the change had manifested

itself in cleanliness and neatness, however temporary. "Must have been dreaming on my feet," Stephanie had said.

Maybe they'd both been dreaming, giving in to a deplorable weakness for imagination. But surely that was carrying coincidence a little bit too far?

The wind rattled the windows, and strangeness filtered into the room from the darkness outside. Paula tossed the blanket to the floor and got up to draw the drapes before returning to her place by the fire. She threw another log on, and the flames hissed and leaped. Their crackle was absurdly loud in the deep silence.

She picked up the diary and read on, her awareness sharpened, her attention focused on that faded writing with an intensity she knew would engrave it forever in her mind.

There were more notes about social engagements, a description of a fur coat she'd bought, sardonic comments about Nick's reaction. There were also frequent references to Buddy. Since most of the entries weren't dated, it was difficult to tell how often she'd been seeing him, though it appeared that it must have been at least twice a week. It also appeared that it must have been someone Nick had known.

> The four of us went to the theater last night. So very staid and proper, and all the time Buddy and I kept glancing at each other and thinking about the things we'd done earlier that afternoon.

But after a while the references to Buddy had started to taper off, possibly because she had begun to find him boring, or possibly because Nick had started to suspect that something was going on. The first supposition was more likely. Stephanie did not seem like the sort of woman who'd give up something she still wanted. She had written about Nick's suspicions lightly, almost dismissively.

Paula put the open notebook on the floor beside her and stared at the flames. She was filled with desolation and something else—an awareness of the malice that seemed to rise out of those old pages like a poisonous miasma.

Oh, Nick, she thought. It should never have happened to Nick—Nick, who was so vibrant and warm and driven by that keen intelligence, that sense of privacy and pride that had little to do with arrogance. It was obvious that Stephanie had used that pride to her own ends. No wonder Nick never talked about her. It must have been a parody of a marriage, a burden that would have been increasingly harder to bear with each passing day. It was just as well that Stephanie had died, she thought in a flare of angry passion.

She shivered, appalled by her own thoughts. No one should die by violence, ever, no matter what they had done or failed to do. She had a sudden memory of one time when she'd gone deer hunting with her brothers. It had snowed the night before, she remembered, and the ground in the woods had been covered with a thick white blanket that crunched beneath their feet as they trod along in their outdoor boots. The tracks of the stag had been very distinct in that new snow, and they had followed them for what seemed like hours. And then, in a breathtaking moment, they had come upon him, standing less than fifteen feet away from them. He had looked up at them with immense eyes. His powerful neck arched at a graceful angle, his swift muscles were paralyzed by fear.

"Shoot," her brothers had whispered. "Shoot."

She had raised her rifle, and then, ever so slowly, had lowered it until it pointed to the ground. "No," she had told them, and they had watched in silence while the stag leaped away.

No, she thought now. It was not just as well that Stephanie had died. But it was just as well that the police had never found this diary of hers, had never thought of looking for it. They would have felt that Stephanie's account gave Nick a powerful motive for her death. It didn't matter that his blood type was different than that found on the knife Stephanie had used to defend herself, because it must be easy enough to hire a killer if you knew your way around.

She forced herself to pick up the diary once again. The fine elegant handwriting looked subtly altered now, the letters thickened and distorted as if Stephanie had literally stabbed her ballpoint pen into the paper.

She had written:

> He's trying to get even with me, trying to get me jealous. I found a woman's sweater on the couch.

Does he really think I'll believe he actually brought another woman up to our apartment? It's all too ridiculous for words.

But she couldn't have believed it was so ridiculous after all, because there were no more notes about shopping trips, luncheons, or dinner parties. The next entry, undated, read:

She has been here. I find small signs of her all over, everywhere I turn. Nick denies it, of course, but she's like a shadow haunting me. Her books, her clothes, her makeup on my dresser. They're trying to drive me insane. I can't stand it any longer. Had an appointment to see L. this afternoon but canceled it to see Buddy instead. I'll have to pay for it of course, but what's half an hour in bed if it gives me a chance to talk to someone who knows Nick? I'll find a way of getting even with them.

Paula closed her eyes. "They're trying to drive me insane." The words closed around her like an insistent fist, and for a moment she found it difficult to breathe. So here was proof that Stephanie, too, had seen signs of an intruder, and that the experience had been next to unbearable.

The last entry had been made in a handwriting so twisted that it was next to illegible.

I saw them. I finally saw them together. I opened the door of our room and there they were, her hair all spread out upon my pillow like dark seaweed, their arms tightly wound around each other, so intent they didn't even hear me when I went into the kitchen to get the knife. When I came back with it, she was gone. How did she slip out? I don't know. All I know is that I have to kill her before they kill me. Because I'll never give him a divorce now. Never. Never. Never.

The remaining pages were blank. Paula stared at them for a long time, as if expecting them to yield a tightly guarded secret that would explain away the horror she felt. Finally she got up and placed the diary on the coffee table, as gingerly as if it were a bomb ready to explode.

Stephanie had seen another woman with Nick, here in this apartment. She had been afraid of being killed. And then, at some later point, she had been shot to death.

And now Paula, too, was seeing signs of an intruder. Was history repeating itself? Did it mean that she would be the next to go?

The strangeness she had felt earlier was multiplied, and the walls seemed to waver, which, added to the silence of the room, had the effect of making her feel that she was gliding through an underwater world where nothing was stable. Where peculiar shapes might be floating just outside her ken.

She'd have to pull herself together. She'd have to take that terrible diary and destroy it, or else hide it where it could never be found, never be read by anyone who might question just why Stephanie had been afraid that Nick would kill her shortly before she had been shot. Not that anyone who knew Nick could suspect him of calculated murder. The very thought was absurd. She knew it with a certainty beyond question or doubt.

But it was equally obvious that he'd been shielding someone. He would have known full well that the police would want to question the woman he'd been seeing, that she had the motive and might have had the opportunity. And yet he'd never told them about her. Perhaps because he cared for her too much, or else because he was convinced that she had an impregnable alibi, thought Paula.

She was so absorbed in her thoughts that she didn't hear the soft footsteps slithering behind her.

Next thing she knew something flew, batlike, up above her head, and she was smothered in folds of something soft while pythonlike arms caught her in their grip. The suddenness of the attack slowed her reactions. In that instant pause that seemed to last an eternity she was aware of something stronger than her own fear. An emotion emanating not from herself but from her attacker. Hatred. A hatred so intense that it seeped through her like corrosive acid, a hatred that paralyzed her, so that for a split second they stood like lovers in an intent embrace.

And then Paula fought back. Her shoulders heaved as

she lurched forward, managed to free one of her arms, and reached up to pull away those smothering folds from around her face. She almost made it, but not quite. She was pushed from behind, and then she was falling and her assailant was on top of her, straddling her from behind, grasping her blinded head, lifting it to smash it down against the floor. Again and again.

She heard a sharp hoarse cry from above her, the cry of a sea gull or a soul lost in hell. And then the soft fabric was being pushed against her nose and mouth so that she couldn't breathe. So I was right, she thought almost detachedly while trying to retain consciousness. She was the next to go.

The attack ended as suddenly as it had began. The choking hands were lifted from her face, and she shook her head groggily. She heard, or thought she heard, the sound of rushing footsteps. She heard the sharp sound of the slammed front door. She sat up tentatively and lifted the enfolding cloth from around her head. She stared at it. It was the blanket she had wrapped herself in earlier and had later discarded.

She stood up. Her legs were shaky, but otherwise she was all right. Nothing felt broken. She made her way to the bathroom on those unsteady legs and switched on the light. She examined her face and throat. They bore no signs of violence, but something had happened to her eyes. They stared back at her with a bruised, sad knowledge that hadn't been there before.

She splashed cold water on her face and went back into the living room. The police. She'd have to call the police, of course, but first she'd have to hide that telltale diary. Her legs felt unsteady, and the room seemed to spin around her in slow, sickening circles. Who had attacked her? Why? Would they come back? Her legs gave way and she half fell across the couch.

It wasn't much longer before Nick came home. He let himself in and called out to her, slamming the door behind him.

"You should have come with us," he told her. "It was a good match. A TKO in the fifteenth round."

He paused, surprised that she didn't return his greeting. His face, ruddy from the night wind, lost some of its color when he saw her.

"Paula," he said sharply. "Paula, what's wrong?"

She didn't answer him.

"Did something happen? Are you sick?" he insisted. His eyes were hard and bright with concern. "What's wrong?" he repeated.

She shook her head slowly. Her mind was functioning quite lucidly at a fantastic speed, but there was a deplorable thickness to her tongue that made it difficult if not impossible to speak. There were pins and needles running through her legs. Her hands felt as though she were carrying fifty-pound weights in each of them. She glanced down at her hands. They looked much the same as usual—thin, muscular, perfectly competent. The only problem was they didn't seem to be functioning right now.

She stretched one of her leaden hands to Nick and got up on her brand-new unsteady rubber legs. As she stood up, she felt the swift rush of something to her head. I'm suffering from a delayed reaction, she thought. She looked up at him.

"Someone just tried to kill me," she said.

And then, to her everlasting embarrassment, she fainted.

12

Conscience does make cowards of us all, Shakespeare had written, but Paula strongly suspected that in today's context it was social embarrassment that more often than not contributed to cowardice. A raised eyebrow and mocking smile are formidable weapons, as she had discovered while she was still in school. People had been known to suffer heart attacks rather than ask help from a supercilious stranger, and the city was filled with senior citizens who struggled by on their Social Security and a starvation diet rather than face the modern stigma of welfare.

Things had changed drastically in the last few decades. Women no longer wept and shrieked in happy compliance with their men's expectations, and fainting was definitely out. Unless there was a physiological reason for it, in which case it might still be condoned.

Fortunately by the next morning Paula had developed a satisfactory fever, one high enough to explain her weakness of the night before. She lay in bed sipping her tea, filled with that false sense of physical well-being that often accompanies fever by way of compensation.

"You've picked up a fine case of flu, my love," Nick told her, sitting by her side. His features looked sharper and more defined, as though he had aged five years during the night. He brushed a strand of hair off her forehead and added, "Why didn't you tell me you weren't feeling well last night? I'd never have gone out with Charlie and left you alone at home if I had known."

She stared at him. What was he talking about?

Last night, when she'd recovered from her brief fainting spell, she'd told him what had happened. Had she been so incoherent that he hadn't understood her? She must have been, judging by his remarks this morning. She had told him that she had been attacked, that someone had tried to kill her. And yet he hadn't called the police, which meant one of two things: either he didn't believe her or he was shielding someone.

She put the second alternative out of her mind. He might keep silent to protect someone, but not if they attacked her. She came first with him and always would. But why hadn't he called the police? She wished she could remember exactly what she'd told him before falling asleep.

She'd slept restlessly, haunted by dreams of dark twisted shapes reaching out for her in the oppressive night. She'd heard winged, batlike forms screeching above her as they swooped downward toward her lifted face. The night had been fearsome and too long.

"I was feeling fine before you left," she told him. "Until someone jumped on me from the back. It all happened so fast that . . ." Her voice broke as she remembered the full horror of the experience. "Why didn't you call the police?" she said. "Why don't you call them now?"

He looked at her flushed, delicate face framed by its dark cloud of tousled hair. "I'm calling a doctor instead," he said. "Someone I know. He's usually in his office soon after nine."

So he *hadn't* believed her, she thought miserably. He must have thought her experience nothing more than a dream or a hallucination brought on by her fever. Or an aftereffect of her accident?

"I don't want to see a doctor," she said, stalling for time. "Besides, they don't make house calls, do they?"

"Not as a rule. But Paul owes me a favor or two. I'm sure he'll come during his lunch hour, if not before. In the meantime I'll spend the morning with you. Would you like that?"

He was smiling at her, but she barely heard him. Her mind raced as she considered various possibilities. If Nick didn't believe her, no one else would either—certainly not the police, who like to see some tangible proof that a crime has, indeed, taken place. She would have to find a way to convince him. But how? And then she thought of the diary. If he read the diary, he would have to believe her. She and Stephanie couldn't both have imagined such similar experiences. Coincidence could only be carried so far.

She slipped out of bed and reached for her slippers.

"What do you want?" Nick asked. "I'll get it for you."

Instead of answering him, she headed for the living room, and he followed her, frowning. The diary, she thought. I must show him that diary. She had left it on the coffee table, she remembered. One look at that awful diary and he would be convinced.

She paused in midstride and looked at the coffee table in dismay. The diary was gone.

She felt as though someone had knocked all the air out of her lungs and she were floating in a cold vacuum in which the only warmth was the fever raging inside her head. She was aware of Nick's supporting arm around her. What if she told him about the diary now?

It would only make things worse, she realized dully. It would merely add fuel to his conviction that the whole experience had been a hallucination caused by her injury and the onset of the flu. She stood quite still within the circle of his arm, and then broke away and picked up a newspaper off the table, as though that were the reason she had come to the living room in the first place. She tucked the newspaper under her arm, and then, still walking through that cold silent vacuum, she went back to the bedroom and slipped into bed.

Why didn't he trust her? Why didn't he believe that she was telling him the plain, unvarnished truth? She would have believed him if the circumstances had been reversed. She looked into his smiling, concerned face and felt she was looking at a stranger.

"I don't want to see a doctor," she said firmly. "And I don't think you should bother staying home. Didn't you tell me you had some important meetings coming up? That things were beginning to pile up on your desk?"

"Yes. But it's nothing that can't wait. Don't you want me to stay with you?"

"It's not necessary," she said, speaking not to the man she loved but to the stranger that he had become. "Besides, I promised Bibi I'd take care of the mail while she was gone. I'm going up there this afternoon."

."Not with a fever of a hundred and three, you're not. I'll

tell you what. I'll call Teresa and tell her you're in bed, ask her to bring the mail down when it comes in. You can go through it at your own pace. If you're up to it, that is. As for the doctor—we'll wait until tomorrow, if you insist."

The results of Nick's call to Teresa were predictable. She would come down to sit with Paula as soon as she had finished cleaning the apartment. She would fix her a nice lunch. Boiled chicken and rice. Nonsense, of course she would come down. The countess would insist on it, she said, as if to clinch the argument.

When Nick hung up, he turned to Paula, grinning and slightly abashed.

"That's a formidable woman," he said. "I'd hate to have her against me on the board of directors. I have my instructions. I'm to stay with you until eleven, and then Teresa will come down and take over. She hinted strongly that my presence would be less than necessary for the rest of the afternoon. Shall I get us some breakfast?" he added.

Paula nodded. Feed a cold and starve a fever, her mother had always said, but her father had argued that all animals, including the human one, know what's best for them. And she was hungry, much to her own surprise.

"I'd like two soft-boiled eggs," she said. "And lots of orange juice and toast." She saw something close to relief in his face.

"I love you," he said, turning to leave the room.

After he was gone, she lay back against the pillows and closed her eyes. The thoughts she'd been repressing until now flooded her mind. She didn't know which was more frightening: the insidious implications of that faded diary or the sudden attack on her, the unexplainable presence of the assailant in the room. She could still feel the horror of her blindness under the suffocating blanket. Had it been a man or a woman? The strength of the assailant pointed to a man, but women could find hidden reserves of strength under duress. Even that furious, high-pitched cry could have belonged to either sex.

Why didn't Nick believe her?

They made it seem so easy in the movies. The woman in danger—and it was almost always a woman—went running to her man with her tale of terror, at which point one of two things would happen: either he was involved in the villainy himself, in which case the woman came to no good end, or else he was a just and upright character who took the entire burden off her shoulders.

The writers of those plots conveniently chose to ignore the myriad intricacies and nuances between men and women. The wish to stand on one's own two feet. The fear of appearing overly dependent. The pride of accomplishment. The reluctance to give up a hard-won independence. The sudden abyss of doubt or misunderstanding that could yawn between them.

She and Nick had known each other for such a short time. They weren't truly married, not in the sense that her parents were married, so adapted to each other and each other's needs that they functioned as one single entity. She and Nick had the potential of achieving that type of marriage, but at this point they were still reaching toward each other, tentatively feeling their way along. There were so many things she still didn't know about Nick. Or he about her, for that matter.

She could remember his face hardening into anger when she had questioned him about his former girlfriends. It was quite obvious that he'd thought she was prying, that he hadn't believed for a minute her tale of a stranger haunting their apartment. He hadn't believed her then and he didn't believe her now. He would if she had any proof, of course, but she didn't. She couldn't stand the memory of the doubt flaring up in his eyes as he removed himself from her to see her more objectively.

Why hadn't he believed her?

When he came back into the bedroom, he was bearing a large tray in his arms. His face held the victorious expression of a man who has survived the perils of the kitchen to prepare a quite edible meal.

He set his own plate and cup on the table beneath the window before handing her the tray.

"Compliments of the house," he said, setting it on her lap. "I added a couple of strips of bacon to whet your appetite."

The bacon was crisp and well done without being burned,

the way it often was when she cooked it. Its pungent smell tickled her nostrils. She took a bite.

"The bacon is delicious," she said.

"Isn't it? If there's one thing I know how to cook it's bacon," he said almost smugly. "Bacon and lettuce sandwiches were my specialty at one time."

They ate in silence, preoccupied with their own thoughts. Nick's face had the guileless, almost blank expression he wore whenever his mind was performing its speediest acrobatics. His thick dark hair had fallen across his forehead, softening the angles of his face. He seemed to be toying with his food. He's already at the office, thought Paula, pondering the day's strategies and routines. She was wrong.

"I think we should move," he said unexpectedly. "I thought I'd call the real-estate agent today and put the apartment up for sale. If that's all right with you, that is."

She was caught off stride.

"Move?" she echoed. Was it possible that he believed her after all?

"Yes. We could buy another co-op, either here or on the East side. Or we could look for a brownstone. We couldn't afford one here in Manhattan, but we might be able to find one across the river in Brooklyn Heights. Do you think you'd like that?"

The understatement of the year, she thought. Would she like it? She would start packing their things today if he said the word.

"Yes," she said cautiously, "I'd like that very much. That one time we walked through Brooklyn Heights I thought it looked like the Village must have been a hundred years ago. But I thought you didn't want to sell as yet. What made you change your mind?"

He gave her a curious look in which sheer male exasperation was mixed with concern.

"You don't remember much about last night, do you?"

"What about last night?" Oh, Nick, what about last night?

"You wouldn't let me leave your side until you fell asleep. She's going to come back, you kept saying over and over again. She's going to come back, and when she does, she'll kill me."

She? thought Paula. She hadn't even been sure of the sex

91

of her assailant, but her subconscious had evidently been busy making its own identification.

"And you thought I'd been having a bad dream."

"A lulu of a nightmare. What else? I've been an idiot not to realize before that you couldn't possibly be happy here. The emotional strain is beginning to tell on you. The last few weeks have been difficult, and from here on it can be only downhill." A sudden passion flared up in his face. "I don't want anything to come between us," he said, leaning toward her as though to protect her by the sheer bulk of his shoulders. "I can't afford to lose you."

He stood up and started collecting their plates and coffee cups. "I won't mind getting out of here myself," he added lightly. "But this time it's your turn to decide where you'd like us to live. Think about it while I'm at the office. And try to get some rest."

At eleven o'clock on the dot Teresa came down and Nick left for the office. Like the official changing of the guard, Paula thought dryly, but she was glad of Teresa's massive, brooding presence. There was a no-nonsense quality about Teresa that was immensely reassuring. No outsider would be foolish enough to risk anything while she was around.

Paula closed her eyes and started daydreaming about town houses with light, airy rooms and that special warmth that generations of people bestow on an old house. There would be a flagstoned garden filled with wisteria and lilac. There would be trees. There would be a beamed attic with skylights that could easily be converted into a sunny nursery. Just in case. Her mind drifted from one dream house to another, and within a few minutes she was asleep.

She woke up to the sound of china rattling on a tray and the smell of something delicious wafting out of a large tureen. Teresa set the tray down on the table and turned to look down at Paula with a disapproval belied by the warmth in her eyes. When she spoke, her voice carried the same mixture of harshness tinged with affection.

"So you managed to get sick," she said. A thick Neapolitan accent colored her words. "Too much running around, too much work. When I was young, a girl did not do anything the first year she was married. She moved in with her husband's family, and her husband's mother took care of the house. It is enough for a new wife to take care of her husband, is that not so? To start making the babies."

Paula smiled at her sleepily. "I'm sure you're right, Teresa. But things are different over here."

"Different is not always good, is it? Never mind. You will be well soon, you will see. I have brought you lunch."

"But we just finished breakfast a couple of hours ago," Paula protested, not too strongly. The aroma of the soup tantalized her nostrils.

"It is good to eat when you are sick," Teresa said firmly. "Food gives you strength. Besides, you have been getting much too thin."

Hadn't somebody said you can't ever be too skinny or too rich? thought Paula. It was obvious that Teresa did not subscribe to the theory. Paula sat up and obediently accepted the tray. The soup was delicious. Teresa sat down and watched her while she ate, as she might have watched a recalcitrant child to make sure it didn't dump the food into the nearest flowerpot. Paula smiled at her between spoonfuls.

"Thank you, Teresa. You're being very good to me. It's almost like being in Vermont once again. When I was a kid, people always brought mountains of food to their sick neighbors. I didn't think it would happen in New York."

"People are people," Teresa said obscurely. Yet it was obvious that she was pleased.

"I hope we can continue to see you and Countess Bibi after we move," Paula added. She hesitated. "Did Nick tell you? We're putting the apartment up for sale. We'll be looking for another place. A house, perhaps. Wouldn't it be lovely to have a house of our very own?"

"It would be very good," said Teresa. She pulled her chair closer to the bed and leaned toward Paula with an animation that split across her normal impassivity like jagged lightning across a sullen sky. "It would be very good if you moved. And soon, I hope."

"Why, Teresa? You sound like you'll be glad to have us out of here."

"I will be," said Teresa, tugging at her skirt with an age-old gesture. "This is not a good place for you. I think it must be different for Mr. Nick. He's away most of the day, and anyway, men are different from women. They do not feel the same things. I will tell you something," she confided, her new animation spreading a faint blush across her heavy-featured face. "When the countess first told me you would be working with her, I did not like the idea."

"Why, Teresa?"

"I thought you would be like the other one. That there would be all kinds of carryings-on." She indicated her disgust by flicking a broad thumb from underneath her teeth. "And then I met you, and I knew at once that you were different. And I started to worry about your living here."

"Whom do you mean by the other one, Teresa?"

"I have already said too much."

"No, please tell me. Do you mean Stephanie, Nick's first wife?"

"Yes. That one. This is not my country, but people are people, like I said before; and I may not speak good English, but I have eyes in my head. She was no good, that one."

She paused for a moment, and when she spoke again, it was on a lower key. "I was not happy that she was killed. No," she said, and crossed herself with a quick gesture. "But I was not really surprised. She was the type who, how do you say it, brings it upon herself. You are very different from her. I am glad you will be moving. And I will come and help you prepare your new place."

Paula had placed the empty soup bowl on the night table. Now she sat up and stared at the other's brooding, intent face.

"But why, Teresa. Why?" she said insistently. "Why did you say this wasn't a good place for me?"

She wondered if Teresa knew something she was not telling, if she knew or suspected anything about last night's attack. But Teresa's face had closed up like a clam, and her former animation had faded to leave something close to animal cunning in her eyes. She sat in silence for what seemed like a long time.

"This is not a good place," she said finally. "I can feel it inside. I said a prayer when I came down earlier. It is not a good place."

Her mouth closed stubbornly and she made it evident that she had nothing more to say. But she didn't leave the room. They stayed together, listening for unwanted noises in the vast silence of the apartment.

13

The next day Paula's fever was gone. She woke up before the alarm went off, prompted by an inner alarm that brought her abruptly from the depths of sleep to wide-awake awareness. Just so must animals wake up when disturbed by a subtle, foreign noise. But the early-morning silence of the apartment was total, only faintly disturbed by the noises of traffic seeping in through the partially open windows.

She slipped out of bed, careful not to disturb Nick, and put on her robe and slippers before going into the kitchen to make coffee. Her muscles were taut, her nerves jangled as though disturbed by some wild, primitive rhythm.

The implications of the attack on her hit her with full force. What would she do now? she wondered bleakly. There was no one she could turn to, nothing she could do to prevent another attack. The new locks had proved useless. She tried to remember if she'd put the chain on after Nick left. She didn't normally put the chain on while Nick was gone, because she wanted him to be able to let himself in if she were in the bathroom or asleep. But even if the chain had been off, had had her assailant managed to get in when the new locks were supposedly burglarproof?

They would be moving soon, she told herself, spooning coffee into the percolator. The real-estate agent had told Nick that he had dozens of clients waiting for an apartment just like theirs, people with impeccable credentials who'd be readily accepted by the board of trustees of Dover House. So they could start looking for another place immediately. If they were lucky, they might be able to move within two or three months. But even if they moved today, that still didn't really settle anything.

Because what would prevent her unknown enemy from following them to their new house?

She turned the flame on under the percolator and started to set the table for breakfast. As far as she could see, there were only two plausible courses of action open to her: she could run back home to her parents, or she could try to find out who had attacked her, and why. In either case she'd have to get that blasted diary back. Whoever had it possessed a very dangerous—and useful—tool for blackmail.

If she could find a small scrap of tangible proof, she could enlist Nick's help, but in the meantime she was on her own. Unless she hired a private detective, of course. A private detective might be a good idea. Why not? Because she had exactly eight hundred and thirty-five dollars in her savings account, that's why not. It would be just barely enough to cover his retainer. And she couldn't very well use the money in their joint account without asking Nick first. So she was on her own for the time being. Not a pleasant prospect.

"Nick, who is Buddy?" she asked after he had sat down, fully showered and dressed, at the breakfast table.

He looked up from the real-estate section of the paper.

"There'll be more listings in the Sunday paper," he told her, before focusing on what she had just said. "Buddy? Buddy who?"

"I don't know. I thought he was a friend of yours."

"Never heard of him. Why do you ask?" he said absentmindedly, glancing through the ads.

"I saw his name on an old appointment slip," she said, treading warily on the thin line of truth. "Something about the theater."

He gave her the even look he assumed each morning with his business suit.

"Was it in Stephanie's writing? One of her friends, most likely. She had a number of friends I never met. Is there more coffee?" he added.

She poured his coffee and then sat down to sip her own. She pulled the news section out and was taken aback to discover that while her eyes were scanning the headlines, her mind was seeing that thin faded handwriting engraved in her memory. "The four of us went to the theater last night," Stephanie had written. "So very staid and proper, and all the time Buddy and I kept glancing at each other and thinking about the things we'd done earlier that afternoon." Had Nick been one of that foursome? Paula had assumed so, and yet she'd had no reason for making that assumption other than her own middle-class upbringing. In her world, when a husband and wife went out at night they did so together. But Stephanie had lived in a totally different world, an unchartered territory to which there were no guidelines and no maps.

After Nick left, she walked restlessly around the apartment, missing him, missing Tereasa's bulky presence, missing the boring but reassuring routine of going to school or the office. She had never felt quite so alone in her whole life. A healthy state, today's psychologists insisted. People should be able to live on their own. Nonsense, she thought. Man was a social animal, as were all living things. She had seen animals sicken and die when isolated from their own kind, and even plants thrived when surrounded by other living things. She remembered her grandmother's companionable and rambling conversations with her dead husband. Would she have been better-off if some well-meaning shrink had convinced her that she was talking into the thin air?

At nine-thirty she tried to call Cindy at the office. Cindy wouldn't be in today, one of the other girls told her. She had called in sick. But when she tried to reach Cindy at home, there was no answer. She let the phone ring for a long time before hanging up. She *had* to talk to someone. At ten o'clock she picked up the phone again and dialed Charlie Nabokov's number.

He worked at home in the mornings. There was an unwritten rule that he shouldn't be disturbed between the hours of nine A.M. and one P.M., and there was a good chance that he wouldn't answer. She could imagine him hunched over his typewriter, ignoring the annoyance of the ringing phone. But he answered on the third ring.

"Paula, my love. What a delightful interruption," he said when she'd identified herself. "I didn't think you'd be up at this ungodly hour."

"I always have breakfast with Nick before he leaves," she explained. Now that she had him on the phone, she felt at a loss. How on earth could she tell him what she wanted from him?

"There's something I'd like to ask you," she said. "I was wondering if I could see you sometime today?"

"Why, Paula, how *timely*. Here I am reviewing Harringer's latest book, and a dreadful thing it is, so dull and bombastic I couldn't possibly force myself to read it. Which is probably why I'm having such a problem writing the review. At any rate, I'd welcome any excuse that would take me away from it. Even for a short while. What did you want to ask me?" The sharp trill of curiosity was vibrant in his voice.

"I'll tell you when I see you."

"Do you want to come down now? I just made a fresh pot of coffee we can share. I promise to tell you anything you wish. If I don't know it, I'll do my best to invent it."

Why did he always have to sound so flippant? She was already beginning to regret her call. But Stephanie had been his friend, had confided in him. If she were to unravel the puzzle, she'd have to start with him.

Charlie's apartment was one floor below. It was smaller than theirs, one bedroom and a huge combination living room and dining room. The furniture was functional and modern. A large worktable with a typewriter and a litter of paper stood between the two living-room windows. The aroma of coffee was rich in the room.

It was the first time she'd been down here without Nick, and now, facing Charlie across the glass coffee table, she had the sinking feeling that she'd taken the first step down a one-way road from which there was no retreat, that her search for information was, in its own way, a betrayal of Nick. A betrayal that she already felt aching inside her. But what choice did she have? None that she could see. The realization made her angry, an anger that in turn made it easier to speak. She looked straight at Charlie.

"I want to ask you about Stephanie," she said.

Something cold and reptilian flickered in his eyes and vanished, to be replaced by a brilliant smile.

"Stephanie? What could you possibly want to know about Stephanie? She's dead," he reminded her, still smiling.

"I want to know about her friends and her enemies. Particularly her enemies. Did she have any enemies?"

99

"You sound like a rookie detective in a novel. Of course she had enemies, don't we all? It would be too boring if we didn't. Jealousy thriving rampant in the heart of the envious, you know, that type of thing. Stephanie was an unusual type of woman, bound to provoke jealousies and resentments. I'm sure there were people who disliked her intensely. I can't think of any specific ones, however. Perhaps you'll tell me why you want to know."

Paula shook her head. Her wide, watchful eyes never left his.

"I can't," she said. "And I don't really want to know. I *must* know," she added.

"I appreciate the distinction, and yet I doubt whether I can help you. How do any of us know who are enemies are? I don't. Do you?"

She remembered the wiry hands gripping her head, the folds of the soft blanket smothering her face.

"I don't," she said. "If you don't know her enemies, how about her lovers? Did she ever talk to you about her lovers?"

"From enemies to lovers. I would say that's quite a jump, if, unfortunately, lovers didn't turn so often into enemies. It's too bad, isn't it?"

She realized he was trying to distract her. Wariness had seeped into his body, so that his pose of relaxation looked like a parody performed by a bad actor.

"I would find it easier to answer your questions if I knew just why you were asking them in the first place," he said slowly. "But you're not about to tell me, are you? If Stephanie had lovers, she never told me about them. Don't forget that I was Nick's friend long before I was hers. What makes you think she had lovers?"

"I found some notes of hers," she said. His wariness was contagious, and her own nerves were taut in response, aware of hidden lies and submerged danger.

"You found some notes of hers? That's most interesting. Most interesting indeed. What did they say?"

"Nothing too explicit. Something about a man or men she'd been seeing."

"Did she mention any names?" he asked sharply.

Paula shook her head. "No," she said. The lie made her

feel older, burdened with doubt and guilt. "She also wrote about an affair Nick had been having."

Charlie's eyebrows rose, and his nose lifted sharply, like that of a fox sniffing the air.

"Did she really?" he drawled.

"Why do you act surprised? You told Cindy that Stephanie was jealous of Nick, that she had seen his girlfriend in the apartment."

She sensed his rush of anger before he spoke.

"Cindy talks too much," he said very softly. "And so, it would seem, do I. But what does it matter? It all happened a long time ago. It's water under the bridge, way past the bridge, in fact. Don't try to dredge it up now. It can lead to nothing but trouble."

"Who was she, Charlie? If you have any idea, please tell me. I wouldn't ask if it weren't important." The desperation in her voice was as loud as the ticking of a clock in a silent room.

"I don't know," he said, "I've often wondered, but I really don't know." He sighed, and she was suddenly certain that he was telling the truth. "I assume you haven't shown those notes to Nick?"

"I wouldn't be discussing them with you if I had."

"Then don't. I think he's managed to forget those years. It wasn't a good time for him. There's no point in dragging it all back."

He stood up suddenly and walked over to her side. Before she could draw back, his hand had reached forward to caress her cheek.

"I would forget all about it if I were you," he said. "But I'm glad you came to discuss it with me. I'm here any time you want to talk. Or do anything else, for that matter." His voice was mellow and seductive, full of an almost tangible suggestion.

She drew back, repelled by his touch. She could feel the imprint of his hand on her cheek like the slimy track of a snail. She had to get away.

"Thank you for letting me take up so much of your time," she told him formally. She stood up. They were standing so close that she could smell the faint citric smell of his after-shave lotion.

"Won't you have another cup of coffee?"

"Thanks, but I must run. I have a million things to do before going up to Bibi's this afternoon."

He followed her on her way out and held the door open for her. She was out in the hallway before she turned around to face him.

"Charlie," she said, "who's Buddy?"

He was standing with his back to the light. His face was shadowed, and she couldn't see his expression.

"Buddy?" he said. "I've never heard of Buddy."

Without another word she turned on her heel and walked toward the elevator. The conversation had been a mistake. She had tipped her hand without learning a thing. Or had she? She remembered a remark Nick had once made in passing about a business meeting. The information people withhold is as significant as that which they give freely, he'd said. Charlie's omissions had pointed toward something, but the point eluded her, tantalizingly close and yet beyond her reach.

14

The weekends meant two uninterrupted days with Nick, a rich oasis among their constant comings and goings. This weekend was no exception. The high crest of fear she'd been riding receded into a distance, and the focus of her awareness altered subtly. She had the peculiar experience of existing on two parallel levels: one fraught with danger and half-realized shapes that reached out to threaten her, the other one—far more solid and real—the everyday world of her life with Nick.

On Saturday they took the subway to Brooklyn Heights and spent the morning wandering through the landmarked blocks. With the frank curiosity of tourists they gazed at the ancient brownstones and toylike carriage houses fronted by intricate shrubbery and short, delicate trees that were bursting into bloom. They looked at the windows of the antique shops, delicatessens, and boutiques that nestled against each other on streets along which horse-drawn carriages had rolled a hundred and fifty years ago. They delighted in pointing out discoveries to each other: the ageless grace of an archway, the worn carvings of stone ornaments, the joy of a glossy, Chinese-red painted door. Two hours of sight-seeing left them enchanted and exhausted.

"Would you like to live here?" he asked her over coffee. A young boy with liquid eyes set deeply in his thin Arabic face had taken their order. An older, heavier man who was obviously his father smiled and nodded at them from behind the counter.

"I'd love it," she said. "But could we possibly afford one of these brownstones: They all look like they'd cost a fortune."

"I'm sure they do," he said. "But we might just be able to swing it if we get a good price for the co-op. If we can find any available houses, that is. It's worth a try. I'll call a few agents next week."

"On Monday," she said.

"On Monday," he agreed. He looked lighthearted and carefree, as though the prospect of moving brought with it the promise of a new beginning. They walked back to the subway hand in hand, and once again she had the sensation of living on two parallel levels. They were having a great time, but only because they had managed to push their fears and their angers far into the background of their minds. Right now their relationship seemed idyllic, but what would happen to it tomorrow, next week, next month? She resolutely thrust the thought out of her mind.

That evening she tried to call Cindy at home and let the phone ring for a long time before hanging up. She tried again the following morning.

"I'm getting worried about Cindy," she told Nick. "I've been trying to reach her since Friday."

"She's probably gone somewhere for the weekend. Didn't she say she was taking ski lessons?"

"The season is almost over. Besides, I don't think she really cared for skiing. She told me she thought she'd stick to indoor sports. Far less dangerous, she thought."

"That depends on the sport, doesn't it?"

"You mean that man she's involved with? You don't like the sound of him either, do you?"

"It's not a question of like or dislike. I doubt I'd trust any man who played around outside his marriage. It's adolescent and messy. Not to say time-consuming and ridiculous."

"Is that so? You mean you've never had an extramarital affair?"

"We've been married less than two months, woman." He grabbed her by the waist and lifted her up into the air. He was not a bulky man and she was still surprised by his wiry strength. His upturned face laughed at her. "Wait until we've been married a year, and we're both old and worn. Then I might start looking for outside fun and games."

She wound her legs around him and tugged at his hair. They wrestled briefly, laughing.

"I don't mean now, you idiot," she told him, catching her

104

breath. "I mean before. Did you ever have an affair while you were married to Stephanie?"

The laughter faded from his face, leaving his eyes as blank and still as the bare windows of an empty house. They'd ended up on the floor, and now they sat up Indian fashion, facing each other. At first she thought he wasn't going to answer.

"No," he said finally.

"Never?"

"Never. We had enough problems as it was."

A nerve twitched at the corner of his eyelid, and the lines running from his nostrils down to his mouth looked more pronounced, as though evoked by unwelcome memories. She had a sudden vision of what he might look like ten years from now.

"You don't like to talk about it, do you?"

"Not much. It wasn't a good time for either one of us." He hesitated, poised on the brink of withdrawal. "I'd asked her for a divorce," he said to her surprise. "She refused. I was getting set to leave her."

"And then?"

"And then she died."

Paula sat very still, waiting for him to continue, afraid that her slightest movement might interrupt his trend of thought. But he stood up abruptly, as though regretting the impulse that had led him to confide in her.

"Let's go out for the paper," he said. "I could use a walk."

The day was balmy, the air smelled fresh and clean. It was one of those rare days when the poignancy of spring is felt more keenly in the city than out in the country, evoking, as it does, the promise of magic still to come. The sun splashed against the buildings and the sidewalks and tinged the light breeze with a golden hint of warmth.

They crossed the street and walked out into the park. Paula looked at Nick. He strode along with that clean economy of movement that was characteristic of everything he did. Shrubs and trees flowered around them. A group of kids ran past them, shouting and laughing at each other. They passed a number of couples talking quietly together, hand in hand.

She felt like a spectator who didn't quite fit into the scene.

The beauty of the day ached somewhere inside her. She would have preferred the dismal drizzle of blustery winter days to this idyllic scene of which she couldn't be a participant. She and Nick walked in step as they always did, well matched. They looked and acted as a perfect couple. And yet there was a lack of trust between them that was undermining their marriage, that threatened its existence as a house is threatened by unsound foundations. There was so much she was holding back from him. If only she could blurt it all out, enlist his help, win him over to her side. But she couldn't trust him to believe her. He would be concerned about her, yes, but he would show it by calling in other doctors—perhaps sending her to a nursing home to rest. She couldn't take the risk.

He didn't trust her either, for that matter. If he did, he wouldn't have lied about that affair he'd had while he was married to Stephanie. "There they were," Stephanie had written, "her hair all spread out upon my pillow like dark seaweed, their arms tightly wound around each other. . . ." There was no reason why Nick shouldn't tell her about that old affair, was there? Unless it still mattered more to him than he cared to admit.

She thought of the diary, of the mangled flowers, of the unknown assailant who couldn't possibly have entered the apartment—but had. She remembered her talk with Charlie Nabokov, and her distinct impression that he'd lied to her, that he, too, knew more than he was willing to tell her. Why? The fear she'd felt earlier returned, all the more powerful for having been repressed.

On Monday morning she tried to call Cindy at the office, and was told that Cindy was still out. No, they hadn't heard from her. Yes, she was still on sick leave. She could probably be reached at home if it was important.

She dialed Cindy's home number. Still no answer. She was just getting ready to hang up when, suddenly, she was seized by the uneasy feeling that Cindy was there, staring, silent and unmoving, at the ringing phone. It wasn't a pleasant thought.

There's little more impelling than the need for action, however futile the action itself may be. Paula didn't even stop to think. She got her wallet and her keys and took a light windbreaker from her closet. She had to see if Cindy was all right.

106

The weather was still deplorably fine, filled with its spurious promise. The traffic was relatively light. She hailed a passing cab and was at Cindy's apartment within twenty-five minutes.

15

The apartment she and Cindy had shared until she'd moved in with Nick was in that part of the West Village that has been developed to its highest potential density, so that at times the very air seems rationed. The streets are twisted and narrow, the ancient houses lean into each other like incestuous cousins at a drunken party. Small stores and restaurants proliferate overnight, go out of business, and are reopened the next day under a different guise. Most of the apartments are small, narrow, dank. The rents are sky-high. Cindy's apartment was rent-controlled, but she was still spending one-third of her salary for the privilege of living there by herself.

Paula paid off the cabbie at the corner and started to make her way through the crowded street. She had always felt stimulated by the Village crowds, had been intrigued by the variety of styles that ranged from chic to streetwise. But today her perceptions were altered by her mood. She looked at the people that she passed and seemed to read a dull desperation in their eyes and animated movements. The hurried rhythm of their footsteps seemed motivated by an inner clock that prophesied that time was running out. She felt claustrophobic in the narrow street.

She walked into the small lobby of Cindy's building and rang the buzzer. No answer. The inner door was locked. She tried the buzzer once again. It was probable, indeed likely, that Cindy wasn't home and that she'd made the trip down here for nothing. So much for instinct, she thought. But her intuition had a deplorable way of being deaf to logic, and she was more than ever convinced that Cindy was up there in the apartment.

She waited until one of the other tenants came in and unlocked the inner door, smiled at him, and followed him inside. She ran up the stairs to the fourth floor and rang the bell. She thought she heard someone stirring inside.

"Cindy!" she called.

No answer.

"Cindy, it's me. Paula."

She heard the sound of footsteps and the door opened, squeaking lightly on its hinges. It had squeaked like that for years and they'd always meant to do something about it but never had.

"Hi," said Cindy. "Come on in."

She looked terrible. Her face was puffy and her eyes were red beneath their swollen lids. Her hair was uncombed. The T-shirt and jeans she wore might have been dragged out from the bottom of the laundry hamper.

"Cindy, what happened? I've been trying to reach you for days."

"Oh, was that you?" said Cindy. She threw herself into an armchair and tucked her feet beneath her. "I thought it might be him."

"Did you have a fight?"

"He left me," said Cindy. "We broke up. Last Thursday." A wintry smile flickered across her face. "But then you always knew it wouldn't last, didn't you?"

Paula stared at her, shocked. She hadn't realized that Cindy had cared that much. Not quite that much. What was it Nick had said about extramarital affairs? Adolescent, messy, and ridiculous. His definitions fell far short of the mark, they didn't cover the full span of very real suffering. Cindy had isolated herself in her apartment like an injured animal licking its wounds. Was that ridiculous? Perhaps. But it was also horrible, the way that illness or death can be both ridiculous and horrible at the same time.

She couldn't bear that small wintry smile on Cindy's face. She wanted to walk up to her and put her arms around her, to hold her and rock her back and forth like a small child. Cindy needed holding. But Paula knew better than to indulge in any such folly—in her present mood Cindy wouldn't tolerate the smallest sign of sympathy.

She cleared some newspapers off the couch and sat down, leaning well back. It was quite possible that Cindy might ask

109

her to leave, but it's harder to dislodge someone once they're seated.

"Tell me about it," she said.

"There's not much to tell, is there? We had a brief fling and then it was all over," Cindy said flatly. She might have been talking about someone she barely knew.

"But you told me his wife had agreed to a divorce."

"I did, didn't I? I spoke too soon. What do they say about not counting your chickens until they're hatched?"

"Cindy, what did happen? You must tell me about it." Paula spoke sharply, trying to break through that wall Cindy had built around herself. "It will make you feel better if you tell me," she added more gently.

Cindy looked at her as if she were really seeing her for the first time. Her mouth lost its rigid line, quivered, regained control. She seemed unwilling to give up the privacy of her grief, just as an animal that has been trapped too long is loath to leave its cage.

When she spoke, it was so softly that Paula had to lean forward to hear her.

"He lied to me," she whispered.

"About what?"

"About everything."

"He didn't ask his wife for a divorce?"

"No. It turns out that they have children after all. A boy and a girl."

"Oh, my God, Cindy."

"He said he couldn't bear the thought of leaving them, of not seeing them grow up. He said he would have told me about them earlier but was afraid I wouldn't see him if I knew. He was right, of course."

"He told you all this last Thursday?"

"Thursday night. He came here for dinner."

Her vague gesture pointing to the living room was that of a spectator indicating the scene of a disaster. Paula was silent.

"He told me if I forced him to make a choice between us he'd have to stay with them. I think he's terrified that I might call his wife. He lied to her, too. He's a one-hundred-percent phony, and yet I still love him. Isn't that ironic? There's nothing special about him, you know. He's not particularly good-looking, and I know at least a dozen men who are at least as intelligent and witty as he is. If not more so. And I've known better sexual athletes. And yet . . . there's something about him that made me care for him." She paused. "I guess he's the only man I ever really cared for," she said.

Her face twisted with pain. She bent over and clutched at her stomach as though to pacify some monstrous baby turning around inside her.

Paula watched her helplessly. "He cared for you, too," she said.

"Oh, yes. He kept telling me that again and again. We got quite drunk. Isn't that funny? We hardly ever drank before. We got quite drunk and then we made love. Afterward, he cried."

"Oh, Cindy," said Paula. It was her turn to whisper.

"I hated him for crying. He knelt beside me on the bed and cried, and all I could think was how much I hated him. I told him so. I didn't cry until later, after he left."

They stared at each other. Paula had the impression that she was looking not at a close friend, but at a mirror image in which she saw herself as she could have been had things turned out differently.

"You must come to stay with us for a few days," she said. "You can't stay here, like this. I'll help you pack your things."

Cindy stood up and shrugged impatiently. She walked over to the coffee table and picked up her cigarettes.

"Don't be silly," she said. "I'm perfectly all right."

"Yes, I can see that."

"No need to be sarcastic," Cindy told her. But she looked down at herself and touched her uncombed hair. "I have been indulging myself, haven't I? But I'm better now. Really. I promise you I'll be all right."

But she wouldn't be. In the evening the apartment would become too empty, the noise from the street too loud in contrast to the silence of the room. She would remember the echo of previous conversations, gaze into her reservoir of memories, and see the shadow of their past gestures like fleeting shapes beneath a bed of ice. No, it would never do. Cindy needed her—and she needed Cindy, for that matter. They could help each other.

"Cindy," she said, "I think it would be good for you to stay with us for a few days. But I was going to ask you to come over for a while even before I knew about—about this. That's why I've been trying to call you. I'd like you there. I'm in trouble, you see."

"What do you mean?" Cindy said suspiciously, with the air of one who knows a red herring when she sees one.

"Someone attacked me the other day."

"Attacked you? What do you mean? Where?"

"In the apartment. While Nick was out with Charlie Nabokov."

"In the apartment? But how did they get in?" Her tone was sharp with disbelief, but she was looking at Paula with attention, her self-centered trance abruptly dispelled.

"I don't know," said Paula. "I don't know how or why. But then a lot has happened that I don't understand."

"Like those strands of blond hair you found in your hairbrush?"

"Yes. And a lot besides. Things I haven't told you. For a while I even thought I was seeing and hearing things that simply weren't there, but Dr. Schneider assured me I've made a full recovery from that accident. And I feel all right. Do you think I'm becoming one of those people who end up on street corners and announce that the end of the world is near?"

"Are you asking me if I think you're going insane?" asked Cindy. This time her smile contained a trace of genuine amusement.

Paula was taken aback. "That's not what I said, but I guess it might be what I meant. Yes."

"I wouldn't worry about it," Cindy told her. "It would take more than a knock on the head to destroy that hardy Vermont common sense of yours. But tell me about the attack. Were you hurt? Was it a man or a woman? And what does Nick have to say about it?"

"I wasn't hurt. I couldn't tell if it was a man or a woman. And Nick doesn't believe it ever happened."

"Good grief. He doesn't believe you? Why on earth not?"

"He doesn't trust my hardy common sense the way you do. I asked him to call the police and he wanted to call a doctor instead. We haven't talked about it since. I'm afraid, Cindy, afraid that it's going to happen again. But I can't discuss it with Nick because it would only make things worse."

And because I don't really trust him, an unwanted voice said inside her. Because there's only two ways someone could have gotten in after we changed the locks: either they were master burglars, or else Nick gave them a set of the new keys.

Silence fell between them. When Paula looked up, she saw that Cindy was staring at her intently, as though wanting to ask a question she didn't know how to phrase.

"I thought you and Nick had the perfect marriage," she said finally. "I thought things were going so well for you two."

"They are, on the surface. But I'm beginning to discover that there are far too many things we can't discuss, vast areas with 'Private' signs posted all over them."

"Oh, Paula, I'm so sorry."

Paula shrugged. They seemed to be taking turns in sympathizing with each other. She said, "Nick's decided he'd like to sell the apartment and look for a house. I'd be more excited about it if I didn't feel that it's not so much a new thing he wants to do as a way of escaping something from the past. I don't know. I expect I'd feel less muddled if I weren't frightened."

"You'd better tell me all about it," said Cindy. "Do you want some coffee? We can make some instant."

The kitchen was small, but a long shelf along the wall with two bar stools beneath it provided an eating area. Paula perched on one of the stools and turned around to watch Cindy at the sink. Time seemed to shift, flow backward, and she felt as though she were still living here with Cindy and they were having a quiet cup of coffee before going out on a date or turning in for the night. From this perspective the last few months receded into a distance from which she could see them more objectively.

"It all started with a torn dress I was going to wear to Bibi's party," she said, and went on to tell Cindy about the small signs of someone having been in the apartment, the hairbrush she'd never found again even though she'd searched the entire bedroom, the flowers torn off their stalks in a living room that looked as if it had been hit by a cyclone. When she got to Stephanie's diary, she heard Cindy's sharp intake of breath.

"What did it say?" Cindy wanted to know.

"I don't remember most of it," said Paula. Some of the passages were graven in her memory, but she didn't want to quote them now, as though the repetition of the words would only recall her initial horror. "Most of it was about lunches and dinners and shopping expeditions. She must have spent a small fortune on clothes. And she was obviously carrying on a couple of affairs."

"It seems to be quite the vogue, doesn't it?"

"Oh, Cindy, I'm sorry. I shouldn't be bothering you with this."

"On the contrary. You should have talked to me earlier, just as I should have talked to you. We could have helped each other. We still can. Tell me about the diary. What else did it say?"

"Well, at some point she appeared convinced that Nick had started an affair of his own and was bringing his girlfriend up to the apartment while Stephanie was out."

"It seems farfetched, doesn't it?"

"It seems impossible, or rather it would if I too hadn't noticed someone had been there. But the worst part is that she was sure Nick was planning to kill her. That's nonsense, I know, but don't you see what would happen if the police got hold of that damn notebook? They might be tempted to reopen the case. And Nick would be the prime suspect."

"Well, why don't you just destroy it?"

"That's the part I'm getting to. I told you I was attacked." She shivered as she remembered the soft fabric blinding her face. "Whoever it was took the diary . . . which means that, somewhere in this city, someone is holding the perfect tool for blackmail."

Cindy got up off her stool and started to wash the dishes piled up in the sink. Her back was turned to Paula. "Have you considered," she said, "that it might have been Nick himself who took the diary? From what you tell me he's the one who stands the most to lose by its getting into the wrong hands. He might have come home early, seen that you had found it, taken it, and left."

"It wasn't Nick," said Paula.

She was certain of it. Nick would have probably destroyed the diary if he'd known about it, but he would never have attacked her in that way. She could still feel that corrosive surge of hatred stemming from the unseen assailant. It hadn't been Nick.

"I would know Nick's touch anywhere," she told Cindy. She took a kitchen towel and started to dry the silverware. The silence that fell between them was filled with almost tangible speculations. Cindy scoured the sink before turning around to face her.

"If I were you," she said, "I'd stay here for a few days. Or else go visit your folks in Vermont. But you won't do that, will you?"

"I can't. Don't you see that if I leave Nick now we might have nothing left when I come back? I must stay with him. What would you do in my place?"

"I'd probably do the same," said Cindy. "If you wait a few minutes, I'll shower and pack a few things. I'm coming with you."

When she came out from the bedroom fifteen minutes later she looked much like her old self. She hadn't bothered with makeup and her face was still pale, but her brushed hair had retained its sheen and her movements were quick, definite, precise. The smell of danger, even at second hand, had served to dispel her apathy. For the time being, at least.

She picked up her weekend bag and took out her keys.

"Let's go," she told Paula.

And then she did an odd thing. She stood in the open doorway and looked at the living room, as a person leaving on a long journey will take a final look at a place where they're leaving part of their vital essence. A look that attempts to salvage every memory, every experience, every word.

Paula was to remember that look for a long time.

16

<hr>

"Gin!" Cindy sang out, and laid her cards down on the table with a flourish.

Nick groaned out loud. He picked up all the cards and shuffled them carefully before dealing the next hand.

"It's a good thing we're playing for pennies. Paula didn't warn me I'd be playing with a card shark," he said. "Are you always this good?"

"Usually," Cindy told him. "Once, in Bermuda, I won a small fortune at the blackjack table. It more than covered the cost of my vacation. Bridge, gin rummy, poker, you name it—I've always been lucky at cards."

Luckier at cards than with men, thought Paula. She herself was a deplorable player. She had decided to spend the evening with a bunch of magazines she'd been meaning to look through. They hadn't pressed her to play. People who played cards with her once seldom insisted that she do so again.

She watched Nick and Cindy as they sat at the dining-room table. Nick's face was intent and frowning, Cindy's totally blank with that peculiar stillness that was the frequent hallmark of the inveterate card player. They looked well together. Their movements were elegant and swift, their voices edged with a sophistication she would never achieve if she lived in the city for the next fifty years.

She found herself wondering again about the women Nick had known before meeting her—a whole procession of tall willowy figures with silken hair and impeccable makeup—the type of women who were always given the very best table in a restaurant even without the formalities of a reservation and who were the darlings of the best stores in town. She thrust the demoralizing thought out of her mind. The problem was

116

that she was losing her self-confidence, had started to lose it the day she had awakened in that bare hospital room to be told she had wrecked the rented car in a freak accident. She was coming along splendidly, they had told her. She would make a full recovery in no time at all. But it was then that the realization of her vulnerability had started its insidious, underground process, and the last few weeks had done little to erase her self-doubts. Had she really made a full recovery, or was she swinging along a vast pendulum between reality and her imagination?

It was Tuesday night. On Monday night, when Nick came home, he had seemed pleased to hear that Cindy had taken the week off from the office and was planning to stay with them. "Great," he said. "Paula could use some company." He didn't add he'd been worried about Paula.

The last two days had been remarkable only for the singular lack of any new developments. There had been no phone calls, no interesting mail, no unexpected visitors. Even Charlie Nabokov had failed to show up for four days in a row, which in itself set some sort of precedent.

Paula had made no headway in discovering who had stolen Stephanie's diary, and why. She didn't, when it came right down to it, have the foggiest idea of just where to start.

All she had managed so far was to convince herself that Charlie Nabokov was concealing something—and who didn't have something to conceal?—and to alternate between distrusting Nick and the evidence of her own senses.

Cindy's presence had been comforting but not particularly helpful. They had spent so many hours discussing the diary and the implications of its theft that they'd ended going around in circles.

"If you think the whole thing started with Stephanie," Cindy had said at one point, "maybe you should talk to her parents. She might have told them something that could explain it all. It's a pity you don't know who or where they are."

"I do, as a matter of fact," Paula had told her. "They live in Chappaqua and their name is Brewster. Mr. and Mrs. Wayne Brewster. There was an article about him in the business section of *The New York Times*. I was surprised when Nick pointed it out to me, because he'd never mentioned Stephanie's family before."

"Well, there you go. Why don't you talk to them?"

"You must be kidding."

"I'm quite serious. They should be glad to help, particularly if this whole thing is connected with their daughter's death."

"What on earth would I say to them?" Paula said dubiously.

"Tell them about the diary. Ask them if Stephanie ever told them about seeing that woman here in the apartment. Find out if they have any idea who she was."

"If they knew anything, they would have said so at the inquest. Besides, what if they ask what else Stephanie had to say in the diary? Can't you just imagine their reaction when I tell them she was sure Nick was planning to kill her?"

"Don't be an idiot. You don't have to tell them anything of the kind. Just say— Oh, hell, there really isn't anything you can say, is there? Not without sounding very odd indeed."

"Or without dragging Nick into it, for that matter."

Cindy allowed herself to look impatient. "Well, why don't you just do the simplest thing and discuss the whole thing with Nick. Tell him everything you've told me. You know how much he cares for you. If he thinks you're in danger, he'll turn heaven and earth upside down to find out who's behind it. Talk to him tonight."

"I can't," Paula said miserably. "I can't discuss it with him."

"For heaven's sake, why not? You make him sound like some modern-day Bluebeard with a secret chamber tucked away someplace. You said yesterday that you can't talk to him because he doesn't believe you. Why don't you give it another try? Are you just being stubborn, or is there some other reason why you won't talk to him?"

Because I'm not sure of the extent of his involvement, thought Paula. Because we've only been together for a short while and our relationship is still tentative and new. Because I'm not sure how much I can trust him. She couldn't say the words out loud. Not even to Cindy.

"Does it matter? Does the reason really matter that much?" she said instead.

"Of course it does. Because you should tell him about the diary unless you've got a damn good reason not to. You owe it to him. And to yourself, for that matter. Particularly if you think he knows who it is."

"What do you suggest I say to him? Nick, I know that you must be shielding another woman."

"Why does he have to be shielding anyone? There could be a number of perfectly innocent explanations."

"Give me one."

"All right. Supposing, for instance, that he asked Charlie Nabokov to pick something up for him here. If he gave Charlie the keys, it would have taken ten minutes to get an extra set made up. And Charlie would be free to come and go at will. I'm only using Charlie as an example, mind you, but he's just creepy enough to be behind the whole thing. For all we know he might be one of the men Stephanie was having an affair with. If the diary was stolen, it could well be in Charlie's apartment at this very minute."

"Wait a second," said Paula. "You keep saying if. Don't *you* believe me?"

Cindy looked embarrassed. She looked at her hand to inspect a nail that, though perfectly shaped, didn't quite seem to merit the attention she was giving it.

"I do," she said. "But you must admit that it does sound peculiar."

The combination of Welsh and Irish genes is fertile ground for a quick temper, and Paula had tried to control hers since she was a child. Her older brothers had stayed well clear of her whenever she had flown into one of her rare, short-lasting rages. She could feel one coming on now. The sudden rush of blood beat at her temples and then drained away, leaving her pale. Her great eyes smoldered in her small, freckled face.

"Ah, yes," she said. Anger made her voice quiver. "Next I'll be seeing butterflies and pink elephants, no doubt. Why don't you come right out and say what you mean!"

"Paula, wait a minute. I didn't mean anything of that kind. It's just that—"

"I know exactly what you meant. You try to convince me to tell Nick all about it and imply I must be nuts all in the same breath. Supposing you saw something that couldn't possibly happen, but did nevertheless. Wouldn't you expect someone to believe you? Such as a close friend. Someone you had thought of as a close friend."

"Paula, there's no need to fly off the handle. I was just raising some questions—"

"You didn't raise them yesterday."

"I wasn't very coherent yesterday, was I?" said Cindy.

Paula caught herself short. She had almost forgotten that Cindy's problems were as troubling as her own. Cindy was making an effort to act as if she didn't care, but it was quite obvious that she did. A million small things gave her away. I should never have involved her in the first place, thought Paula.

"I'm sorry," she said. "I guess it's beginning to get to me."

Her anger ebbed away, to be replaced by an all-pervading sadness. A sense of sorrow she couldn't quite define. Sorrow for Cindy, whose blond beauty hadn't helped her win the thing she wanted most; for herself, because she had no idea of what her next move should be; for Bibi Marcovaldi, whose pride rebelled against the crippling effects of her arthritic pain; for Nick, whose first wife had cheated on him and who in turn had become involved in something that still held him now. Even for Charlie Nabokov, who hid God knows what secrets behind that foxlike, unattractive face. What had happened to all the happy people she'd once known?

On Wednesday Bibi Marcovaldi called to say she'd be flying back home the next day, and that same night Paula's parents called from Vermont. She was in the bathroom when the phone rang. Nick answered it from the kitchen, and she heard the low murmur of his conversation before he called out, "It's for you, hon. Your parents."

She picked up the extension in the bedroom.

"There you are, darling," said her mother. "So nice to hear your voice. We tried to call you all weekend, but you were never in."

The sound of static, followed by her father's deprecating cough.

"We tried to call you twice," he corrected mildly. "How are you, baby? We miss you."

The connection wasn't as clear as it normally was, and they sounded farther away than usual. Or was it just her state of mind?

"I'm fine," she said. "I thought of calling you, but then I decided to wait until I had something more definite to tell you. I have news for you. We're going to move, but I don't know when. We were out on Saturday looking at houses. We're going to sell the apartment as soon as we find a house we like and can afford."

"That *is* great news, darling." Her mother's relief flooded across the wires. "Such very good news. I've never liked the idea of your living in that apartment. You say you don't know when you'll be moving? I'll be glad to come down and help you pack."

"Hey, not so fast, Mom. It might take us months to find a place, and when we do, Nick says it will take two or three more months before we go to closing. The real-estate agent said she could sell the apartment tomorrow, but there's no point in selling it before we have some place to move to. It might take us a while. You know how expensive most houses are these days."

"I have some money put aside," her father said. "It's yours if you need more money for a down payment."

"Oh, Daddy. I think Nick's equity in the apartment will more than cover the down payment. It's more than doubled in value since he bought it five years ago. Besides, I don't think he'd accept. He never took a penny from Stephanie's folks when they were married."

"That's neither here nor there," her mother started to say with marked disapproval, but her father interrupted her.

"It would be strictly a business proposition," he said lightly. "You could repay us over a number of years at the usual rate of interest. Discuss it with Nick and think about it."

"We will, Daddy. And thanks. I'll let you know what happens. What's new with the two of you?"

But her mother was not to be distracted.

"Couldn't you sell the apartment and sublet somewhere until you find a house you like?"

"Oh, Mom." Paula sighed. "It would mean two moves, and

121

putting our furniture in storage, and a lot of time and money besides."

"Your father told you we'd be only too happy to let you have some money," her mother persisted. "The sooner you leave that apartment, the better, as far as I'm concerned. It's not a good place for you."

Paula's skin prickled. Who had told her the same thing just recently? Teresa. "This is not a good place," Teresa had said.

"I had this weird feeling today," her mother continued. "I was at the pottery wheel working on a vase, a very simple little thing, really, but try as I could, it just wouldn't turn out. And suddenly I had this feeling that something was wrong with you. That something very bad was about to happen. Are you sure you're all right?"

Paula was silent, taken aback, as always, by her mother's sixth sense. It was downright uncanny. Maybe it was time to tell them what had happened, but if she did, it would have to be all or nothing, and if she told them everything before discussing it with Nick, their marriage would be as good as over.

"You could come to stay with us for a few days," her father suggested.

It was strange that he, the rational man of logic, had nevertheless developed a healthy respect for his wife's premonitions.

I want to go home, thought Paula with a swift yearning that took her aback. I want to be with them. But she had promised herself that she would never run away again. And her home was here.

"We'd love to visit you, and soon," she said. "But not right now. I expect we'll be busy looking at houses for the next few weeks." She knew the call was getting to be expensive, but she felt unwilling to sever the connection between them. As long as she had them on the phone, she could almost feel their presence in the room. "I love you," she said quickly, half embarrassed. Verbal demonstrations of affection were unusual between them.

Her mother had her facts right but her timing wrong, she decided later. Something bad *had* already happened, and now that she was on her guard it wouldn't happen again. She and

Nick would regain their former closeness, and they wouldn't keep secrets from each other. Not ever. Not ever again.

Everything will be fine, she told herself, and wished desperately that she could believe it.

17

Bibi Marcovaldi looked around the room with satisfaction. The remarkable blue eyes caressed the bookcases, the small fireplace, the old Oriental rug, before turning to Paula with undisguised affection.

"More tea?" she said, picking up the teapot. Her hands were steady as she poured. The crippling arthritis had gone into one of its brief periods of remission.

"It's good to be back home," she said. "You wouldn't believe the Washington scene. A lot of sound and fury signifying nothing—is that how the quote goes? Everyone sitting around most earnestly and judiciously making serious promises only the most naïve believe will ever be kept. And the food. My dear, you wouldn't believe the drink and the food. Quite understandable in its own way, of course. One couldn't possibly face those conversations on an empty stomach. Talking of food, you simply must try one of these pastries. Teresa tells me she made them just for you."

Paula reached out obediently and bit into one. The soft cream filling melted in her mouth. She could detect the subtle taste of almonds and something less definable.

"I believe Teresa wants to fatten you up," Bibi was saying. "She's quite alarmed at the amount of weight you've lost. She scolded me this morning, saying I've been working you too hard."

Paula finished the pastry and leaned back in the wide chair, holding the teacup in both hands. Its warmth felt good against her palms. She looked at Bibi. There was something about the faintly malicious prattle of her gossip, the deceptive innocence of those immense blue eyes, the arrogant tilt of the small elegant head, that was immensely reassuring, as though nothing uncivil or primitive would have the impertinence to rear its head in her presence. She and Teresa are older than any of us, thought Paula, and yet they have an endurance we all lack.

"You've been working me too hard? Hardly that," she said. "I didn't realize until you were gone how little work there really is for me to do. You've been creating work for me, haven't you? Trying to keep me busy."

Bibi Marcovaldi's mobile face was capable of many expressions, but embarrassment wasn't one of them. She shrugged lightly and smiled.

"My dear," she said, "even if it were true, I am too old and wily to be trapped into any such admission. And it so happens that it isn't true, particularly on those days when I don't function the way I should." She glanced at her slightly twisted hands. "As a matter of fact," she added, "before I met you I called one of those agencies and told them I was looking for someone to assist me. They informed me that what I wanted was a social secretary. They would have somebody for me in no time, they said. Sure enough, she showed up the next day, a bright young woman with an unfortunate voice. And far too many teeth and eyelashes. And the sensibilities of a metal filing cabinet. Very efficient, though. She took a look at this small room and assured me that with only a little bit of effort we could turn it into a modern, businesslike office. It was too abysmal for words." She shuddered delicately to indicate just how abysmal the experience had been.

Paula laughed out loud. "Bibi, you're impossible," she said.

"Quite so," said Bibi with approval. "And the fact that you can tell me so shows that we are friends. I look forward to our afternoons together. So you see, you're the one who's helping me out, not the other way around." She paused. "But I expect you're anxious to get back to your own job?"

"Not really. I was at first, but I've been gone so long I'm not sure of how well I'd fit in. Or if I'd still like the work, for that matter. Isn't that awful? I'm twenty-six and I still haven't decided what to do with myself."

"Twenty-six? My dear, you're just a child."

"Not really. My mother had three children by the time she was my age. But Nick's been encouraging me to go back to school to learn a trade that I would really like. I might at that, if we can still afford it after we buy the house."

"Ah, yes. I'm delighted to hear about the house, and so is Teresa. She's already planning the housewarming dinner she wants to cook for you. You've quite won her over. Would you care for some more tea?"

"No, thanks, Bibi. I told Cindy I'd be down by five o'clock."

"You should have asked her to join us."

"I did, as a matter of fact, but I think she wanted to be alone for a while. She's still trying to pull herself together. It's not easy. I went through something similar myself once," she confided.

"And so did I," said Bibi. "So did I."

The old face softened and seemed to reflect the image of past loves and hatreds, old passions that whispered at the back of the mind like dying leaves on an autumn tree. And then she smiled and the illusion passed.

"I'll see you tomorrow afternoon," she said.

It was good having Bibi back. It was good having Cindy in the apartment, for that matter, thought Paula on her way down. She wondered how Cindy and Bibi Marcovaldi would get along. Very well indeed, she suspected. They were both real. There was no pretense to either one of them. But why this sudden wish to bring everyone together into one large, happy family? At this rate she'd be trying to form a commune, a stronghold of familiar faces to stand between her and . . . and what? A shadowy figure leaped into her consciousness. She stood stock-still, stricken.

She would have to find a way to control her fear, or else it would become like a virus that would eat away at the tissue of her life. On any one day the newspapers were filled with stories of people who were mugged, beaten up, raped . . . or even murdered. Did the ones who were lucky enough to survive ever manage to forget the viciousness in the eyes of a husband or lover, the insanity flaring from the face of a junkie, the demented demands of a rapist? The sudden crash of a blow, the tearing, the twisting flash of pain? Did they ever manage to forget the humiliation and the fear? They would have to if they were to resume normal lives. And so would she.

126

There was a chance that whoever had been in the apartment, whoever had attacked her, had been there after one thing and one thing only. The diary. Not necessarily for purposes of blackmail, but because it contained something incriminating. If so, they would stay away now that they had it, and she and Nick would have a chance to once again start leading normal lives. Later, when their marriage was on a more solid footing and they had grown used to depend on each other, perhaps he would tell her whatever it was he had been holding back. In the meantime she must stop jumping at shadows.

That evening Nick took her and Cindy out to dinner, and afterward they walked to the East Side to see a movie that had been drawing rave reviews. The soft night air was balmy, the people they passed looked carefree, laughing, sharing a gay holiday mood. The ancient spring rites persisted in the city.

The next day dawned equally perfect. When they woke up, the room was tinged with amber tones of sunlight, and the warm breeze stirring the curtains was laden with the promises of summer.

"My last day of playing hooky," said Cindy after Nick had left for work. "Let's go shopping this morning, shall we? I think I'd better show up at the office on Monday. My boss must be getting restless."

"Aren't you afraid you might lose your job?"

Cindy shrugged lightly. "What if I do?" she said. "I'm a good stenographer, one of the best ones around. My typing is fast and letter-perfect. It's not glamorous work, but I make as much money as any lawyer or teacher just out of school. And I can get a job anytime, anywhere. Good secretaries are hard to find these days." She paused. "Besides, I *have* been sick," she added.

"And now? Are you feeling any better?"

"Of course. I'm feeling fine."

"No, really. Please tell me how you feel."

"It's going to take a while," Cindy said. Something wounded looked out of her eyes. "I don't think there's been an hour when I haven't wanted to call him. I look at the phone and think it would be so easy. Just pick it up and dial. And then I'd hear his voice."

"But you didn't call him."

"No, I didn't. Staying with you helped. I might have called him if I hadn't been with you. And it's getting easier. I thought I'd go home sometime tomorrow."

"Must you?" said Paula. She was caught off balance, as though a support she'd been leaning on had been snatched away.

"I have to go back home sooner or later, don't I? And face it on my own. But listen, Paula. About that other thing. Nothing's happened this week, so it might be all over. If it isn't, call me, and I'll be right back. But have you considered that whoever it was might have been looking for that diary all along? There might be something in it they didn't want anyone to see. Now that they have it they won't bother you again."

"I was thinking the same thing," said Paula. "We may never find out who it was, but I don't really care. As long as it's all over." She felt buoyant and carefree with a sudden rush of happiness.

They walked down to Fifth Avenue and started window-shopping. The summer displays were in full bloom. Glistening silks, soft cottons, bright wraps and bikinis, improbable hats and shoes that might be worn by a gymnast with a good sense of balance. The windows of Tiffany's and Cartier's glistened with their king's ransom.

"No, not a king's," Cindy amended. "Aren't all kings poor these days? An oil tycoon's, perhaps. Or a corporation president's."

They walked across to Madison Avenue and tried on a number of dresses in a French boutique. The clothes were elegant and striking, but not as striking as the price tags. They walked out without buying anything. The supercilious eyes of the salesgirl told them she'd known they wouldn't buy anything all along.

Shortly before one o'clock they managed to hail a cab and went back to the apartment. It had been a happy morning and they were sorry to see it end, filled with that odd sense of letdown that follows a party or leave-taking.

"I've got to go up to Bibi's," said Paula. "She'd like you to come up for tea around four o'clock. Won't you come? She said she'll never forgive you if you don't."

"Sure, why not?" said Cindy. She grinned. "It's my last day. I might as well make the most of it."

"Good. I'll call you as soon as we're ready."

But it was Cindy who called her an hour later. Paula was sitting at Bibi Marcovaldi's small desk, reading a letter that was almost abusive in its request for a contribution. She was trying to decide if it deserved an answer when the phone rang. She picked it up absentmindedly.

"Marcovaldi residence," she said.

"Paula, please come down." The voice was so low and intense that it took her a second to recognize it.

"Cindy, is that you? What's wrong?"

"Oh, my God, Paula, I know who it is. I think I know. Please come down. Hurry."

"I'll be right down. But won't you tell me what's happened?"

"I can't right now. I can't even believe it's true. But you must hurry. I can't stand it much longer."

The intense whisper sent a thrill of fear down Paula's spine. She pressed the receiver more closely to her ear, as though to establish better contact.

"Cindy, listen carefully," she said. "I'll be right down. Don't do anything until I get there. Do you understand? I'm on my way."

She heard a faint gasp and then a ringing in her ear. Cindy had hung up. She jumped up and hunted for her handbag, got out her keys. She caught a glimpse of Bibi's startled eyes, of something stark in Teresa's dark face. "Cindy's in trouble," she told them over her shoulder. She ran out into the hallway and pressed the elevator button. Again. And again. The indicator showed the elevator was down on the first floor. She couldn't wait for it.

She ran toward the staircase and opened the fire-escape door. Why can't I run downstairs two steps at a time? she thought inanely. Let Cindy be all right, she prayed.

The door of the apartment was locked. She inserted her key in the first lock, and suddenly she knew, with a certainty that defied all reason, that Cindy was not all right. That she would never be all right, never again. Her hand was quite steady as the second lock clicked open.

The apartment was just the way she'd left it. One of the

windows facing the park was wide open, allowing the mellow breeze to pour through the room. The morning newspaper lay neatly folded on the coffee table. There was no sign of Cindy. Paula was halfway into the living room before she saw the words scrawled across the mirror hanging above the fireplace.

"I can't stand it anymore," they said. They'd been written with a crayon or a lipstick. A lipstick red as blood.

Paula closed her eyes for a second and then walked slowly toward the open window. She looked down. A group of people had gathered around a doll-like, broken-looking figure lying on the cement. A small figure with glistening bright hair surrounded by a puddle the same color as the writing on the mirror. An ambulance screeched up the street and stopped in front of the building.

How fast they are, thought Paula. How efficient. She saw someone wave the crowd away. She saw someone else cover the small still figure with a blanket.

She continued standing at the window until Teresa's strong arms pulled her away.

18

"They do it all the time," said the older cop. "All the time, all over." He shrugged his massive shoulders, as though to disclaim all responsibility for such colossal folly. "Sometimes it's an affair gone sour, like your friend's. Sometimes it's a job they lose, or a fight with their parents. I have a daughter her age," he added more gently, rubbing a powerful hand across his plain broad face. "She has a husband and two kids. They live in Queens."

His colleague had been busy taking notes. He was a young man with a soft voice and dark bright eyes in a starved-looking face. He said, "Did Miss Michaels seem particularly despondent? Did she at any time threaten to take her life?"

"On the contrary," Nick told him. "She was unhappy, of course, but she seemed to be getting over it. My wife told you that they went shopping together this morning." He turned to the older cop. "We had absolutely no reason to believe she was planning suicide, Sergeant Plover."

"Plower. With a W. It's seldom planned in advance, you know. And it often happens after a party or visit with friends. A sudden lift, a few laughs, and then the letdown that follows is all that much worse. That last-minute call to Mrs. Girard also fits the pattern, for that matter. They often call for help at the last minute. Do you know the name of the man she was involved with?"

"I believe his first name was Bill," said Nick. "Do you know his last name, Paula?"

"She never mentioned it," said Paula. "I think she was trying to protect him. He's married, you know. He lives somewhere in New Jersey."

"That doesn't narrow it down very much, does it? There must be thousands of men named Bill living in New Jersey who indulge in their little flings while in town. He'll probably read about your friend's death in the paper tomorrow. And five will get you ten that he'll be involved in another affair within six months."

Paula let the conversation flow around her. She had made her statement earlier and now she sat silently, speaking only when asked a direct question. She was thinking about Cindy's last telephone call. "I know who it is," Cindy had said. "I think I know." What had she meant? She looked at the people in the room and saw them as clearly as a frozen tableau. Nick looked pale but totally composed, so that it would have been difficult for a stranger to guess he was under a strain. Bibi Marcovaldi was sitting very straight, her face impassive, those huge eyes of hers for once devoid of any expression. Teresa was standing in the dining-room doorway, her breasts pillowed against her folded arms. The stern disapproval on her face was belied by slow tears crawling like insects down her cheeks. Sergeant Plower and his starved-looking colleague were gathering their things. They looked ready to leave.

"Cindy didn't kill herself," Paula said suddenly, coming out of her trance.

"You mean an accident?" Sergeant Plower said kindly. "It's possible, of course. It would be possible. Except for that short message that she left behind."

He gestured at the mirror above the fireplace. The police photographer had taken his shots and Teresa had washed it as soon as he was done, so that it sparkled clean and new. But the message on it seemed indelible, never to be forgotten. Any more than she could forget the writing in that diary, thought Paula.

The policemen said their good-byes and left, taking the keys to Cindy's apartment with them. They said they would notify her closest relative, a sister she'd disliked intensely who lived somewhere in Iowa. They could come back if they had any more questions. They were grateful for the help Paula and Nick had given them.

"Do you have any brandy?" Bibi Marcovaldi asked Nick after they left. "I think Paula could use some. So could I, for that matter."

"And you, Teresa?"

"No, thank you. It is kind, but no."

He brought a glass over to Paula and she took it, but when he put his hand on her shoulder, she shied away from it. As though it were a stranger's touch. As though he were intruding on her privacy. The brandy flamed in her throat, sent waves of warmth down to her chest and the pit of her stomach. But it didn't touch the icy particle embedded inside her. She stood up. She felt clearheaded and was faintly surprised when she stumbled. Before Nick could reach her, Teresa was at her side and put her strong arms around her.

"My poor *bambina*," said Teresa, stroking her hair. "My dear *bimba*. It will be all right, eh? You will see. It will be all right."

Paula relaxed against her. Teresa's warm body smelled faintly of detergent and subtle kitchen spices. Above Teresa's wide shoulder she could see Bibi's and Nick's stark, intent faces.

"I think you should take her away," Bibi told Nick. "To a hotel, or up to Vermont. Away from this building. It will not be good for her to remain here now."

They exchanged a long look.

"Of course," said Nick. "You're absolutely right. I'll call around for some reservations right away. And next week we'll try for a place we can sublet until we find a house."

"*No*," said Paula.

They stared at her.

"No," she repeated. "I asked Cindy to stay here with us. And now I'm going to stay. No matter what. So please forget about the reservations."

They started to argue with her, and it was strange, because while she could see every detail of their faces, their words sounded all jumbled up together, so that she couldn't quite make out what they were saying. She watched them with the helplessness and determination of a deaf-mute. It was Teresa who took charge.

"Come to bed, *piccola*," she said. "There, little one. Teresa shall make you all comfortable in bed and bring you some hot tea. And later you shall sleep. You will think what it is you want to do later. Later, *bambina*."

She took Paula's hand and led her into the bedroom. It should have been embarrassing to be undressed and put into

133

bed like a small child, but it wasn't at all. It was comforting and nice. And it was nice to be under the covers. She felt warm, except for that sliver of ice embedded deeply in the hollow of her stomach.

Nick and Bibi Marcovaldi were talking in the living room. Now that she couldn't see them, she could make out their words quite distinctly, as though her nervous system could monitor only one of her senses at any given time.

"Perhaps I should have a doctor in to see her," Nick was saying. "I don't like the way she looks."

"It's the shock," Bibi told him. "She needs warmth and quiet and complete rest. Trust Teresa to look after her. Teresa's instinct is infallible in these things." There was a short pause. "It *is* a shocking thing," Bibi added. "Poor Cindy. So very young, and beautiful as well. Did you have any idea at all that she was thinking of suicide."

"None whatsoever. I would have bet anything against it. We could tell that she was terribly upset, of course, and deeply unhappy. But she did seem to be getting over it. She was a survivor, or so I thought. There was a single-mindedness about her that made the idea of self destruction totally preposterous. And yet we should have seen the warning signs. We were responsible for her."

"Am I my brother's keeper?" Bibi murmured. "We are all to some extent. But only to a limited extent. Ultimately we all bear the responsibility for our own actions."

Paula shifted against the pillows. "I know who it is." Cindy hadn't killed herself, she wanted to tell them, but she was unable to get up and go into the living room to face them. Besides, did it really matter what they all thought? The important thing was that Cindy would still be alive if she hadn't come here. "Cindy," Paula whispered, but there was no answering echo in her mind. She closed her eyes. The sound of their voices continued from the living room.

"I'm afraid," said Nick. "Afraid for Paula. She hasn't been herself the last few weeks, and this may well be more than she can take. I think I should get her away from here. But you heard her. She refuses to go."

"Perhaps she has her own reasons," Bibi suggested.

"Perhaps she does. But in that case, why doesn't she share

them with me? She's changed. I've watched her changing a little more each day. And there is nothing I can do about it."

"She's changed? In what way?"

Another brief silence, as though Nick were marshaling his thoughts or trying to overcome his natural reluctance to breach their privacy.

"I remember when we first met," he said finally. "We knew each other for six months before we were married. Six months and a week, to be precise. She was different from anyone I'd ever known before."

"She was raised in the country," Bibi pointed out.

"Yes. You should meet her parents. They must have been married for thirty years at least, and their marriage shows it. Steady as a rock. But there's also a freshness about them, a joy that's hard to describe. It's as if they renewed each other every day."

"And the same thing happened with you and Paula?"

"Yes. At least I believed so. At first I thought she was too young for me, even though we're only three years apart. And then I realized there was nothing naïve about her awareness or that keen delight she takes in everything around her. I felt like a man who's crawled out of a cave into bright sunlight. I decided never to look back, to let nothing disturb that bright new world we'd managed to create. But recently she's been drawing away from me. I can feel her holding back. I'm afraid of losing her. If I haven't already done so."

"My dear," said Bibi Marcovaldi. "My dear." Her tone echoed the desolation in his voice.

It's true, thought Paula with her newborn insight. She had been drawing away from him, and now there was a vast distance between them. Was it her fault for not trusting him? Or his for not believing her? Not that the reason mattered. What mattered was the slow process that was separating them as inevitably as if they'd been on two trains headed in different directions. *Something had come between them.* And something was holding her here in this apartment with the strength of a powerful magnet. She could no more leave here now than she could change the color of her eyes or skin. She would have to stay here for better or for worse. "Cindy," she whispered again, and this time there was an answering echo in her mind. She slept.

When she woke up, she smelled something delicious from the kitchen, and guessed that Teresa must have fixed dinner for them all. She put on her dressing gown and joined them at the table. They ate quietly and thoughtfully, without much conversation. Through unspoken accord they didn't mention Cindy, though Paula gathered that while she was asleep a number of reporters had come and had been turned away by the old doorman. No one brought up the funeral arrangements. No one mentioned that it might be a good idea to move away for a few days.

It wasn't until after Bibi and Teresa had left and she and Nick were both in bed that he brought up the subject once again. He was leaning on his elbow, his head cupped in his hand.

"Are you sure you couldn't use a change of scene?" he asked.

"I'm sure," she said. There was such finality in her voice that he didn't press the point. He continued to look at her, and for the first time since she'd met him he seemed at a loss for words.

"Paula?" he said finally. "I love you."

"I love you too," she said.

But when he reached to comfort her, she felt the same shrinking away she'd experienced earlier, and though she tried to hide it, he must have sensed it too. He drew away from her and turned his head so that she couldn't see his face.

"It's late," he said, looking at the alarm clock. "You need a good night's rest. Shall I turn out the light?"

Turn out the light? Even as a child she had never been afraid of the dark, but suddenly she couldn't bear the thought of the room plunged into shadow.

"Please leave it on for a few minutes," she said. "I'll read for a while."

He fell asleep before her. And now it was her turn to lean up on her elbow, to look down at his sleeping face as though it were a beloved photograph of someone she might never meet again. She ached to hold him. She wanted to touch his dark springing hair, to trace the sculptured outline of his cheekbones, to smooth away the small tick at the corner of his eyelid.

Death dictates renewal, she had once read, but she was still taken aback by the surge of passion that swept through her, leaving her breathless and unsteady. Her blood drummed through her veins. All she'd have to do would be to lean over and kiss him, to let her naked breasts brush across his chest, and he'd wake up ready and aroused as his arms slid around her. My God, how she wanted him to hold her. To have him ease that rushing need. To soothe away the loneliness.

It would be so easy, and yet she couldn't do it. She could hear his even breathing, see his sleeping, vulnerable face, but she was separated from him as effectively as if a wall of Plexiglas had risen up between them. Nick. Cindy. Stephanie. Their names whirled through her mind like images in a nightmare. After a while she got up and turned out the light.

Sometime during the night she dreamed she heard the sound of soft laughter coming from the living room.

19

The store was narrow and long and brightly lit. An imposing array of rifles and shotguns was displayed in glass cases along the walls. Pistols and revolvers lay beneath the thick glass tops of the counters running down one side of the room. Two men in business suits were debating the merits of a rifle under the watchful eyes of a salesman. A second salesman dressed with all the flair of an undertaker and wearing an expression to match looked up when she walked in.

"May I help you?" he said, though his tone seemed to imply that he personally doubted it.

"Yes," said Paula. "I'd like to buy a handgun."

"A handgun? Of course. Would you prefer a revolver or an automatic?"

"A revolver, I think." She and her brothers had sometimes used her father's revolver for target practice, and she had learned to clean and oil it after each use before replacing it in its chamois wrapping.

"A revolver it is, then," the salesman said. He was speaking in hushed tones, as though unwilling to breach the quiet of the carpeted room. "We have them in all calibers and price ranges, of course, starting with a small twenty-two caliber, a handy little gun that takes up little room, up to a forty-four Magnum. But first—may I see your license?"

She stared at him blankly.

"A license?" she said, feeling foolish. "What type of license?"

"A police license, of course. Didn't you know you need one before you can buy a gun in New York?"

"No, I didn't. I thought you were supposed to register it later, after you bought it."

His expression became even more doleful.

138

"You must be from out of state," he said, and looked at her closely, as though to memorize her face for a potential police lineup. "Here," he said finally, writing on a slip of paper. "Go down to One Police Plaza. You know where that is? Way downtown, around Chambers Street. Apply for a permit. If and when you get a permit, we shall be more than happy to help you select the gun best suited to your needs."

She took a subway downtown and lost her way in the narrow winding streets. When she finally found 1 Police Plaza, she had to wait almost an hour before she was allowed to talk to the oversized woman who presided over her desk with all the charm of a Marine drill sergeant facing new recruits.

The woman had a blond head of perfectly coiffed hair, several layers of makeup, and three muscular chins that rippled down toward her powerful chest. She listened to Paula impatiently.

"Do you own your own business?" she interrupted her halfway through her request.

"No," said Paula.

"Do you carry large sums of money in the course of your work?"

"No. No, I don't."

"Well, in that case, would you tell me exactly why you think you should have a gun?"

"For self-defense," said Paula.

"For self-defense?" said the woman. She leaned forward, and her massive breasts flattened across the desk top in the process. Something close to friendliness crept into her eyes. "Let me give you some advice, honey. Leave the guns to experts. If we gave a permit to everyone who wanted a gun for self-defense, the whole city would be walking around armed to its teeth. The best self-defense for a girl like yourself is to stay home at night. And keep a good, hefty bolt on your door."

She leaned back in her chair, the brief friendliness gone.

"You can put your request in writing," she added, "and it will be reviewed through proper channels. But I must warn you that I don't think we'll be able to help you. To get a permit you must show due cause," she said, relishing the words. "It goes without saying that you must show due cause."

There were probably a hundred places where she could get

139

a gun without a permit, thought Paula, but they most certainly wouldn't be listed in the Yellow Pages. She stood still on the sidewalk, unaware of the curious glances some passersby gave her, or of the cab that slowed down and almost stopped before rejoining the congested traffic.

So that was that. It was ironic that any gangster, any minor hoodlum, any streetwise teenager could get his choice of weapons for the asking, whereas the average citizen was denied equal opportunity. Just the other day she had read about a store owner who had shot one of two murderous thugs who had broken into his shop, and had been arrested for illegal possession of a weapon. And yet it had been the thug who had fired the first shot. It made no sense, as far as she could see. She had thought a gun would provide her with some measure of security, because she knew that her danger was both imminent and real. Stephanie and Cindy were both dead. She felt absolutely certain that she was slated to be next.

She could go visit her parents for a while, just as Nick had suggested. Or she could merely pack a bag and check into a hotel. She could do neither. Partially because she felt responsible for Cindy's death, and partially because the unseen face of danger had mesmerized her and was making her run in ever smaller concentric circles that would lead . . . where?

Once, as a child, she had watched a television documentary and stared at the screen while a mouse was digested by a boa constrictor. The documentary was well done, detailed, and unforgettable. She could still see the small furry rodent fixed in its place by those reptilian eyes, could still remember the soft slithering sound the snake had made as it moved gracefully and slowly toward its prey. There had been no need for it to hurry. The mouse hadn't tried to escape. It had been unable to move by so much as an inch.

It took her an hour to get back uptown. When she reached Dover House, she hesitated before going in, until the doorman saw her and greeted her with a wide smile. He had already told her how sorry he was about Cindy's death. His remarks had been sincere, devoid of the disapproval she had seen in the faces of a number of her fellow tenants. They had made it obvious that they disapproved of suicide committed in such a spectacular manner. It wasn't good for the reputation of the building. It brought a certain notoriety. It brought down real-estate values.

Paula walked through the lobby half-defiantly, readying herself to meet one of those icy, disapproving stares. Instead, she was met by Bibi Marcovaldi's dazzling smile.

"Paula, my dear child, how good to see you," she said. "You look exhausted. I do hope you're not coming down with something. The weather is so beautiful these days, the very worst time of year for colds, don't you think? Have you had lunch? Why don't you come up and chat with me while I arrange these flowers," she added. "The shop around the corner managed to find some lilac for me."

"They're beautiful," said Paula, touching one of the delicate, fragrant branches protruding from their wrapping.

"My very favorite," said Bibi. "Next to mimosa, of course. And a small wild flower I have never found anywhere away from home. A golden flower called ginestra."

She turned around and led the way toward the elevators. She walked slowly, leaning upon her cane, but even so Paula had trouble in keeping up with her. She was seized by the dizziness she'd been experiencing on and off since Cindy's death. The lobby spun around her in wild crazy circles, and she was glad when she could steady herself against the elevator door.

"Would you like more shrimp salad?" asked Bibi, raising her napkin to her lips.

"No, thanks," said Paula. "Though it was very good. I'm getting spoiled by Teresa's cooking."

She took a sip of the chilled white wine. She had told Bibi that Cindy's sister was flying out to pack Cindy's things and close up the apartment. Cindy's body would be flown for burial in the family plot out in Iowa.

"Cindy's sister didn't sound very friendly when I called," Paula told Bibi. "I offered to help her clean the apartment and she refused. I had the feeling she holds us to blame for Cindy's death."

"She probably blames herself," said Bibi. "Didn't you tell me they hadn't talked for years? Perhaps it's just as well you didn't meet. What would you say to each other? It is always difficult. One either says too much or not enough."

"Perhaps you're right."

"Of course I'm right. Tell me. What have you been doing with yourself the last few days?"

They hadn't seen each other since the afternoon of Cindy's death. Through unspoken consent they had understood that Paula would need some time to herself, and Bibi had arranged for a young painter she knew to help her out with her correspondence. He'd been only too glad of the chance to earn some extra money, and Paula had been relieved to be released from the responsibility of the daily schedule. There were things she had to plan, things she had to do.

Yet she missed the routine, the *safety* of the afternoons she'd spent with Bibi. Yesterday she had spent the day by herself, and by midmorning the silence of the apartment had become oppressive. In spite of herself she had started to listen for small noises. Everything was still. Or was it? At one point she thought she heard a sigh from the living room. The echo of a footstep. The faint rattling of china in the kitchen.

It had been her imagination, of course. But supposing someone *had* come to the door. Supposing she heard the sound of a key slipped into the lock and saw the door open slowly to admit . . . whom?

"This morning I tried to buy a gun," she heard herself saying.

"A gun?" said Bibi. It sounded like a sigh.

They stared at each other. A shaft of sunlight streamed through the open window. Something flickered in Bibi's immense eyes. Her thin face looked old and lined in the harsh light. Time hovered, suspended between them. And then Bibi sighed.

"So it's that bad, is it?" she said.

"Yes," Paula said simply.

"And you still won't consider going to visit your parents?"

"If I went now, I might not come back. I can't go."

"No. I see that you can't. I probably wouldn't either. Tell me. Have you talked to Nick? He's very concerned about you, you know."

"Oh, yes, I know. I'm worried about him, for that matter. It's odd, isn't it? We both care for each other, and yet it's as if we spoke a different language, or as if a barrier stood between us. I did try to talk to him once. He got angry. He doesn't want to talk to me about the past."

"What do you mean by the past?" Bibi asked sharply. "Do you mean Stephanie?"

Paula looked at her. How much should she tell her? She had come to think of Bibi as a friend, almost a contemporary. Yet there were at least two generations between them . . . and they came from different countries, almost different worlds.

"Yes," she said slowly. "He won't talk to me about Stephanie. It's almost as though he had locked that part of his life away."

"That's understandable, surely. You must know by now he wasn't happy with Stephanie."

"Yes, I do know that. And yet, you see, I have the strong feeling that everything that's been happening is somehow involved with her. Or with her death."

"What *has* been happening, Paula?"

Fleeting motes of dust danced in the light between them. The sound of traffic came muted from outside. She had to talk to someone. Cindy was dead. And who else was there? She had lost track of her friends from out of town. If she called her parents they would come down and collect her as if she were a child. There was no one else other than this old, unusual woman sitting so quietly in her chair.

"What has been happening?" she said. "Odd things. Peculiar things. I don't know if you'd believe me if I told you. Did I ever tell you that I had a grandmother who had what she called the second sight? Any psychiatrist would have declared her insane, but none of us thought she was. And yet I've wondered about myself. Because, you see, there's absolutely no way anyone could have entered our apartment. And yet they did, a number of times. There's no reason I can think of why anyone should hate me. And yet I've felt that hatred, there are times when it surrounds me like a fog. Does it sound mad to you?"

Bibi sighed again and leaned forward to touch Paula's hand. Her fingers were cool and dry.

"I'm old enough," she said, "to realize that nothing is impossible. But why do you link these things—and I shan't ask you to go into details unless you want to do so—to Stephanie and her death?"

"Because," Paula whispered. "I read some notes Stephanie had written before she was killed. Her experiences seemed to parallel mine. While reading her diary, I had the odd impression that I was looking into a mirror image. I don't believe she was killed by a random burglar. I think it was someone she knew. Someone Nick knew."

"I think I understand. You think that whoever killed Stephanie killed Cindy as well, don't you? That is what you meant when you said Cindy hadn't killed herself."

"Yes," said Paula. "I know that you and Nick have been friends for a long time. I know I shouldn't ask you this. But if you know, please tell me. Was Nick seeing anyone while he was married to Stephanie?"

"You mean did he have a mistress? I would doubt it very much, and I have known quite a few men during my time. Why? Do you think he's still involved with another woman now?"

"No!" Paula cried out, and realized she was protesting too much. "No," she repeated more quietly. "We love each other. We spend all our free time together. There's no way he could still be involved with someone else."

"And yet you went out and tried to buy a gun. I gather you were unable to get one. You need a permit to buy firearms in New York. Would you mind telling me why you want a gun?"

"Because I'm afraid," said Paula.

There, it was out. The admission brought her relief, but at the same time it made her fear more real, as though the words had given it body and substance. Once again she remembered the small white mouse waiting quietly and helplessly for the snake to strike. She closed her eyes to shut out the all-too-vivid image. She heard Bibi Marcovaldi calling out to Teresa, heard Teresa's response. They were speaking in Italian and she couldn't understand their urgent conversation. When she opened her eyes, she saw Bibi and Teresa looking at her. There was a gun in Teresa's hand.

20

Paula's heart skipped a beat. Teresa held the gun casually, but in a manner that made it unmistakable that she was used to handling firearms. Her heavy face was almost but not quite devoid of expression. She crossed the room and placed the gun in Bibi's outstretched hand.

Bibi took it from her and broke it open to examine the chamber. The weapon looked incongruous in the thin, blue-veined hand.

"You both seem familiar with firearms," said Paula. Her voice sounded faint in her own ears.

"We are," Bibi told her. "Are you?"

"Yes," said Paula. If Bibi didn't choose to elaborate, neither would she.

"With handguns?"

"Slightly. My father owns one. I think it was different from yours."

"The principle is the same. This is a thirty-two-caliber Baretta. It's old but in good condition. It has six chambers. It's fully loaded, as you see. The safety catch is down here. I should warn you that it has a tendency to fire slightly to the right. The sight is a fraction of a millimeter off, I believe."

She reached out and laid it on the table next to Paula.

"Keep it for as long as you need it," she said.

"But why?" said Paula.

"Because we have another one," Bibi told her as lightly as a housewife assuring her neighbor that she can easily spare a cup of sugar. "And I don't really think we need both, do you? We have a permit for both of them," she added.

"Yes, but why are you letting me have it?" Paula insisted. "Just like that, without any conditions, without questions asked?"

145

"Because I trust your common sense," Bibi said simply. "And because once, a long time ago, I made a bad mistake. A mistake I swore I would never make again."

"Do you want to tell me about it?"

"It's an old story," said Bibi. "It happened many years ago. Before you were born, in fact. It's Teresa's story, actually, but I don't think she would mind if I were to tell you now."

Her eyes assumed that inward look Paula had noticed several times before, like searchlights probing something in the past. Her face was as remote as a photograph in an old picture album.

"It happened during the Second World War," she said. "There have been many wars since then, but that was my war. Much has been written about it. Perhaps too much. Or perhaps not enough. It was a peculiar time, to put it mildly. Loyalties were mixed. Friend turned against friend, child against parent, and the other way around. Loyalties tend to become mixed in times of stress."

She paused, and Paula remembered what Nick had told her about Bibi's activities in the underground movement.

"Many weird characters cropped up at that time," Bibi continued. "One of them was a priest. A defrocked priest. That means he had been excommunicated from the Church. He had quite a large following, nevertheless, because of a singular talent. He claimed he could tell whether any one person was alive or dead. If they were alive, he could also tell where they were at that time. What country. What town. You must understand that people were scattered all over during the war. Some of them in the army. Others in concentration camps. People flocked to this priest to find out what had happened to their missing relatives."

"He must have become rich."

"He never took a penny for his services."

"Then how did he live?"

"Who knows?" There was a Gallic shrug in her voice. "Perhaps he begged in the streets. Perhaps he was a spy for the fascists, or communists, or both. Perhaps he had money of his own. The fact remains that he was supposed to be quite good at what he did. And when she heard about him, Teresa went to him. It may be difficult for you to imagine now, but Teresa was young and lovely in those days. There were many men after her, but she was interested only in one. His name was Carlo. He was as slim and dark and vigorous as she was. They would have had fine children. They were very much in love."

"And Teresa went to the priest to find out where Carlo was?"

"No. She knew where he was. He was right there in Rome. No, she went to have their fortune told. She took a picture of Carlo along with her, as instructed."

"Did the priest read their cards?"

"No. His method was simpler, and much more dramatic. He used a pendulum. A small iron crescent hanging from a string. He had a large map spread across the floor. Teresa told me that it was a map of the entire world, but that it also included two unmarked areas. One was colored white, the other gray. The white indicated death, the gray immediate danger. He would stand above the map, pendulum in hand, looking at the picture brought to him. After a while the pendulum would start to swing until it pointed to a specific section of the map."

"And in Carlo's case it pointed toward the gray area," said Paula, more as a statement than a question. She was caught up in this old world Bibi was recreating for her. "Carlo was in the danger zone, wasn't he?" she said.

"Yes. Teresa was terrified. She begged me to get him out of town. I laughed at her. I was young myself in those days, suspicious of anything that wasn't logical, demonstrable, pragmatic. Superstitious nonsense, I told Teresa. Carlo was in no danger. He had partisan sympathies, that's true; he even attended occasional party meetings. But he wasn't really active in the movement. He wasn't an activist, as you say today. He had no time to be. He worked twelve hours a day in the vegetable shop he'd inherited from his father. There were people who needed our help more, I told Teresa. People whose danger was at once more immediate and more real."

"What happened?"

"Carlo was seized and executed one month later. We found out that a cousin of his had turned him in. The cousin took over the store after Carlo's death."

She fell silent, staring at the dancing motes of dust. Her

face had the expressionless look of someone who's learned to live with old, unhealed wounds.

"What did you do?" said Paula.

"Do? I did nothing. It was too late to do anything. What I should have done would always remain undone. I should have helped Teresa when she asked me, not because of what that odd, deranged man had told her, but because she *asked* me. I was her closest friend, and I let her down. That would be the last time, I promised myself then. Never again."

"And is that why you're helping me out now?"

"Perhaps," said Bibi. "Do you want to talk about it further? Do you want to tell me exactly what's been happening, what you suspect?"

"Not right now. Not until I've had a chance to talk to Nick. I must talk to Nick first," said Paula. "If I can. I must try to reach him. If I can't, our marriage is as good as over."

She stood up and picked up the gun. It felt surprisingly light and compact in her hand. She slipped it into her shoulder bag.

"What did Teresa do?" she asked Bibi. "What did Teresa do about the cousin who turned her boyfriend in?"

Bibi was standing up with the help of her cane. She glanced up at Paula with unconcealed surprise.

"What did Teresa do?" she echoed. "Why, my child. What do you think she did?"

When Paula went downstairs, she picked up the phone and called long-distance information for the number of the Brewster residence in Chappaqua. To her relief the number was listed. The first time she dialed it the maid answered and informed her formally that Mrs. Brewster was out. She had to call twice more before she reached her.

When she did, Mrs. Brewster sounded as though she'd just emerged from a cold bath. Her tone was glacial. Yes, she understood who Paula was, but surely they had nothing to discuss? A diary? Oh. She hadn't known her daughter had been keeping a diary. Very well. She still failed to see what they had to talk about, but if Paula insisted, she would see her tomorrow. Paula was to come out at two o'clock and bring the diary with her. She hung up before Paula could explain that the diary was gone.

Paula replaced the phone in its cradle and stared at it for a long time. Her fingers tingled. She had felt something akin to electric shock at the sound of Mrs. Brewster's voice, a sense of déjà vu that defied all logic, since she'd never talked to the woman before. Stephanie was their only common denominator. *Stephanie*. It all centered around her. Paula was sure of that, just as she was sure that whatever had happened to Stephanie was happening to her, too. She was being swept along down the same track by a force too strong for her to fight against. Talking to Stephanie's mother might help her to understand where she was heading.

She would go up to Chappaqua tomorrow. But first, tonight, she would try to talk to Nick.

21

"You did *what?*" said Nick. His face was white with anger. In the deepening twilight the shadows under his eyes looked like dark bruises. "Whatever possessed you to do such a thing? I don't want you to have anything to do with her. With any of them, for that matter. I want you to call her back right now and say you've changed your mind."

Paula was shaken. She had never seen him this angry before. His hands had clenched into fists. If she had been a man, he would probably have hit her.

"I didn't do it because I want to, but because I must," she explained, speaking softly so as not to add fuel to his anger. "There are some things I must ask her about."

"Such as what?" She sensed the effort his self-control was costing him.

"Such as what happened to Stephanie. The things she did and said before she was killed. It's just barely possible she confided in her mother, isn't it?"

"I see," he said harshly. He got up to get a pack of cigarettes. He had cut down on his smoking after meeting Paula, but now he was back to two packs a day. "You just can't leave the past alone, can you? Can't you see what you're doing? You won't get anywhere by raking up old wounds."

"Do you think I like it any more than you do?"

"Then why don't you stop it now, once and for all?"

"Because whatever happened to Stephanie didn't stop with her death. It's still going on. It happened again last week. Nick, I'm convinced that Cindy didn't kill herself."

"That's a fairly normal reaction," he said more gently. "None of us like to think that someone we loved took his or her life. But you can't get around that note she scrawled across the mirror. Like it or not, it was not an accident."

150

"I don't think it was an accident. I never did."

"You don't think it was suicide or an accident. What was it, then?"

"I think it was murder. I think Cindy was killed by whoever killed Stephanie."

A wintry smile twisted his lips and made him look like a stranger.

"That must be it," he said. "A burglar with a compulsion to enter this apartment. To kill whoever he finds here. What do you suppose keeps bringing him back? The view, perhaps? We do have a lovely view."

She almost hated him then.

"It's not a laughing matter," she said.

"No, it isn't. But even if you were right by some wild chance, even if Stephanie's death were somehow linked with Cindy's, do you really think that you can find out anything that the police didn't?"

"I might. Because, you see, I know some things the police never knew."

"Such as?"

"Such as the fact that Stephanie thought she was in danger. That she felt threatened long before her death. She was afraid she would be killed, and then she died. Is that sheer coincidence?"

"How do you know what Stephanie was or was not afraid of? Have you been holding a séance?"

She bit back the quick rejoinder that came to her mind. They would get nowhere by striking out at each other.

"Let's not fight, Nick," she said.

"I'm not fighting. I'm understandably curious about your source of information."

"I read Stephanie's diary," she told him.

His face went totally blank. When he spoke again, his voice sounded remote, as though he had retreated to some far distance where he couldn't be reached. In some way his remoteness was more frightening than his anger had been.

"A diary," he said. "So Stephanie left a diary. It must make interesting reading indeed. I expect she wrote about me?"

She hesitated. How much could she tell him without hurting him further? She was angry with him, yes, but she didn't want to wound him. She knew he no longer cared about Stephanie, hadn't for a long time. But he would still be vulnerable to her betrayals, her mockery. She had been his wife, after all.

"She wrote about you, yes," Paula said slowly. "And other people as well. She wrote about the things she did, the friends she saw. Her world sounded miles apart from mine. And yet . . . there are parallels. You remember when I told you someone had been coming into this apartment? You insisted I go see Dr. Schneider. Well, it turns out Stephanie was imagining similiar things, if you still insist it was imagination. She actually *saw* someone else here. A woman. A dark-haired woman in her room, her bed. With you."

He was silent. It was getting too dark for her to see his face, but she could make out the outline of his shoulders as he hunched toward her, his elbows on his knees, his head in his hands. How well did she really know him? She brushed away the small insidious voice whispering inside her, and wondered if he could hear the drumming of her heart.

"There are things I should have told you," he said finally. "Things I'd much rather forget. About Stephanie. She was convinced I was seeing another woman, was bringing her up here whenever I had a chance. Not a thing that any man in his right mind would do, needless to say. There were constant scenes, one long argument we lived with night and day. That's probably why I reacted the way I did when you said someone had been here. I thought it was starting to happen all over again."

His voice was empty of feeling, the voice of a man recounting an old nightmare. Was he telling the truth? Paula sat very still, afraid of interrupting his trend of thought.

"I'm fairly sure she was seeing other men," he said, "and to tell you the truth, I didn't care. By that time there was nothing left between us. I couldn't even blame her. She was lonely, bored. And she had other problems I won't go into now. Maybe that's why she thought that I, too, was seeing someone. She was wrong. I wasn't. Not for any moral reasons, but simply because I had enough problems at that time."

The silence stretched between them like an aerialist's rope on which they hung, precariously balanced.

"Do you believe me?" he said, his voice so low she could barely make the words out.

Did she believe him? She wanted to. But in that case how could she explain what had happened? If Nick hadn't been involved with someone, who else would have had any reason to come into the apartment? And who was the woman Stephanie had seen? It made no sense. She had the feeling that the fate of their marriage depended on her answer.

"I believe you," she said. But she still couldn't bring herself to reach out, to touch him. The darkness was oppressive, and she got up to switch on the lights. They blinked at each other like two strangers. He got up to face her, and she had to will herself from taking one step back.

"Do you realize that it might have been power of suggestion?" he said.

"What do you mean?"

"Simply that you read Stephanie's diary and, having read her ravings, started to imagine the same things. Dirty ashtrays. Used glasses. Torn newspapers and flowers strewn around the room. You took two and two and came up with five. All because of the diary."

"No," she said. "I found the diary later. After it all happened."

"Happened? Then it's no longer happening, is it? Since we changed the locks. Power of suggestion once again. You felt secure once we changed the locks."

She stared at him, stricken. He was right. Since the locks had been changed, she had seen no traces of anyone in the apartment; so, if it had been a game intended to drive her out, it was over. Or the stakes were higher. Much too high. Since the locks were changed, she had been attacked and Cindy had died. Cindy had been murdered. "I know who it is." The game had become deadly. It was like playing hide-and-seek with a homicidal maniac.

"So it's all over," he was saying. "Over and done with, and you can forget about that damn diary. I would like to see it, by the way."

"You can't," she told him. "It's gone."

"Gone?"

"It disappeared the night I found it, the night you and Charlie went to see the fights. Someone came and took it."

For a fleeting second she relived the horror of the blanket thrown up over her head, the feel of the soft cloth against her face, shutting out air and light. "I told you someone attacked me," she reminded him. "You thought I was delirious."

But he was no longer listening. She was standing close enough to him to see a vein throbbing in his temple and notice the slight twitch in his eyelid. His eyes had become darker, opaque.

"So you won't let me see it," he said flatly.

"Nick, I can't. I don't have it. It really was taken," she said urgently. "Don't you think I'm telling you the truth?"

"I think you no longer know the difference between fiction and truth," he told her, turning away. "I'm going out for a walk. Don't bother waiting up for me."

He was almost at the door before he turned around to face her. He looked like a man reeling from a sharp blow.

"I wonder how much more you haven't told me," he said, and then he was gone.

She started to walk around the living room, pacing back and forth, picking up a book or magazine only to lay it down again. She wanted to cry but couldn't, could think of nothing she could do to ease the pain inside her. What was happening to them? They had become strangers to each other, worse than strangers, because they had lost the potential of both friendship and trust.

He was right, of course. There was a lot more she hadn't told him. He didn't know that she had questioned Charlie Nabokov one time—not unless he'd found out from Charlie himself, and she didn't think he had. He didn't know that she had borrowed a gun from Bibi Marcovaldi, that even now it lay under some papers in the top drawer of the desk in the living room. And, most importantly, he didn't know about her conviction that something cold and alien had entered their lives, something she was beginning to glimpse like a malevolent face barely seen in the fog.

She waited for him until midnight, but he didn't come back.

When she finally went to sleep, she dreamed that she and Teresa were running away from faceless men in uniform. "Faster," Teresa kept saying. "Run faster. This is not a good place." And then somehow she was on her own running down a long corridor, and there were footsteps behind her, closer, ever closer. . . .

She woke up. The sound of footsteps continued and Nick walked into the room. Without saying a word he sat down on the bed and put his arms around her.

22

There might be etiquette books that provide detailed instructions on what to wear when visiting one's husband's former mother-in-law, but she doubted it. Not that it would matter what she wore, if Mrs. Brewster's voice when she had talked to her over the phone were to be used as a yardstick. But it would still be best to dress conservatively. She put on a gray flannel skirt, a sweater, and a tailored tweed jacket, and went over to inspect herself in the mirror before rushing out to catch the train.

Chappaqua is one of the most luxurious of the suburban "villages" that honeycomb Westchester County north of New York City. The train that led there, on the other hand, was rickety and ancient. It looked like a train borrowed from a museum. It was practically empty and Paula had her choice of seats. She chose one by the window and stared out at the countryside. It seemed hauntingly familiar, as though she had taken this same train many times before. Had Stephanie taken this same train when visiting her family? It seemed probable. She was beginning to identify too closely with Stephanie—an unhealthy state under the circumstances.

When she reached Chappaqua, she walked up to one of the cabdrivers waiting at the small train station and gave him the Brewsters' address.

"That will be five dollars," he said pensively, chewing on a wad of gum.

"All right," she said.

"Maybe more. Depends on how long it takes."

"All right," she said.

She had expected to feel nervous, but all she felt was an odd excitement. She stared at the gently rolling hills and the houses half hidden by the lush, spring-green trees without really seeing them. In a few minutes she would be at Stephanie's house. She would see the place where she had grown up and she would meet her mother. Why did it seem important? It was almost as though Stephanie were sitting at her elbow. The thought was disturbing.

They pulled up into a curving driveway that led up to a deceptively simple house nestled against the hill, and she again experienced that strong feeling of déjà vu. It was almost like coming home.

The illusion disappeared one minute after she rang the doorbell. She had expected to see the maid, but the woman who came to the door was unmistakably Mrs. Brewster. She was very slender and immaculately groomed. Her light-brown hair and the way she held herself made her seem surprisingly youthful. Yet there was nothing youthful about her set expression or her cold, watchful eyes. It must have taken her decades to develop that shuttered look.

"You must be Mrs. Girard," she said, giving the last name on ironic intonation.

"Please call me Paula."

"Come on in, Mrs. Girard," she said. She led the way into a small sitting room facing the garden and turned around to look at Paula. Her eyes were the cold leaden gray of a winter sky. They stared at Paula with remote politeness.

"Please sit down," she said.

Paula sat down as instructed. She wished she hadn't come. Nick had been right. She must have been out of her mind to call Mrs. Brewster, to expect any help from this woman who so obviously resented her for taking her daughter's place.

"And now," said Mrs. Brewster, "perhaps you'll be good enough to tell me what this is all about. You must agree that it's a most unusual visit?"

"Yes," said Paula. "And I'm sorry to disturb you. I really am. But I had hoped—I hope that you can help me. As I told you over the phone, I found a diary that your daughter kept at one time."

"And you read it?"

"Yes?"

"I see." Her glacial tone matched the look in her eyes. She reached for a pack of cigarettes lying on a small desk and took one out with quick, nervous fingers. She lit it and inhaled deeply.

"Do you make it a practice of reading other people's diaries?" she said.

Paula's face burned. "No," she said. "But some things had happened—I'd been upset by some things that happened, that I thought were connected with your daughter—or rather, with someone your daughter knew. Someone who resented Nick's marrying me. And so, when I found her diary, I read it. It wasn't mere curiosity, I assure you."

"A convenient-enough excuse. Though I still fail to see how Stephanie's diary could be connected with your problems."

"Oh, but you see, it was. Stephanie was being bothered by much the same things before she died. Weird, unpleasant things."

There was a moment of complete silence, and then Paula thought she heard a muffled movement behind the closed door leading to the hallway. Was someone listening in to their conversation? She was taken aback when Mrs. Brewster laughed, a high brittle sound.

"Stephanie was always overly imaginative," she said. "She could build a mountain out of a molehill more quickly than anyone else I've ever known. It would appear that you have the same faculty. What exactly are the things that you say bothered my daughter?"

"She thought that someone, someone she didn't know, had access to the apartment. Did she ever discuss it with you? Do you have any idea who it might have been?"

"No. Stephanie seldom chose to confide in me. A stranger with access to the apartment? It sounds highly unlikely. Preposterous, in fact. A case of overactive imagination, I daresay. Or premonition. She was killed during an attempted burglary, as you must well know."

"Can you be so sure?"

"Of course I'm sure. Do you have any reason to suspect otherwise?"

Paula leaned forward, staring at the older woman, trying to penetrate that smooth, cold expression.

"Mrs. Brewster, a close friend of mine was killed in the apartment a week ago."

Something flickered in Mrs. Brewster's eyes. Her face blanched beneath her makeup, leaving patches of blusher high up on her cheeks. She made an odd little gesture with her hands and walked to a chair facing Paula's. She sat down on it heavily, as if she had suddenly aged by twenty years. The cigarette she held smoldered in her hands.

"It's not a very lucky place, is it?" she said. Her attempt at irony lacked conviction.

"No," said Paula, handing her an ashtray, "it isn't."

"Your friend—was she killed in the same way as my daughter?"

Paula shook her head.

"No. The verdict was that she jumped to her death. While under mental and emotional strain."

Mrs. Brewster froze. The muscles of her face tightened until it looked as rigid as a statue's. The look she gave Paula was the same cold look with which she'd greeted her at the door.

"Then there's absolutely no connection between her death and Stephanie's," she said.

"But Cindy didn't kill herself, Mrs. Brewster. I know she didn't. I told her about Stephanie's diary, and—"

"It sounds as though everyone has heard about my daughter's diary," she said, looking at Paula with a dislike so intense it was akin to hatred. Her mouth turned downward in a bitter grimace. "You will please turn it over to me. At once."

Nick, too, had wanted the diary, Paula remembered. She shrugged helplessly.

"But I no longer have it, Mrs. Brewster. It disappeared. That's one of the reasons I came to see you, because—"

"I think I know why you've come to see me," Mrs. Brewster said. The sharp edge of anger trembled in her voice. "There is a word for it, and the word is blackmail." She stood up. "I'll call the police if you ever bother any of us again."

Paula stood up also. "Mrs. Brewster," she said. "I can assure you that—"

"I don't want your assurances. You've heard what I've said. We have connections in this state," she added, her anger mounting with each word. "We are protected from this sort of thing. Haven't we suffered enough? The scandal, the gossip, the rumors. Enough. Stephanie was nothing but trouble from the time she was born. But now she's dead, and it's over. Get out before I call the police."

"Mrs. Brewster—"

"Now." Her voice cracked. She was beginning to lose control.

Paula walked out in a daze until she reached the edge of the driveway. She stood there for a minute, trying to decide which way to turn. It was going to be a long walk to the train station. The sun dazzled her eyes. She'd forgotten her sunglasses. Her head was spinning as she headed south.

She had been walking for less than five minutes when she heard the car behind her and moved to the side of the road to let it pass. But the car pulled up next to her and stopped. It was an old convertible painted a bright and shiny red. The girl behind the wheel was also shining and bright. She was twenty at the most. She looked vaguely familiar, though Paula had never met her.

"You're Paula Girard, aren't you?" she said.

"Yes. And you . . ."

"I'm Nancy Brewster. Get in, will you? There'll be hell to pay if my mother sees us together." She leaned across the seat and opened the door to let Paula in.

23

Nancy Brewster bore a striking similarity to her mother, or rather, to the way her mother must have looked thirty years ago. She had the same high, narrow cheekbones, the fine arched eyebrows beneath a rounded forehead, the curved, short upper lip. But her face was mobile and expressive, and her long hair streamed behind her like a sun-burnished flag.

She was a relaxed, competent driver. She kept her hands lightly on the wheel, her eyes fixed on the road. She didn't speak until they reached a flat plateau overlooking a wide natural reservoir. She parked the car and turned off the engine before turning around to face Paula.

"This is pot haven," she said.

"Pot haven?"

"You know. This is where all the high-school kids come to turn on after school and on weekends. The cops keep chasing them away, of course, but they always come back. It adds to the excitement."

She spoke wistfully, as though remembering a better and happier time. It couldn't have been more than a year or two since she was part of that group herself. As if to prove it, she took out a pack of cigarettes and removed a slim joint tucked away between the cover and the cellophane. She lit it and inhaled deeply.

"Do you smoke?" she said, offering it to Paula.

"Not right now," Paula told her.

She caught a whiff of the sharp acrid smell of the marijuana. The mellow breeze felt warm against her face, and the water of the reservoir sparkled in the sun. It's almost summer, she thought, and wished she could shake off the feeling of unreality pressing upon her. She turned to Nancy Brewster.

161

"I didn't mean to upset your mother," she said. "I should have realized how strongly she'd resent talking to me. Her former son-in-law's new wife."

Nancy Brewster shrugged lightly. "Oh, that's not it," she said. "Mother never gave a damn about Nick. She couldn't care less about him or what he does. I do. I've been curious to meet you. I used to have a real crush on him, you know. Sissy used to tease me about it. Not that I ever told her, but she was good at sensing things like that."

She grimaced, and for a fleeting moment Paula was reminded of Mrs. Brewster's bitter, set look.

"Then why?" she asked Nancy. "If your mother didn't resent Nick's remarriage, why was she so angry when I came to talk to her? Why would she be angry if she saw us together? Was it because I opened up old wounds?"

She watched while Nancy brushed a long strand of blond hair off her face. Something clicked in her mind. She had a sudden flashback of long golden strands of hair caught in the bristles of her hairbrush. Nancy? No, that was silly. Nancy Brewster was no more than a child, though there was nothing childlike about her expression.

"It's very simple," said Nancy. "Mother always hated talking about Sissy, even when she was alive. And now she won't talk about her at all. I used to think she resented Sissy for having been born. And now she resents her for getting herself killed. I heard what she said to you earlier. I was listening at the door. Does that shock you?"

She didn't really expect an answer, and Paula kept silent, afraid to interrupt her trend of thought. Suddenly Nancy turned around and stared at her directly. Her irises, darkened by the marijuana, looked like deep pools.

"I'm sorry about your friend," she said. "The one who died at your place. Were the two of you close?"

"We were very close," said Paula.

"And you think someone killed her?" said Nancy in the matter-of-fact tone she might have used to discuss the weather. "Someone who knew Stephanie?"

"Perhaps. Did Stephanie ever talk to you about her friends? Or her enemies, for that matter?"

"Sissy never discussed anything with me," she said. "We never really got along, you know, and later on, after she got

162

married, we lost track of each other altogether. Except for family holidays and things. That was her first marriage, of course."

Paula's heart skipped a beat. She wondered if she'd heard right.

"Her first marriage? You mean Stephanie was married to someone else before she married Nick?"

"Of course. Didn't you know? It only lasted a few months, however. She met Nick soon after getting a divorce."

"Did you know her first husband?"

"Larry? Sure. His full name is Lawrence Jaffe. He's an architect. He's got a quick temper, and he and Sissy used to fight like cats and dogs. But he's a gorgeous-looking man. Sissy sure knew how to pick them, I must say that for her."

"Does he live in Westchester?"

"I don't think so. I doubt it. He used to have a loft down in the Village. Still does, for all I know. But why do you want to know about Larry?"

Larry. L. "Had an appointment to see L.," Stephanie had written. Could she have continued seeing him after her marriage to Nick? Nancy was looking at her, waiting for an answer. Her eyes seemed old in her childlike face. And then, unexpectedly, she smiled.

"You're not much older than me, are you?" she said.

"Sure I am. By five or six years at least."

"That's hardly any difference at all. We grow up pretty quickly in the suburbs. Half the kids I know are on dope, and the others—well, I guess I don't really know any of the others. The point is, I've been trying to imagine how I'd feel if I were in your place and found one of Sissy's crazy diaries. I have a pretty good idea. They used to give me the willies."

"You've read one of her diaries?"

"Sure. Sissy always kept a diary, ever since I can remember. She used to keep them locked up in her desk drawer, but what she didn't know was that I had a key. I used to read them whenever I had a chance, and dream about them afterward. Regular nightmares. The things she wrote about! Crazy, insane things. There was a reason for it, of course."

Paula felt cold fingers traveling up her spine. She shivered in the warm sun.

"A reason?" she asked softly.

"Didn't you guess? Sissy was crazy. Out of her mind. A schiz. She had her first breakdown when she was in her early teens. And a number of times afterward. She was in various clinics at least half a dozen times. The last time was just before her divorce from Larry. Nick didn't know. Not until they were safely married, that is."

"Oh, my God," whispered Paula.

She thought of Nick, trapped in a marriage from which his conscience wouldn't let him escape. It must have been sheer horror to live with a woman so precariously balanced on the edge of sanity. It explained so much. His refusal to discuss his first marriage or his own role in it, the haunted look that crossed his face whenever Stephanie was mentioned, his dismay when he became afraid that his second marriage might be headed in the same direction. That's why he couldn't believe me, thought Paula. That's why he would never be able to believe anything that was implausible at best, at worst impossible. He must have heard many such stories before.

"They're trying to drive me insane," Stephanie had written. Textbook paranoia? Or had she been reporting what had actually happened, desperately holding on to her slim grip on reality?

"I'm sorry," said Paula.

"Sorry? About what?" said Nancy Brewster. Her face was turned away, hidden by its fall of silken hair.

"About your sister. About her illness. Her death."

Nancy turned to face her.

"It's just as well Sissy died," she said. "I have an aunt—my mother's oldest sister—who's been in an institution for the last twenty years. That's what would have happened to Sissy had she lived." She paused and looked out at the water of the reservoir. "These things are supposed to be hereditary," she said, and flung her hair back as though she didn't have a single care in the world. She smiled. "I keep wondering if the same thing will happen to me. Do we ever recognize the first signs, I wonder?"

Paula felt a rush of pity for the girl beside her. She reached out and touched her shoulder.

"You mustn't even think about it," she said.

"Wouldn't you?" Nancy Brewster asked, and Paula was silent.

She was on the train headed back for New York when she first heard the sly, quiet whisper. "Stephanie," it said. She turned around, startled, but there was no one sitting behind her. "Stephanie." The sound was originating in her own mind in response to a presence as tangible as if Nick's former wife were sitting right beside her. They seemed to be traveling down parallel roads heading for the same destination. "Stephanie." It was almost as if Stephanie were still alive, waiting, and she, Paula, had no choice but to take the steps that would lead to their inevitable confrontation. It was ridiculous, of course. Or was it? Nancy Brewster had said that insanity was hereditary. That was still being debated, Paula knew, but if it happened to be true, then other things might be hereditary as well. Such as her grandmother's "second sight." She had a sudden recollection of her grandmother sitting in her rocking chair, calmly gossiping with her dead husband. Centuries of Welsh legends and superstitions crossed her mind. Was it ridiculous, or were the dark tendrils of her ancestry beginning to blossom and bear fruit? "Stephanie." The rhythm of the name was echoed by the sound of the wheels along the tracks, became amplified until it was a shout. "Stephanie! Stephanie! Stephanie!"

She was glad when they reached New York and she got off the train, but her new feeling of awareness did not leave. She suspected that time was running out, and knew that there was no turning back, nowhere she could hide. She was caught in the maze of her nightmare and the concentric circles were getting ever shorter.

When she walked into the apartment, she felt the blood draining from her head. She stood quietly and looked around the living room.

It was worse, much worse than the time she had walked in to find everything in a shambles, newspapers and flowers strewn around by a furious hand. Now the apartment looked neat, but it had been rearranged. The table and chairs that were normally up against the windows had been moved to one side of the fireplace, next to the bookcase. The heavy couch was in its usual place, but the two rocking chairs had been switched around. There were new curtains on the window. Not new curtains, she realized dully, but the old ones she had taken down and stored in the guest closet during her brief attempt at redecorating.

Slowly, still in a daze, she walked into the bedroom. The dressing tabletop was bare. Her perfumes and makeup lay scattered on the floor, swept off by a furious hand.

She looked at the closed closet doors. Could someone be waiting there for her, ready to jump out when she came near? She could make a run for it, of course, but if someone were waiting for her, she'd never be allowed to get as far as the front door. She stood still, undecided. Her heart was pounding erratically and her face and hands were wet with sweat. Moving as slowly as someone in a dream, she walked over to the sliding closet doors and opened them with an un-steady hand.

There was no one there. Nick's clothes were still hanging where they'd always been, but her things had been torn off their hangers and lay at the bottom of the closet in an untidy heap. Without quite knowing what she was doing she started to pick up her crumpled dresses and suits and to put them back on their hangers. "They're trying to drive me insane," Stephanie had written in an outburst of panic and hatred. And now the same thing was happening again. But surely whoever had done this was insane herself? Yes. She could feel it all around her in the room, an alien, insane force pressing against what little self-control she still had left.

She brushed her hair off her forehead with her arm. It was unusually warm for this time of year, and the weatherman had predicted a heat wave for tomorrow. She was sweating and cold at the same time. Nick, she murmured, as if in prayer. Nick.

She walked over to the living room and dialed Nick's office number. Her reflexes took charge, and she was able to ex-change greetings with his secretary without revealing a trace of her immense shock. And then Nick was on the line. As soon as she heard his voice, her defenses crumbled.

"Nick, please come home," she blurted out.

"Hey, hon. Is something wrong?" His concern was immediate.

"Oh, my God, yes. Please come home, Nick."

"But what's wrong, Paula?"

166

"Everything. When I came back from Chappaqua . . ." Her voice broke.

There was a silence between them. And then he said, "You mean you went to see them after all?"

"Yes. And when I came back home—"

"You decided you'd made a mistake," he said. His tone was sharp and angry. "I told you not to go," he reminded her. "I *asked* you not to go."

"Nick, you must come home," she pleaded, almost incoherent in her panic. "You must see for yourself what happened. We must talk, we must—"

He interrupted her again.

"Later," he told her curtly. "We'll talk about it later. I'm not that eager to find out what my dear former mother-in-law had to say. Don't bother fixing dinner for me, by the way. I'll probably be here till at least ten o'clock. I'll have a sandwich sent up."

He hung up before she had a chance to reply.

She stared at the phone as if it were a lifeline he had just cut off. She needed help. Whom else could she call? Bibi Marcovaldi? Charlie Nabokov? Her parents?

It would be so easy. She could lift up the phone and tell them she was taking the six-thirty bus for Rutland. She would be home soon after midnight. And then what? Whoever was persecuting her could easily follow her. She remembered a biblical story she'd read as a child. Appointment in Samarra. The story of the man who'd escaped Death in one small town only to find it waiting for him in another. If she went home now, she'd be exposing her own family to danger.

She was so tired.

And there was so little she could do except sit back and let things take their own course. She could feel them picking up speed, like a berserk train gone out of control. Whoever had been trying to drive Nick and her apart had finally succeeded. Someone who had reason to hate her? Someone who had been involved with Stephanie?

Stephanie. It was odd, but the more she found out about Stephanie, the more she became aware of her, almost as if her thoughts were giving the dead woman a new life. If she didn't watch herself, she'd soon be talking to her the way her grandmother had talked to her grandfather so many years ago. If only there were something she could do—but there was nothing she could do except sit and wait, she thought dully. Sooner or later she would meet her enemy face to face, but by that time it would be too late.

She walked over to the desk and opened the top drawer. The gun was still there. Could she bring herself to use it if she had to? She honestly didn't know. And supposing the next attack on her came when she was out in the street, or in the hallway, or shopping in a store? The gun wouldn't help her then.

No. The only way she could stop that berserk train in its tracks was to identify her enemy before she struck again. But how? There was no one else left for her to talk to and no leads she could follow. Unless . . . unless she tried to reach Lawrence Jaffe, Stephanie's first husband. He might be able to supply a clue that would point her in the right direction. He might not be willing to talk to her, of course, particularly if he were the L. that Stephanie had mentioned in the diary. But what could she lose by trying?

She picked up the hefty Manhattan phone book and started leafing through the pages. It was quite likely that he had moved by now. Or else that he had an unlisted number. But his name was there. Jaffe, Lawrence. 715 Washington Place. He won't talk to me, she thought, even as she dialed his number.

The voice that answered was low, pleasant, and masculine. Yes, this was Lawrence Jaffe, he said. Who was this? She had some explaining to do before he understood who she was and why she wanted to see him.

"Stephanie and I were divorced a long time ago," he pointed out. "I really don't know that there's anything I can tell you about her."

She took a wild chance. "But you used to see her afterward, didn't you?" she said. "After she was married to Nick."

She could sense his hesitation.

"I did," he said finally. His voice had altered slightly. "It's something I prefer not to think about. I can see no reason to dredge it up again."

"Oh, but there is. Please listen to me. I've been troubled by something connected with Stephanie's past. Badly troubled. I wouldn't bother you otherwise. Can't you please spare me half an hour?"

"You make it sound serious."

"I can't tell you how serious."

She had herself under control now, but he must have sensed her underlying desperation because when he spoke to her again, his voice was kind.

"Very well," he said. "What time is it? Five o'clock. I must deliver some papers to a client, but I'll be back between six-thirty and seven. Let's say seven o'clock. Can you find your way here?"

"Oh, yes," said Paula. "I used to live in the Village at one time. I'll be there at seven. And thank you."

After she hung up, she continued to sit in the chair, aware of the ticking of the clock in the silent room. Time went by so slowly when one was waiting, but at least she had one more thing left to do, one more card left to play. And what if that card proved to be worthless? Then she would have lost, and the game would be over.

At precisely six-thirty she left the apartment and walked toward the subway.

24

Lawrence Jaffe was tall, angular, and thin. He might have been good-looking, but it was difficult to tell because of the short, thick beard that covered most of his face and the long shock of hair that fell down to his eyebrows. The eyes that gleamed between this hairy growth were as light and shining as a wet pigeon's egg.

"No man likes to admit he's acted like an idiot," he told Paula.

He had insisted she join him in a drink and had settled her down on the low couch that ran the length of an entire wall. His own drink lay untouched on a sturdy worktable as he paced the length of the large, sparsely furnished room.

"Does her husband—your husband—did he ever find out?" he asked.

"I don't think so," said Paula. "But he was pretty sure there were other men."

"The poor bastard. I should know, I was in his shoes for over six months. When the divorce came through, I swore if I didn't see Stephanie for fifty years it would be too soon. And then, a year later, she showed up at my door. Just like that. And I was stupid enough to let her in. That time. And the next time. And the next."

"Were you still in love with her after all?" asked Paula.

He stopped his pacing and stared down at her. Something gentle glowed in his eyes, and he seemed close to smiling.

"You're very nice," he said in an apparent non sequitur. "No, I wasn't in love with her. Then, earlier, or later. She was a twenty-four-carat bitch—a condition that had little to do with her mental health, mind you. She was at her bitchiest when in full possession of her faculties."

"But in that case—"

"Why did I marry her?"

"Yes. And why did you continue to see her later . . . after she married Nick?"

"Oddly enough, her bitchiness was one of the reasons. Don't frown at me; I'm serious. It might be easier for you to understand if you were a man. I mean, to understand my physical reaction. She was also attractive, but I know any number of women who are equally attractive, if not more so. You, for instance."

"Me?" asked Paula, surprised. It seemed an odd time for compliments, unless he was just trying to make her feel at ease.

"You," he asserted. "I used to paint before I realized I was almost, but not quite, good enough. I should have liked to have painted you. You have an unusual face—that fine, delicate bone structure and those large smoky eyes—do your folks come from Ireland?"

"My father's did. My mother's came from Wales."

"I should have known. Have you ever noticed how people pick up protective coloration from their geographic origins? The Swedes and Norwegians, as pale as their snowy landscapes. The lush, languorous look of the Mediterranean races."

"And the black vivid colors from the African continent?"

"Precisely. If I had ever painted you, it would have been in the classic style. On a vast moor or against craggy hills. Your hair is neither brown nor black, is it? I would have painted it the color of clouds before a storm, or of dark seaweed glowing in the sun."

Paula's heart skipped a beat. "Her hair all spread out upon my pillow like dark seaweed." She shivered and felt cold sweat breaking out on her forehead.

"What's the matter?" he said. He pulled out the stool beneath his worktable and sat down, his long legs splayed out in front of him. He leaned toward her. "I'm not making a pass at you, you know."

"I know," said Paula. "It's just that what you said reminded me of something—something I read recently. But you were telling me about Stephanie."

"I was, wasn't I? Her protective coloring was pure American suburbia. Glossy, expensive, arrogant in its self-assurance.

171

And yet, beneath it all, lay something feverish—a dark fever-ish quality that smoldered like a volcano about to erupt." He paused. "An addictive quality," he added.

"You sound as if you miss her."

"No, I don't miss her. On the contrary. Would you be shocked if I told you I was relieved to hear that she was dead?"

He was looking directly at her to gauge her reaction, and Paula had to force herself not to look away. How awful, she thought. How awful to be killed and have no one miss you—not your relatives, not your friends, not your lovers. Had anyone cried when Stephanie died? It seemed unlikely. How many others beside Lawrence Jaffe had felt relieved by her death? And had one of them killed her?

Whoever killed her is out to get me, Paula thought bleakly.

"Did she ever confide in you?" she asked. "About other men she was seeing? About . . . other things that might have bothered her?"

"Why?" he asked abruptly. "Why does it matter now? You told me you were badly troubled by something from Steph-anie's past. I'm beginning to think that was an understate-ment. Don't you think you should tell me what the trouble is?"

"I can't," she said, taken aback.

"Can't you? I've answered all your questions so far. I think it only fair that you answer mine."

He was putting her on the spot. She knew that he had liked her at first sight and responded to her as instinctively as if they had known each other for a long time. As if they were old friends. She needed friends badly at this point. But how would he react if she were to tell him how her world had turned itself upside down almost overnight, leaving her with-out an anchor or familiar signposts? What would he do if she told him that she was afraid someone was trying to kill her? He would draw back in disbelief. As Nick had. She couldn't risk it.

She shook her head. She said, "I can only tell you that someone—someone Stephanie must have known or seen—seems to resent my marriage to Nick. I must find out who it is. I had hoped you could tell me."

She was startled by his laugh, which sounded both bitter and amused.

"Very well," he said. "I think I always knew that someday someone would question me about Stephanie. I dreaded the thought. And yet in an odd way it's a relief. Do you suppose that's why Catholics go to confession?"

He took a sip of his drink and smiled at her.

"I would like to help you if I could," he said. "The problem is, you see, that Stephanie and I did little talking while she was here. She didn't come here to talk."

"No, I expect she didn't."

"She never discussed any of her friends with me. Except for— Wait a minute. Yes, she did mention someone. A man called Buddy."

Easy, she told herself, easy. Don't let him guess the name means anything to you.

"Buddy?" she said.

"Yes. He was a friend of Nick's, she told me. She seemed to be amused by the fact he was a friend of Nick's. His closest friend, she said."

"Do you remember his last name?"

"I wouldn't remember even if she had mentioned it. All I know is that apparently she was sleeping with him—when she wasn't here with me, that is—and that he lived in the same building as they did. I think she told me in the hope of making me feel jealous. He was a free-lance writer, I believe."

Of course. Buddy. Charlie Nabokov's face had gone quite blank when she had asked him about Buddy. Nick's buddy. His closest, oldest friend. She felt the faint beginnings of nausea and stood up before it overwhelmed her.

"You've been very kind," she said formally.

"Hey, you're not leaving?"

"I must go home," she told him. "Try to sort things out."

"If you stay longer, we can sort them out together."

He had stood up when she did and was leaning above her, smiling and distressed. He seemed honestly reluctant to see her leave.

"Thank you," she said. "But this is something I must work out on my own."

"Are you sure? Are you sure you don't want to tell me what's bothering you?"

173

"I'd like to, but I really can't."

"Because if it's something to do with Stephanie I might be able to help, given more time to think about it. I knew her better than most people."

"I thought you wanted to forget all about her."

"I did. I do. But the past won't always stay conveniently buried the way we'd like it to. Take this case, for instance. When Stephanie was alive, she managed to destroy everything she touched. It's odd that she manages to do so even after death. I have the feeling you're facing something very unpleasant."

She didn't say anything.

"When you called earlier," he told her, "I thought to myself, Here it comes. It's catching up with you at last. If it's blackmail, you'd better face up to it and have it over and done with. And instead I'm beginning to wonder if someone isn't blackmailing you. Are they?"

"No," she said. "At least I don't think so." She wasn't sure if terrorism might not be used to pave the way for blackmail.

"Will you do one thing for me? When it's all over, will you call me and let me know how it all came out?"

That's the least she could do, she thought, looking up at his kindly, bearded face. She knew he didn't want her to leave, and she herself was reluctant to leave, for that matter. There was an element of safety in this bare-looking, functional apartment. She held out her hand. His clasp was as warm and steady as his gaze.

"Let me know what happens," he insisted. "And good luck."

She looked down at their joined hands. His fingers were muscular and thin, the nails cut very short. There was a thick ridge of white scar tissue between his index finger and his thumb. The skin around it had puckered and turned brown. He saw her questioning look.

"Stephanie," he said shortly. "One of the less pleasant of our domestic scenes. She used to be handy with a knife."

He stood at the door and watched her as she ran down the stairs. When she reached the first stairwell landing, she looked up at him and saw him lift his hand in a gesture of farewell.

It was hot outside. A tropical wind was blowing from the south and the hot moist air mingled with the exhaust fumes

174

from the buses to form an oppressive smog. She started to walk back toward the subway. Was it just the smog that pressed against her temples, making them throb, or was she surrounded by an atmosphere of evil? There were no electronic or chemical devices to measure evil, any more than goodness or kindness could be measured. And yet they existed, side by side, affecting people's lives as much if not more than any economic or political factor.

Evil. Had it been evil or merely weakness that had caused Charlie Nabokov to have an affair with his best friend's wife? Had it been evil or weakness that had induced Stephanie to betray Nick over and over again? Or had she been seeking revenge for that woman she had seen with Nick in their bed? "Her hair all spread out upon my pillow like dark seaweed." What had Lawrence Jaffe said about her own hair?

"I would have painted it the color . . . of dark seaweed glowing in the sun. . . ."

So the woman Stephanie had seen might have looked a bit like Paula. Another coincidence. *Unless . . .*

The sudden thought exploded in her mind with a force so strong it sent her reeling. She grasped on to a wall for support. For a split second everything was illuminated in that jagged flash of lightning, and she saw past, future, and present blended into one. Could *that* be the explanation? It was, it had to be. Everything fit. And then the light faded, and she became aware of the curious stares of the people passing her along the street.

No, she thought. No. It was preposterous, impossible. She was allowing her nerves and growing panic to play tricks with her mind. She took a deep breath and tried to pull herself together, but she was still shaken as she made her way toward the subway.

When she got home, she heard the sound of music from within the apartment. She looked guiltily at her watch. Nine o'clock. Nick had come home earlier than he'd said he would, and would demand to know where she had been. Her headache had gotten worse. She pulled out her keys to open the door and braced herself, quite literally, to face the music.

25

<hr />

Having braced oneself for a direct confrontation if not an out-and-out fight, it is disconcerting to have one's impetus checked by the other person's total and complete lack of response. Somewhat like pushing one's shoulder against a door one had thought jammed, only to have it open easily and find oneself sailing into the room. She had prepared herself for Nick's recriminations over her visit to the Brewsters. She was, in fact, quite ready to match his arguments with her own, because, after all, wasn't he letting her down just when she needed him most?

She had expected to face his seething anger the minute she walked in. She had not expected him to look as though the wind had been knocked out of his sails. He looked weary, his shoulders slumped in an appearance of defeat. His eyes had the slightly unfocused look of a man who's trying to come to grips with a shock outside his field of experience. There was a glass in his hand and a bottle of Jack Daniels at his elbow.

"There you are," he said. "I wondered where you were. Did you go out to get a bite to eat?"

"No, I didn't. I went to see someone. How about you? Did you have dinner?"

"I had a sandwich at the office," he told her. His tone was absentminded. It was quite evident that food was the furthest thing from his mind.

She watched him cautiously, expecting him to ask her whom she'd gone to see. But if he'd heard her remark he gave no sign of it.

"It's hot in here," she said, stalling for time. Her head was throbbing badly. "Couldn't we turn on the air-conditioner?"

"I'm afraid not. Haven't you heard the evening news? The

electric company has declared a brown-out. They couldn't have been expecting a heat wave this early in the year."

He drained his glass as casually as if it contained water and set it down on the table. He'd been furious with her a few hours ago when she'd told him she'd gone up to Chappaqua after all—was it possible that his anger had spent itself so quickly? Or was he postponing the subject until later? She was under so much pressure that she couldn't bear the suspense of waiting.

"I'm sorry I upset you by going to see the Brewsters," she said hesitantly. "I would never have done it under normal circumstances, but as it was . . . I don't know. I guess I thought I could learn something to help me understand what's been happening."

"I bet Mrs. Brewster didn't prove too pleasant."

"You'd win your bet. It was awful. She accused me of coming up there simply to blackmail her. She must be one of the most unpleasant women I've ever met."

"It sounds like she hasn't changed. It was a wasted trip, then?"

She was disconcerted by his mildness. What had happened to change him since she'd called him at the office? Was he finally beginning to pick up on her own feelings of dread? It seemed unlikely.

She sat down in the chair across from him. "I talked to Stephanie's kid sister," she said. "Nick, why didn't you ever tell me about Stephanie's nervous breakdowns?"

His shoulders moved slightly in what could have been a shrug. He leaned forward and poured some more Jack Daniels in his glass. In all the months she'd known him she had never seen him drinking after dinner.

"It was a bad time," he said. "I wanted to forget about it. I was wrong. I should have told you. And I should never have dragged you into all this. Would you like a drink?"

"Yes, please," she said. A drink was the last thing she wanted, but it was better than letting him drink alone. They'd been doing far too much on their own, lately.

He appeared to share her feeling.

"There are times when apologies are meaningless," he said, "but that doesn't mean they shouldn't be expressed. I'm sorry,

177

Paula. I'm just beginning to realize what you've been going through."

Why? Why now? What had made him realize it now, she wondered. She didn't want his apologies. She wanted to feel safe once again, and to feel close to Nick. To share the closeness that had once promised to be a lifetime thing. But there was something she had to tell him so that there would be no more secrets between them.

"I went to see Lawrence Jaffe earlier this evening. Stephanie's first husband."

She braced herself for a new outburst of anger, but it didn't come. He merely looked puzzled for a minute, as though he'd forgotten that there was another man who'd shared his ill luck.

"I never met him," he said. "What's he like?"

"He seems very nice. I liked him a lot, which surprised me, because I didn't like some of the things he had to say. But he wasn't able to tell me what I wanted to know."

He regarded her steadily. The skepticism she'd grown accustomed to seeing on his face had been replaced by something else: a bare, expectant look that made him appear oddly vulnerable.

"What do you need to know, Paula?"

"I already told you," she whispered.

"Tell me again."

"I need to know who hates me, and why. Who's behind all the things that have happened. I'm so afraid," she said, still whispering. "I don't know what to do anymore. Oh, Nick. Do you know why I called you at the office this afternoon? When I came home, the furniture—" Her voice broke.

"Yes. I noticed you rearranged the furniture," he said.

"Oh, but I didn't."

"You didn't?"

"No. It was like this when I came home. I didn't really think you had done it. But I hoped you had. Who did it, Nick? It's like a nightmare that won't stop. What's happening?"

"I don't know. But I do know this. Whatever's been happening we must make it stop."

"You do believe me, then?" she asked with a terrible, forlorn hope.

178

He closed his eyes. When he opened them again, she saw such pain in his face that her heart twisted inside her.

"I believe you," he said.

So he was back on her side. Her relief was so overwhelming that it took her a few seconds to realize that something must have happened to change his outlook. She watched him as he stood up and started pacing up and down the room like a trapped animal seeking the dimensions of his cage.

"I've been a fool," he said abruptly, "and I don't have much patience with fools. Listen to me, Paula. When you first hinted that I might have given some woman a key to this apartment, I felt annoyed. Justifiably, I thought. If there's anything worse than a fool it's a self-righteous one. It didn't occur to me that you felt insecure and ill-at-ease. When it finally did, I realized that it couldn't be pleasant for you to live here in this apartment. You were still rocky from the accident, I thought; you couldn't be faulted if your imagination was working overtime. I asked you to see Dr. Schneider, if you remember. I thought you might be having a relapse. I called him after you saw him."

"You did? You never told me that."

"It would appear there's quite a few things I haven't told you. Schneider assured me you'd made a fine recovery, and went on to give me a small lecture on overprotectiveness. If there was anything bothering you, it was probably real, he said. He acted as though he knew you better than I do, and I resented it. If you were healed, there could only be one logical explanation for what you'd been telling me, I thought. You were bored and were playing games like a spoiled child with too much time on her hands."

"Oh, Nick."

"That's what I thought. I'd been through it all before, as you know by now. You mentioned a nightmare a while back. That's how it felt, a recurring nightmare that would never stop. I know you had somehow connected Cindy's death with Stephanie's, but that was part of your obsession, I believed. I thought you were overly curious about Stephanie, obsessed with her, in fact."

"I was," said Paula. "I don't know how or why it started. But it's gotten worse."

He was going to tell her something terrible, she knew with

179

mounting certainty. She wished it weren't so hot in the room. She looked with longing at the silent air-conditioner.

"It wouldn't have started if I had told you everything right from the beginning. But I didn't. And then I grew to believe that you were amusing yourself by playing detective and making things up to make the game more interesting. An improbable stranger haunting our apartment. A nonexistent diary. A missing hairbrush. Someone wreaking havoc in a fit of rage. You were like a child inventing monsters, I thought, or a would-be scientist recreating dinosaurs out of the thin air."

"But now?"

"I've found one of the dinosaur's tracks. And as a result nothing else seems impossible."

"What did you find, Nick?"

He walked over to the desk. When he came back to her chair, his face was ashen gray, glistening with sweat, and she was briefly reminded of a friend of her father's who'd suffered recurring bouts of malaria.

"The diary," he said. "Stephanie's diary. It was on the coffee table when I came back home."

He was holding it with his index finger and his thumb, as though it were an obscene object he didn't care to touch. *The diary was back.* She had put it on the coffee table the night she'd read it, just before that swift, silent attack that had rendered her helpless. Her throat constricted and she felt a bout of nausea. She reached out and took the diary from Nick. In spite of the heat his hand was icy cold.

"Did you read it?" she asked.

"Just the first few pages. Just enough to realize that what I'd always suspected was true. She was sleeping with everyone in town, and not because she enjoyed it—not the physical part of it, I mean—but because it gave her some sick, perverse feeling of power."

"Does it still hurt after all this time?"

"Hurt? No, it doesn't hurt. It just makes me feel dirty. What I probably need is a long, hot shower. I gather one of the men she was seeing was someone I know. Fellow called Buddy. Must have been a casual acquaintance. I don't even remember him, thank God."

Buddy. Should she tell him that Charlie Nabokov and Buddy were one and the same man? She wanted no more

THE INTRUDER

secrets between them, and yet she was certain that Charlie's betrayal would hurt him more than Stephanie's ever had.

Later, she thought. She would tell him later, when things were back to normal. Not right now.

"Who do you think brought the diary back?" she asked instead.

"I expect the same person who took it in the first place."

"But why, Nick? Why? What on earth is going on?"

"I'm not sure," he said. He had resumed his pacing. "Either someone is playing a hoax, a vicious hoax, or—"

"Or what?"

"Or it's a question of malicious sabotage. Sheer terrorism intended to frighten you and sever our relationship. I don't believe it's coincidence that the things you've experienced parallel Stephanie's sick ramblings. I believe it was arranged that they would, and that they would seem unlikely and absurd enough to drive a wedge of mistrust between us. It almost worked, didn't it?"

She didn't know how to answer him. The memory of her isolation from him was too vivid, and though he had finally come over to her side, she still felt a barrier between them. Would they be able to tear it down? He had stopped his pacing and was looking down at her, waiting for her to answer.

"You're the best thing that's happened to me in a long time. The best thing that's ever happened to me," he told her. "Have I lost you?"

She met his look and held it. All the promise of their early days together passed in that glance between them, and she remembered the warmth of their nights together, their laughter as they walked down the street hand in hand, the plans they'd made for the future. She had wanted his children and had believed they would stay united whatever happened. She still wanted that future.

"I love you," she said.

"But you're no longer sure you can rely on me."

"I don't know," she said. "It feels like we've been separated for so long . . ."

His face had become expressionless, but something lonely and wounded looked out of his eyes. He held out his hand to her. He said, "Shall we give it another try?"

His hand felt warm now, and familiar in hers. The physi-

181

cal contact started to mend the broken circuits between them on a deep, primal level, and then grew in potency so that all her awareness lay within that touch. Without quite knowing how she got there, she found herself within the circle of his arms. As he pressed himself against her she could feel the pounding of his heart. She rested her cheek against his shoulder. It was so long since she'd been home. She didn't want to move. They lost track of time as they stood there welded in that embrace. And then she felt his erection pressing against her stomach and felt herself responding. She drew back, half giggling and half crying.

"Now?" she said.

"Not now," he agreed, and brushed a strand of hair off her forehead. "But soon. It's been much too long."

"It has, hasn't it?"

"It has indeed. But first we're going to discuss what we're going to do about this . . . this insanity."

"What can we do when we don't even know who's behind it? I tried to find out, without success, as you know. I'm afraid I'd make a very poor detective."

"You did better than most people would have. And all the time you were there out in the open, like a sitting duck, getting no help from me. It's not something I'm going to forget. Ever. But right now is no time to indulge myself in the luxuries of guilt. You said you were a poor detective. Well, lady, we're going to hire ourselves the best there is. I know the name of a couple of men who've had excellent results in industrial sabotage. One of them owes me a few favors—I'll ask him to look into this, and I'm sure he'll come up with some answers."

He paused and took her hand. "You'll have to tell him everything that happened. In some detail. Do you mind?"

Did a man stranded in a barren desert mind when help showed up on the horizon?

"I don't mind," she said, and thought it the understatement of the year.

"Very well. I'll call him tomorrow and tell him where he can reach us."

"What do you mean? He can reach us here or at your office, can't he?"

"You don't think I'm going to leave you on your own until

this thing is settled, do you? Not on your life. I shudder to think that it *could* have been your life. Tomorrow morning, my love, I'm going into the office to tell the powers that be that I'm taking a few days off for personal reasons. While I'm gone, you can pack a few things for us, enough to last us for a week or so. If I know Joe, he'll have the whole thing settled by then. In the meantime you and I are going to check into a hotel. As Mr. and Mrs. John Smith. Unless you can think of some more original aliases. How does that sound to you, my love?"

That was one thing about Nick. He didn't believe in half measures, which probably accounted for much of his business success. He hadn't believed in the existence of the diary, but now that he had seen it for himself he automatically accepted everything else she had told him. He would take every step he could think of to get to the bottom of it.

She watched him as he headed toward the phone.

"Who are you going to call?" she asked. "At this hour?"

"Bibi. From now on, until we find out who's behind all this, I want someone with you at all times. If I know Bibi, she'll be more than glad to keep you company while I'm at the office. I might be gone most of the day—there are a number of pending projects I should discuss with the partners before I take the week off."

She opened the diary and started to page through it. The words she'd memorized seemed to leap out at her:

> The four of us went to the theater last night. So very staid and proper, and all the time Buddy and I kept glancing at each other and thinking about the things we'd done earlier that day.

It was odd that the faded handwriting should still have the power to evoke that chilling malice from so long ago. Paula shuddered as the familiar chill started its slow tingle at the bottom of her spine. How would Nick feel when he found out what the notation meant? And yet Stephanie was also deserving of some sympathy. Someone had been playing tricks with her mind, and it took someone evil indeed to play with the deranged mind of a sick woman.

She turned the pages absentmindedly, and then, suddenly,

she froze. *It couldn't be.* It was impossible, beyond the realm of reason or of logic. But there it was nevertheless. Someone had made new entries in the diary since she'd seen it last, in a handwriting that looked identical to Stephanie's. But Stephanie was dead. She was dead. She'd died years ago, hadn't she?

"Nick," Paula called faintly.

He said a hurried good-bye to Bibi and rushed over to her side.

26

Only a handwriting expert can tell for certain whether two separate documents were penned by the same hand, and it is not uncommon for the experts to disagree with each other when called to the witness chair to testify in a trial or a case involving probate. There was no doubt, however, that the distorted lettering of the most recent entries in the diary closely resembled the older, faded ones. To an inexperienced eye the forgery was impeccable.

It was quite obvious from Nick's startled expression that he thought so too. "Are you sure these pages were blank before?" he asked, though the freshness of the ink supplied its own answer.

"I'm sure," said Paula. She leaned back against the couch and closed her eyes. For a few seconds she had stood within Nick's arms she had felt safe and loved. And now reality had returned with a vengeance, and she felt stunned by its horror. She said, "I still remember the last thing she had written. She'd never give you a divorce, she said. Never. Never. Never."

Nick sat down next to her, the diary on one knee. He reached out to hold her hand and started reading silently.

"Read it out loud," she urged him.

He looked at her dubiously, wondering if she could take any more shocks. She seemed close to exhaustion. She'd had to cope on her own all this time while he had hung out skeptically on the sidelines. If they came through this, he'd make it up to her, he promised himself. If it took a whole lifetime.

"It's something about a dress," he told her.

"Would you please read it out loud?"

He still hesitated, because the calculated malice of this forgery was totally outside the realm of his experience, while at

185

the same time that twisted writing had unleashed a flood of memories he'd managed to forget. His hold on Paula's hand tightened. He read:

"He's had her here again. I saw her dress out on the bed, oh, she would have looked so fine in it, his pretty lady, but not so fine after I finished with it. That thin chiffon came apart like gray smoke within my hands."

Paula's eyes had sprung open, but otherwise there was no change in her expression, so that he wouldn't have realized the extent of her shock if he hadn't felt her hand growing noticeably colder within his.

"That's my dress," she said dully. "The dress I was going to wear to Bibi's party. Remember? It seems so long ago. When I went to change, I found the dress had been ripped right down the middle. I thought I must have torn it the last time I wore it. And not noticed. Or forgotten about it."

"Did you tell anyone?"

She tried to think back. Her memories were all jumbled together like pieces of a puzzle tossed by a careless hand.

"I don't remember," she said. "I think I told Cindy." Had she told Bibi as well? It was possible, but the idea of Bibi writing that forgery was so ludicrous it wasn't even worth considering. The same applied to Cindy, for that matter, and besides, Cindy was dead. She would never write anything again. Nick read on.

"Why can't I ever see her when her things are all around me? She comes and goes like a ghost, and yet there are signs of her everywhere. While I was brushing my hair the other day I realized it was her brush I was holding in my hands. Later I threw it out. God, how I hate her. How I hate them both."

Paula had sat up straight. Her tension was such that a lightbulb placed in her hands would probably have glowed through that reflected energy. She was sure she knew what was coming next. But the next entry was short and inarticulate.

"I wish I could talk to Mother, I just don't understand, and I just wish . . ."

My God, thought Paula, that poor pathetic woman. She could sense her palpable desperation. It seemed so real she had to remind herself that it was only a forgery, the game of a vicious prankster. Unless . . .

"Go on," she urged Nick.

"There's no need to," he said. "I'll turn it over to Joe tomorrow morning. We don't have to torment ourselves with this drivel."

She looked at him curiously. He wasn't nearly as unaffected as he would like to appear.

"Don't we?" she said.

"Why should we?"

"Because we can't just put it to one side and ignore it. It would be as difficult as ignoring the ticking of a live bomb. Besides, I think I know what comes next."

She listened to the passage with the fatalistic acceptance of one who's awakened from a repeated nightmare only to find that it had been no dream, but stark, brutal reality.

"She's everywhere. They're trying to drive me back to that god-awful place, that clinic—why do they insist on calling it a clinic? A nut house is a nut house is a nut house. A nut house by any other name is still a prison or a zoo. I wish I were dead, I wish she were dead, I wish they were all dead. Today I saw that enormous bunch of daffodils he gave her. To my dearest Paula, said the card. He never gives me flowers anymore. I tore the petals off the stalks one by one and I pretended they were butterfly wings, the nails of her hand caressing Nick, the laughter of the children mocking me in school. I tore the place apart. Nick must have cleaned it up. Why didn't he say anything about it?"

Nick paused abruptly. Paula noticed rivulets of sweat running down his forehead. He looked like a man running a high fever.

"This is obscene," he said. "The work of a maniac."

"She mentioned my name," Paula whispered. The night

weighed heavily around them. "I was afraid she would mention me by name."

"We don't know that it's a she," Nick pointed out, as if their only salvation lay in logic. "We don't know who forged this, but we do know it could have been a man just as easily as a woman. Joe will find out."

He snapped the notebook shut and flung it down upon the table as if it were a poisonous snake ready to strike. Paula leaned forward and picked it up.

"Is that the end of it?" she asked him, though she already knew the answer.

"There are a couple more entries. Filth. Not worthwhile reading."

"But you did read them, didn't you?"

He didn't reply.

She opened the diary and started leafing through the pages, searching for the horror she knew lay in wait for her. Was it mere curiosity? No. She had to know. Anything was better than this twilight world without sense or reason. She felt Nick's hand on her arm.

"Don't," he said, but his voice sounded remote. She reached the last page and read out loud:

"I finally found her. There she was, so wide-eyed and fair—odd, I always thought that her hair was dark—and she stared at me, as though I were fate itself catching up with her. It was fun, really, so wonderful to see that dreadful fear in her eyes, her face crumbling in disbelief. Didn't she realize I would catch up with her eventually? She rushed over to the phone to talk to someone, as if a phone call could help her—and then I followed her as she backed up to the open window. It was so easy. I can still hear that wild cry of hers as I pushed her off the sill. I can't stand it anymore. I wrote across the mirror with the lipstick. It was her lipstick. A nice touch, I thought, but when I went over to tell Buddy, he wouldn't answer the door."

The twisted handwriting seemed to become more distorted as Paula looked at it, and she realized she was seeing it through a film of tears. Cindy. Is that really what had happened to Cindy?

"Stephanie killed Cindy," she told Nick.

She was aware of his hands rubbing her shoulders and the back of her neck, his fingers digging deeply into her tense muscles. The human system is capable of absorbing a certain amount of horror and of pain, and after that, it stops functioning. She had reached that level. Nick's insistent hands restored her to the present.

"Stephanie killed Cindy, didn't she?" she repeated.

"No," Nick replied. His voice was calm, as though her temporary frailty had restored his own secure foothold on reality. "No, of course she didn't. Stephanie died years before Cindy did, remember? Whoever wrote this did so in cold blood. In a manner calculated to distill the greatest possible amount of psychological terror. It's most effective, I admit. But it's still just a forgery."

"There's only a few more lines," said Paula.

> How many of them are there? What's happening? I thought I had taken care of her once and for all, but this evening I saw her sleeping next to the fireplace. Am I really insane? She was no match for me. She looked like a kid with that dark mop of hair across her face. I had my hands around her throat, but then she was gone . . .

That was the end of it. The following page was mercifully blank. Paula closed the notebook and handed it back to Nick.

"There are things in here I've told no one," she said. "No one at all."

"So it was obviously written by the same person who was behind it all."

"Yes. But there's another possibility we haven't considered. *I* could have written it. Not consciously, of course, but— Do you believe in automatic writing?"

"Stop it," he said, shaking her by the shoulders. He pulled her up against him. "Stop it," he murmured. "I've doubted you long enough, and now is no time for you to doubt yourself. We'll get to the bottom of this in a few days. You'll see. Joe will find the person or persons behind it and—if they're lucky—he'll turn them in to the police before I get my hands on them."

They sat holding each other for what seemed like a long time. The clock in the hallway struck the hour, and Paula looked at her watch. It was two o'clock. The room was very silent. Strangeness poured in from the wide open windows facing the park.

"Do you want to go to bed?" Nick asked her. His face was haggard with fatigue and he was having trouble keeping his eyes open.

"Yes," Paula told him. "We should try to get some rest."

She didn't think she could sleep that night. It might be different tomorrow night, of course, after Nick had assigned a detective to the case and they were off somewhere in a hotel, registered under different names. It might be different then, but she doubted it, because whoever hated them enough to have devised this elaborate scheme of terrorism wouldn't be stopped by a simple change of name and address.

No. They would be found and hunted down, and then— And yet it was their one and only chance. They'd have to take it.

Nick's head felt heavy on her lap. She sat in the brightly lit room, listening to the ticking of the clock while waking nightmares imprinted themselves on the retinas of her eyes.

27

It didn't take her very long to pack. A suit for Nick, a couple of dresses for herself, slacks, shirts, underwear, Nick's shaving kit—was she forgetting anything? She felt light-headed from lack of sleep, and though it was barely ten o'clock in the morning, the air was already sultry and oppressive. It would be a hot day. She took a last look at the suitcases on the bed and went into the living room, where Bibi Marcovaldi sat calmly sipping a cup of coffee.

Bibi was wearing a gray linen dress with white piping at the collar and sleeves, and seemed totally unaffected by the heat. She looked, in fact, as though she had just stepped out of a cool shower into a comfortably air-conditioned room. If only she *could* turn the air-conditioning on, Paula thought longingly. But when she'd turned the news on earlier that morning, she'd heard that the electric company was urgently warning all consumers to keep their use of all appliances to a minimum. They had already cut down the energy output, for that matter, because when she'd turned on the light in the bathroom it had glowed yellowish and dim, with just a fraction of its usual brightness.

"Sit down and have some coffee," said Bibi, pouring her a cup.

"It's much too hot for coffee."

"My dear child, everyone drinks hot coffee in the tropics, it's ever so much more effective on a hot day than an iced drink. It equalizes things, you know," she murmured vaguely.

"Perhaps they drink warm liquids because they don't have refrigerators."

"There is always that possibility, isn't there? You look tired, my dear. I'm very pleased that you and Nick are going

191

away for a few days. The change will do you good. A vacation usually does."

"A vacation?" said Paula. "It doesn't feel like we're going on a vacation. It feels more like we're being evacuated from a pending disaster."

"Quite sensibly so. I'm glad that Nick finally came to his senses and is taking things in hand. It's quite fortunate, actually, that Nick found that awful diary. He didn't believe it existed, of course, and once he saw it, he was ready to accept everything else as well, wasn't he? He blames himself for not taking you more seriously before. For not believing the things you had to tell him."

"I guess it's not so surprising, after all. For a while I myself had trouble deciding if I was dealing with reality or imagination. I felt I must be dreaming half the time."

"Yes. That must have been part of the plan, don't you think? A plan quite carefully calculated to instill psychological terror, to make you feel you were surrounded by something always a fraction beyond your reach."

Before leaving for the office Nick had told Bibi he would assign a detective to the case, and then he'd shown her the latest entries in the diary. Whoever forged them must have also been responsible for persecuting Paula, he'd said, since no one else would have known all the details. Bibi had agreed. Her composure had wavered, as if for once she was dealing with something outside her field of experience. If Nick had showed her the diary in an attempt to convince her that Paula must not be left alone, he had succeeded.

"As far as I know I have no enemies," said Paula. "And yet there must be someone who hates me very much. I keep wondering why, what I could have done to make anyone hate me to this extent."

She tried to keep her voice matter-of-fact, but a forlorn note escaped and hung in the room between them like the most ancient of all human cries, the eternal lament of the innocent faced by a hatred all the more frightening because not understood.

"You're dealing with someone insane," Bibi told her gently. "Someone very cunning and insane. That's why it's just as well that Nick is taking you away until that detective discovers who's behind it."

Someone insane, and a killer as well, thought Paula. She wished she could believe in the promise of safety, but the heat and her lack of sleep combined to sensitize her to some evil force around her, so that once again she was convinced it didn't really matter where they went. They would be hunted down.

She sipped silently at her coffee. Both Nick and Bibi agreed that they were dealing with someone who was insane. As Stephanie had been. Was that, too, a coincidence? Had she and Stephanie shared a common enemy, or had someone used Stephanie's sick ramblings, as Nick called them, and built her plot around them?

She remembered her discussions with Charlie Nabokov, with the Brewsters, with Lawrence Jaffe, and suddenly the image of Stephanie grew so vivid that Paula wouldn't have been surprised if she'd suddenly materialized out of the thin air. She shivered and felt her thin cotton shirt sticking to her back. She leaned toward Bibi.

"What if those entries in the diary weren't forged at all?" she said. "They looked and sounded as though Stephanie had written them. What if she did?"

A very odd look indeed crossed Bibi Marcovaldi's ancient face. The wide blue eyes seemed to grow even wider, and then became opaque as Bibi's thoughts turned inward.

"Stephanie died over two years ago," she pointed out. "Are you telling me that you believe in ghosts?"

"I don't know what I believe. My grandmother used to talk to her dead husband—can I be sure that he never answered her? She was convinced that he was there, and I'm beginning to get the same feeling about Stephanie. A feeling that seems to be growing stronger every day. Even now I feel that she's here in this room. That she can hear every word we're saying. It's as though I've conjured her up out of my own mind."

"My dear," Bibi murmured.

"I know. I know it's impossible, and yet it would explain everything. Nick told me he never had another woman up here while he was married, and I believe him. Yet Stephanie kept seeing someone in this apartment, someone who, based on her description, could have just possibly been me."

"What are you getting at, Paula?"

"Could Stephanie have been haunted by the future as I am by the past?" Paula whispered.

Bibi sighed and grew silent. "An interesting idea if you believe in the continued life of the individual after death," she said finally. "A belief I've mercifully been spared."

"Yes. But when you told me about Teresa's priest, the man who warned her that her boyfriend was in danger, you seemed to believe that he could foretell the future." She saw something flicker across Bibi's face. "You still believe it, don't you?" Paula insisted.

"Perhaps I do. Yes, I do believe he had that faculty. But that was quite different, you see. A friend of mine, a physicist I've known for many years, once told me that psychics are people who are just a little more farsighted than most of us, whose vision extends across various dimensions. He said that time is just a dimension, and compared its flow to that of a stream running among curved banks. The future and the past are coexistent, Isaac Cavafy said. A psychic is someone who can see both ends of the stream from where he stands."

"He was talking about the relativity of time, wasn't he?"

"Yes, I expect he was. No one else I ever knew made it seem quite that simple. But he was talking about psychics who might be able to see the full range of temporal dimensions. He wasn't talking about life after death. He never talks about religion, though I suspect that in his own way he's a deeply religious man."

"And what do his fellow scientists think of his theories?"

"A man as solidly entrenched in his field as Isaac is allowed a few eccentricities," said Bibi.

It's odd, thought Paula. We grow up believing certain rules implicitly, and when they're suddenly changed, our whole world turns inside out and we no longer have a familiar foothold. Just so must the contemporaries of Copernicus have felt when he first suggested that the earth revolved around the sun and not the other way around. Just so must they have felt deprived of their security until, in self-defense, they had turned on him viciously to condemn him.

"If time is like a stream flowing among curved banks," she said, "isn't it possible that at some point that stream might overflow its banks and the waters merge? The future and past meet?"

"It's possible," said Bibi. "But a wide area divides the possible from the probable."

The conversation was a strain on Bibi Marcovaldi. She was the most modern and sophisticated of women, yet she had spent her childhood in a countryside where prehistoric legends were still recounted around the fires at night, after the doors and the window shutters had been tightly closed against the evils of darkness. She seemed to grow older as she sat in her chair, as though the fingers of long-forgotten ages were stretching out for her.

She said, "Don't torment yourself, Paula. You're desperate and frightened, just as somebody intended you should be all along. You're reaching out for straws. Nick will find out who's responsible for this whole wicked scheme. It will be all right, you'll see."

Does she really believe that, Paula wondered, or is she merely trying to allay her own fears as well as my own?

"Shall we play some backgammon?" Bibi suggested. "It helps to keep busy."

"Of course," said Paula.

And then the phone rang shrilly in the room. They looked at each other, startled, their taut nerves jarred by the unexpected sound. It's probably Nick, thought Paula, or one of the real-estate agents calling about the apartment. But now her feeling of premonition was working overtime. Don't answer it! it told her. Pretend you're not here. She picked up the phone on the eighth ring.

"This is St. Luke's Hospital," said a woman's voice. "Could I please talk to Paula Girard?"

"This is she," said Paula.

"One of our patients has been asking for you. He's regained consciousness long enough to give us your name and phone number. The doctor thinks you should come out to see him."

"Who? See who?"

"Charles Nabokov. Is he a relative of yours?"

"No. We're . . . friends."

"Yes, I see. I don't want to alarm you, but his condition is considered serious. He was taken to the intensive-care ward right after surgery."

"What happened to him?" asked Paula. The telephone receiver felt slippery in her hand. "Has he had an accident?"

"He was stabbed on the street early this morning. He's under sedation, but still insists that he must talk with you. The doctor feels that he might rest better if he sees you."

"I'll be right there," said Paula, and hung up. She turned around to look at Bibi, but couldn't see her distinctly because of her own tears. It was odd that she hadn't been able to cry before, and that now she should cry for Charlie Nabokov, of all people. Charlie Nabokov. Buddy.

"I must go to the hospital," she told Bibi. "Charlie Nabokov was stabbed on the street earlier this morning."

"I'll go with you," said Bibi, and stood up with obvious effort. She leaned heavily on her cane. Her earlier appearance of freshness and well-being had been an illusion. Her small frame seemed shrunken and her hands were trembling.

"No," said Paula. "I'll be all right. Really. I know Nick doesn't want me to be by myself, but I'll be surrounded by people at the hospital. And there's something else you could do for me."

"Anything, my child."

"Would you call Nick at the office and tell him where I've gone? He might be out, of course. He was going to see that detective he knows sometime today."

"If he isn't there, I'll keep trying."

"Yes. Tell him I'll wait for him at the hospital. Charlie has nobody else, you see." She hesitated. "He's Nick's closest friend," she added.

Bibi Marcovaldi leaned forward and kissed her on the cheek, a soft dry touch as light as a butterfly's. She returned the brief hug and turned away to look for her wallet and her keys.

28

———————

"Charlie," Paula whispered urgently. "Charlie."

He was lying very still on the narrow hospital bed, his eyes closed, his thin arms at his sides. An intravenous tube was dripping its lifesaving fluid into his left arm. The sharp bones of his face were straining under a skin so colorless that for a panicked moment she thought he might be dead. And then she noticed the slow rise and fall of his chest.

"Charlie!" she said again.

His eyes opened slowly, as though burdened by the weight of his lids. She saw awareness in them and something else as well: a feeling of relief so profound that it made her catch her breath. She reached out and touched the thin hand lying so still upon the white coverlet.

"I'm glad you came," he said, his voice barely audible. And then his eyes moved and he saw the nurse standing at her side.

"Alone," he said. "I must talk to Paula alone."

The nurse, a pretty blonde who looked as though she had just come out of nursing school, hesitated. It was obvious that she would have liked to have had specific instructions from a doctor. She didn't like leaving her patient, but after all, it was the doctor in attendance who had told her he should be allowed to talk to Paula.

"Very well," she said. "I'll give you fifteen minutes. Call me if you need me," she whispered to Paula in a quick aside before leaving the room.

Paula pulled up a chair and sat next to the bed. Charlie's eyes had closed for a minute, and when they opened again, there was none of his usual mockery in them, only an immense sadness mingled with that peculiar look of relief.

"I had to tell you," he said. "I wanted you to know. It was me all along."

"What do you mean?" whispered Paula.

It was him all along? Did he mean that he was the one who'd been coming into the apartment, the one who'd attacked her and taken Stephanie's diary? Cindy had once pointed out how easy it would be for him to take Nick's keys and have a copy made. It would have taken no longer than ten minutes.

It was a much simpler and less frightening explanation than the one she had reached. She thought of the torn dress, the golden strands of hair, the trace of lipstick on the glass in the kitchen sink. She'd been certain the intruder was a woman, but then she might have been intended to think just that.

He was staring at her as though willing her to understand while he gathered energy for his next sentence. It was obviously painful for him to speak.

"What do you mean, Charlie?" she repeated.

"Stephanie," he said. He spoke so faintly she had to lean forward to hear him. "Stephanie and me. You guessed, didn't you. You were right. It was Stephanie and me all along."

"You mean you were lovers?"

He tried to smile with a trace of his old mockery.

"Lovers?" he said. "We slept together, if that's what you mean. We were accomplices, not lovers. Stephanie was not the most lovable of women."

"But then why, Charlie? Why? You were Nick's friend and Stephanie was his wife. Nick was the one bond you had in common."

"It was enough," he said. "I loved Nick, and hated him as well. Can you understand that?"

Paula shook her head. Her life had been so simple until recently. People either were friends or they were not, and if they were, they might argue on occasion, but their loyalty was intrinsic, unshakable. Love and hate combined? Unconsciously, not meaning to be cruel, she withdrew the hand that had been holding his.

He smiled again, a faint grimace that brought a shade of color to his cheeks.

"You don't understand," he said. "How could you? Nick

198

was everything I never was and always wanted to be. He was on the tennis team at school. His swimming trophies filled our room. Whenever some girl called, it was always for him. Always. And they called all the time. He'd fix me up with dates. Do you know what that's like? I can tell you. It's like being a poor relation who makes do with his rich cousin's hand-me-downs."

He paused. He'd been speaking laboriously but with a mounting excitement that left him exhausted. Paula tried to hide her sense of pity and revulsion. The man was seriously wounded, with his life in danger. Who was she to judge him?

"You must take it easy," she told him. "We can talk about it later."

"Later?" he said. "There may not be a later." His voice was dull now and very low. "I know what you must think of me. I share your opinion. I wanted to break it off soon after it started, but Stephanie wouldn't hear of it. She threatened to tell Nick if I broke off with her, and later—when I said, all right, tell him and be damned—she threatened to kill me." He paused, gasping for breath.

"How did you know about us?" he asked. "How did you know that she called me Buddy?"

"I didn't know," said Paula. "Not then. I thought there was something you were holding back, but I didn't know what it was until I talked to Larry. Her first husband."

"So he was involved with her, too."

"Yes. He wasn't happy about it."

"Who was?" He sighed deeply. It was a rhetorical question to which he expected no answer, a question to which he himself had been able to find no reply. He closed his eyes.

"I've had no peace since then," he murmured. "Night and day. Never. And so, because they can't hang a man more than once, I tried to make you. You hated me, didn't you? Me. Everything I stood for. And even if you hadn't, it wouldn't have helped. The whole rotten mess haunts me, pursues me like the unrelenting hounds of hell. Or of my conscience. Who knows? It's been worse lately. The last few nights I thought I heard her knocking at my door."

Paula reached out and took his hand again. "Charlie, don't think about it. Not now. What happened this morning?"

"This morning? I don't know. It was too hot to sleep, so I

got up early to eat breakfast out. I was at Seventy-fifth and Broadway waiting for the lights to change when I felt something push against me. A thin sharp pain beneath my shoulder blades. That's all. When I came to, I was in the operating room. I would be all right, one of the doctors told me. And then they clamped something over my face and I was out again."

"Oh, Charlie, I'm so sorry."

"You are, aren't you? You're a sweet child. You know, of course, that I tried—I tried to start the same thing all over again with you."

"Hush, Charlie. I know."

"I want you to tell Nick. Everything. In addition to everything else, I'm a coward. I couldn't bear to tell him myself. But if you tell him, and if he can bring himself to do it, I'd like to see him. Have him come to see me. He's the only friend I have, you see."

He was gasping for air. The color that had momentarily stained his cheeks had faded away, leaving his face waxen. His eyes closed and a low moan escaped from his chest.

Paula ran to the door.

"Nurse!" she shouted. "Nurse!"

The young blond girl came running down the short hallway, took a look at Paula, and rushed to Charlie's side. She lifted his arm and placed her fingers on his pulse.

"He's in no condition to take any more excitement," she told Paula. "He must rest for now."

She looked at Paula accusingly, as though Charlie's condition were somehow her fault, as though patients should be protected at all costs from outside interference. But it wasn't that simple, thought Paula. People who entered the hospital didn't leave their everyday cares and anxieties at the doorstep like so many unwanted bundles. They carried them inside like barbs beneath their skin. As Charlie had. And Charlie's guilt would have to be eased somehow.

She picked up her shoulder bag and was almost at the door when she heard Charlie call her name. She walked to the side of his bed and leaned over. His eyes were closed and his voice was quite weak now. But the words were distinct.

"She called me Buddy," he said. "Just before I felt that

stabbing pain someone called me Buddy. Peculiar, isn't it? No one but Stephanie ever called me by that name."

Paula walked out into the hallway before looking at her watch. It was almost two o'clock. She found a dime in her wallet and walked over to the phones. Nick was out, the secretary told her. No, he hadn't left a number where he could be reached, but he was expected back later in the afternoon. Was there a message? Paula told her she would call back, and dialed Bibi's number. Teresa answered. Bibi was resting, she said, but she'd left definite instructions to be called if either Paula or Nick tried to reach her.

"How is Charlie?" was the first question Bibi asked Paula.

"I don't know. He doesn't look good. He's anxious to see Nick, but he wanted to talk to me first."

"I haven't been able to reach Nick yet, but I told his secretary to have him call me as soon as he gets in. Are you coming home now?"

"I think I should stay here, at least until I can talk to one of the doctors. Charlie's in a bad way, Bibi. Supposing he takes a turn for the worse? I can't just leave him here surrounded by strangers."

"No. Of course you can't."

Paula went downstairs to the cafeteria and put some unappetizing-looking food on her tray. The taste of the food matched its appearance: the salad was wilted and dry, the soup watery and tasteless. Or perhaps she just wasn't hungry, she thought, munching absentmindedly on a roll. Nick must have reached his friend. He was probably talking to him right now. A couple of years ago Nick had recommended Joe to a client of his, a major corporation plagued by industrial espionage. Joe had been able to plug the leak, and his business had flourished as his reputation had grown. "That's one I owe you," he'd told Nick. "Just let me know when there's something you want done." Nick was certain he'd be willing to help them—the point was, would he be able to? And was there any connection with what had been happening to them and the attack on Charlie? If so, Stephanie was the only common denominator. "The last few nights I thought I heard her knocking at my door," Charlie had said.

The roll tasted like sawdust in her mouth. She pushed the tray away and went back upstairs. The door to Charlie's room was open and she looked in, but he was asleep. She walked down the hallway until she reached the desk of the nurse who appeared to be in charge.

"I'm Paula Girard," she said. "A friend of Charlie Nabokov's. Can you tell me how he's doing?"

The gray-haired, round-faced woman must have heard similiar questions dozens of times each week.

"Mr. Nabokov is doing as well as can be expected," she said routinely. "Would you be able to give us the name and address of his closest relative?"

"He has no relatives. Just us. I expect my husband will be here fairly soon. I'll wait until he comes."

The woman gave her a sharp look, and something in Paula's face seemed to arrest her attention. Her own expression gentled.

"There's no need to do that," she said. "If you give me your phone number, I'll call you if there's any change."

"That's very nice of you, but I think I'll wait," said Paula.

She sat in one of the chairs in the long corridor and started to doze. She hadn't realized she was so tired. The unrelenting tension of the last few days, her lack of sleep, the heat, the shock of seeing Charlie's bloodless face, had all combined to put her in that state of suspended animation in which, uneasily balanced between waking and sleep, she was only partially aware of white figures bustling along the hallways, of carts bearing unconscious passengers being pushed along on silent wheels, of the unending, insistent voice on the loudspeaker system. Someone moaned softly. She was walking along an endless maze. . . .

Someone touched her shoulder and she jumped. It was Nick. She didn't think she'd ever been so glad to see anyone before. She threw her arms around him and held him tightly, as if his steady heartbeat were the only shield between her and these white and malevolent surroundings. Why couldn't there be soft music instead of that ominous voice on the loudspeaker calling the doctors to God knows what tasks? Why couldn't there be pastels instead of white, why were so many of the rooms filled with those dreadful, scentless mortuary flowers?

"Have you been here all afternoon?" Nick asked.

"Yes. I saw Charlie earlier, but nobody will tell me how he really is."

"I'll find out," said Nick. He held her at arm's length and studied her face. "You look exhausted," he told her. "I want you to go straight to Bibi's and lie down for a while. I'll pick you up as soon as I'm done here, and we'll go to the hotel. I made the reservations."

"Which hotel?" she asked him.

He shook his head. "You'll find out when we get there. Joe told me not to tell anyone, anyone at all. And if Bibi asks you, it will be easier for you not to tell her if you don't know."

"*Bibi?* Don't tell me he thinks she's involved. Its just plain impossible!"

"Of course it is, or I wouldn't ask you to stay with her. But I can see Joe's point. Why go to a hotel if we're going to take an ad out in the paper to advertise the fact? And as for Bibi—it's better for her if she doesn't know. Better and safer. Joe is going to assign two people to the case first thing tomorrow morning."

"It's all so ugly," said Paula.

"Yes. Joe called it unpleasant, which are strong words for him. He has a gift for understatement, to put it mildly. I left the diary with him, by the way. He doesn't have much hope of finding any fingerprints, but he'll have it checked out anyway."

And supposing the only fingerprints he finds are ours and those of a dead woman? Paula drew closer to Nick, and they formed a small island of warmth in the cold sterile hallway where the white-clad nurses rushed around in their silent, crepe-soled shoes.

"Nick," said Paula. "Before you see Charlie there's something you should know. He's got something to tell you, something— I don't want you to be hurt any more than you've been already."

"I think I have a fair idea of what it is," said Nick. He looked at her small exhausted face and his own tightened. "You don't like Charlie, do you?"

Her silence was as eloquent as any reply she could have made.

"And yet you stayed here, waiting, all afternoon."

"There was no one else," said Paula.

They hugged each other briefly, and when she moved away, she missed the protective shield of his body against her own. "Go on," he urged her. "Go to Bibi's." But she stood where she was, watching him, until she saw him enter the room where Charlie had been moved from the intensive-care unit.

29

The air outside seemed to shimmer with heat. It was probably somewhere in the low nineties, but it seemed even hotter as layers of humidity and exhaust fumes settled between the tall buildings with the thickness of fog. There was no saving breeze. It was well past the rush hour, but the streets were still crowded with people bearing that half-injured, half-insulted look New Yorkers acquire when the weather refuses to follow the basic ground rules of any given season. The daylight was beginning to turn to dusk, and the whole city was bathed in an odd purplish light the color of an old bruise.

Paula was wondering whether to treat herself to the luxury of a cab, but a look at her wallet convinced her that it was not a luxury that she could afford. She had exactly three dollars plus the loose change in her pocket. It might be enough to cover the fare, but if it didn't, she wasn't prepared to face an irate taxi driver to ask him to wait while she ran upstairs to get some more money. Even the bravest New Yorkers hesitate to provoke a cabdriver's irritation. Sometimes the doorman had a few dollars to lend; but sometimes he didn't.

She headed toward the subway. She was still fascinated by the subway system, by the train roaring out like a prehistoric monster from the depths of the tunnel, by the speed and economy with which one could travel from one end of the city to the other. If only it were less crowded during the rush hour and the whole thing could be maintained in a better state of repair, it would be the ideal way to travel. There was never enough money for repairs, she knew, never enough money to replace the worn tracks and old, rickety cars. What would happen to the city if the whole subway system wound down like a gigantic, broken toy?

She ran down the subway steps and bought a token. The

subway platform felt like a subterranean oven, making the street seem like an oasis of coolness by comparison. It was all relative, she expected. The platform was crowded, which meant she hadn't just missed a train. She looked at her watch. Seven-thirty. Trains ran less frequently after the rush hour.

She was making her way toward a relatively uncrowded area when she thought she heard someone calling her name. She looked around but didn't see anyone she knew. And then the call was repeated: "Paula! Paula?"

She turned around, startled, and walked straight into a man reading a newspaper. He gave a brief grunt of annoyance, but when she smiled at him apologetically, he returned her smile, and for some reason she felt heartened by that brief human contact. She stood on her toes and scanned the crowd, but she still didn't recognize anyone she knew. And why should she? Whoever it had been must have been calling to somebody else. Her name was not all that uncommon, after all.

The crowd parted, shifted, and she found herself standing on the edge of the platform, surrounded by a solid phalanx of hot, sweating people. She'd be at Bibi's soon, she thought. She would lie down in the quiet guest room for a while and then Nick would come and take her to some out-of-the-way hotel whose very anonymity would help to restore their sense of perspective. Oh, Nick, she thought with a swift rush of tenderness. He was probably talking to Charlie now, while she stood here. How would he react to that mixed burden of envy and guilt that Charlie would be laying upon his shoulders?

She would have insisted on waiting for him if she hadn't realized that he would need a few minutes on his own to reorient his thoughts and his emotions. To rearrange his face into a decent mask suitable for presentation to the public. Nick was not a man to wear his feelings on his sleeve, and though she would have liked to have been able to help him, she respected his need for privacy. So much had changed for them, but at least they still understood each other's needs. They would find their way back together, given the chance.

A distant rumbling down the darkened tunnel told her the train was heading in.

And then she felt someone's palm against her lower back, and shrugged in annoyance. It wasn't the first time she'd been felt up or pinched while standing in a crowd, and on one occasion a man with an erection had pressed up against her until she managed to disentangle herself and get off at the next stop. But this was no sexual weirdo, she realized suddenly. Because as the noise of the incoming train increased so did the pressure on her back, and she tried to shift and turn away but she was jammed in a solid wedge of people and there was no place for her to go except forward, where the subway tracks yawned beneath her. Horror gripped her, and her legs didn't seem to be working properly. Neither did her vocal cords, for that matter, because when she tried to cry out she couldn't make a sound. And then the bright headlights of the train came into sight and she tried to regain her balance until a violent shove sent her falling directly in the path of the train.

At the last minute someone snatched her back with such force that she was flung back against the surrounding crowds.

She lay on the cement platform. Her fall had been cushioned by the people who stood aside now and looked at her curiously before pushing their way across to the open doors of the subway cars. She had fallen on her right elbow and sharp shooting pains were radiating up and down her arm. A young bearded man in jeans knelt down beside her, and when she looked up she saw a black man in a well-cut business suit leaning above her, his kindly face furrowed with concern.

"I hope I didn't hurt you," he said.

So he was the one who'd pulled her back. In the nick of time. She looked at his face and tried to imprint it in her memory. But for the speed of his reflexes she'd be lying mangled beneath the train, another headline on page two of the newspapers.

"Thank you," she said, knowing the word inadequate. Her lips felt numb, the way they did after a shot of Novocain at the dentist's. She took his extended hand and pulled herself up to her feet.

"Are you all right?" said the bearded man. "It's this blasted heat."

"I'm all right," she said, and was aware that the black businessman was still holding her hand and looking at her in a hesitant manner, as if wondering what to do with her now that he had saved her.

"It's the heat," the bearded man repeated. "It's enough to make anyone woozy."

"But I wasn't . . ." she started to say indignantly, and then stopped herself abruptly. There was no point in telling them about the murderous shove intended to send her stumbling in the path of the train. And if she *did* tell them, they might insist on calling a policeman and there would be questions and routines to go through—pointless routines, because whoever had pushed her had long since left the platform. Besides, it was undeniable that she did feel woozy.

"It is hot," she said instead, "but I'm all right now. Really. And I must get home. Another train should be coming soon."

And indeed they could hear the rumbling of another train headed in their direction through the tunnel.

"Thank you," she said again, and the black businessman released her hand. But he had evidently decided that his course of action should be based on the theory that we're responsible for the lives of those we've saved.

He said, "I don't think you're in any condition to go home by yourself. Can you call someone? Your husband or a friend?"

She shook her head. His question underlined the extent of her isolation. Bibi was confined to the house by her arthritis, Cindy was dead, Charlie Nabokov was wounded in the hospital—she was losing friends much faster than she could make them.

"In that case I'm going to put you into a cab," said the businessman.

"I'll be all right, really. . . ." The train was pulling in at the platform.

"I have a daughter older than you are," he told her, frowning, as if the fact gave him some obscure authority beyond dispute.

He took her firmly by her uninjured elbow and led her upstairs and out into the street. A cabdriver answered his summons and pulled over to the curb. Her newly found benefactor opened the door and helped her inside.

"Where do you live?" he asked.

She told him, and then she heard him tell the driver and

saw him hand the man some dollar bills. She wanted to protest, but if a man has just saved your life, isn't he entitled to also pay your cab fare? He smiled at her and lifted his hand, either in farewell or in benediction, or both. And then the cab pulled away and she was left with the image of his thin, kindly face.

The human system can absorb just so many shocks and no more, and she had reached that saturation point where the nerves are numb and the mind is closed to the further implications of danger. It is the state that allows soldiers to return again and again to the horrors of battle. It is also the state in which the mind, unable to see the broader scope, becomes acutely aware of all trivia, and so Paula was very conscious of the hot air that streamed in through the open car windows, the faint repeated rattling of one of the rear doors, the wide, flattish head of the man behind the wheel. At least he wasn't feeling talkative, thank God, or perhaps he was particular about whom he talked to and felt her undeserving of attention.

She did, indeed, look a mess. Her right elbow protruded from the torn sleeve and the painful contusion was covered by a layer of dirt and something that looked like a trickle of dried blood. Her skirt was filthy, covered with dust and something else she preferred not to speculate about, and heaven only knows what her hair must look like. She would have to shower and change before going up to Bibi's. What on earth would the doorman think when she walked past him?

It was amazing how one continued to worry about appearances even when living on the edge of a nightmare, she thought. She remembered how once when she was a child her parents had taken her to the funeral of her father's uncle, and how her great-aunt, puzzled by her vast loss, had fretted and cried over a torn stocking. "But my stocking is torn," the old lady had kept saying, "my stocking is torn. . . ." And that had somehow struck Paula as the saddest thing of all.

The apartment was dark when she walked in, and she walked to each room and systematically turned on all the lights before stripping off her clothes and stepping into the shower.

She turned the water on full blast and let it stream over her upturned face, her hair, her naked body. The clean cool water brought her a measure of revival, as if in rinsing herself off, she was cleansing herself of the palpable hatred that surrounded her.

She soaped her body twice and then shampooed her hair. Her movements were automatic, almost leisurely, because there no longer seemed to be any reason to hurry. She was convinced now that it no longer mattered where they went or when, because it was already too late. Or maybe it had been too late from the beginning? Charlie Nabokov had been stabbed that morning, and just now someone had tried to push her off the subway platform in front of that incoming train. She had been pulled back just in time, but what about the next time? Or the next?

She had stepped into a trap from which there was no escape.

She dried herself thoroughly and put on her long white terry robe before she went into the living room to dial Bibi's number.

"Teresa?" she said. "I'm downstairs. Would you tell Bibi that I'll be up as soon as I've dressed?"

"We've been waiting for you," Teresa told her with a heavy note of reproof.

"I'm sorry, Teresa. I had to shower before coming up. I'll be there in a few minutes."

"Your husband just called to see if you are here yet," said Teresa. "He has seen Mr. Charlie and he's meeting you up here, he said. Are you hungry, *bambina*? I can get dinner ready for you in no time."

"I think we'll be eating out, Teresa," Paula told her. "But thanks. I'll see you soon."

She was walking back toward the bedroom to get dressed when the phone rang again, with that shrill angry sound it seemed to have acquired during the last few days. Was it really louder than it used to be, or did it sound louder because the apartment had grown quieter, as the countryside grows calm and quiet when waiting for a storm?

"Hello?" she said, picking up the receiver.

"Paula," said Nick, "I've been trying to reach you. I thought you were going straight to Bibi's."

"I was," she said, "but I needed to shower and change. I just talked to Teresa and told her I'd be up in a few minutes." She hesitated. Should she tell him about the incident in the subway? Not right now, she decided. She'd wait until they were together and she could tell him face to face. She wished that he were here with her right now. She wished he didn't sound so very far away.

"Teresa told me you saw Charlie," she said. "Is he feeling any better?"

"He's going to make it. The doctor said his condition has stabilized. I think he does feel better for having talked to us."

"And you? How do you feel?"

"I'm fine," he told her. "I was pretty sure of what he was going to tell me before I got there, but still, I'm not sure I was prepared for that outpouring of guilt or that repressed hatred. I've known that man since we were in school, and suddenly I've realized that I've never really known him after all." He spoke in a dry, matter-of-fact manner, but some leaden undertone told her how much the experience had cost him.

"I'm sorry," she said.

"So am I. Particularly for Charlie. The odd thing is that I can't hold it against him, that I have the feeling that when this whole thing is cleared up we'll continue seeing him as if nothing had happened."

"You're probably right," she said.

And then some sixth sense, some feeling of menace in the sullen air around her, made her add, "Nick, are you still at the hospital?"

"I'm in the lobby. I thought I'd try to reach you one more time before coming home. Why?"

"I think you should insist that someone stay in Charlie's room, that someone be with him at all times."

"He won't be allowed any more visitors," Nick pointed out.

"It's still too easy for people to get in and out of there. We're dealing with a maniac, you said—an insane, calculating mind. And Charlie is totally helpless. He can't defend himself."

"You're right," he said immediately, and she realized he had already come to the conclusion that the attack on Charlie was part of the pattern fusing itself around them. "I should have thought of it myself. I'll ask for a nurse to be assigned to Charlie's side for twenty-four hours a day, and tell them we'll guarantee all expenses."

"And then you'll come home?"

"I'll come straight to Bibi's. I'll meet you there within half an hour."

The sound of his voice had been as intimate as a physical touch, and when she hung up, she felt as desolate as if they had said good-bye before a lengthy separation. Half an hour seemed like an eternity. Ten minutes ago she had been moving in the slow, leisurely fashion of one who knows the ending is inevitable, but now she was possessed by that sense of urgency that paralyzes action through its very intensity.

Half an hour. Would he really be here in half an hour, would they have a chance to be together after all? She should have warned him not to take the subway. She should have suggested that he take a cab. But would he really be any safer in the street? Charlie hadn't been. And there was always the chance that when he stepped into a cab someone would be there. Silently waiting for him.

She was getting paranoid, she decided. Nick was the type of man who was fully capable of taking care of himself, and in the meantime she would do her part. She couldn't let her lack of sleep and that destructive tension she'd lived with for so long affect her in this way. She reminded herself that as of tomorrow there would be two capable, experienced detectives assigned to the case, and once they discovered the identity of the person responsible for this nightmare, they would call in the police. And she and Nick could start picking up the pieces.

She walked into the bedroom. The open suitcases on the bed looked like a promise of the future she knew she wanted desperately, the combined future of their lives together. Oh, Nick, she thought. The strength of her yearning was such that it sent a rush of adrenaline through her bloodstream and shocked her out of the lethargy that had threatened to overcome her.

She went to the closet and chose a cool, sleeveless dress and a pair of sandals. She was moving swiftly now, as if to make up for the time she'd lost before. Hurry, she kept telling herself. Hurry. She'd just taken a bra and bikini panties out of her drawer when the light went out.

Her heart jumped against her rib cage. Had the light bulb burned out? But the lights in the living room and hallway seemed to have gone out as well. A burned-out fuse? The fuses had burned out the night Stephanie had been killed, she remembered suddenly, and the thought was like an additional layer of darkness in the dark room.

She stood totally still until her widened pupils started to discern the familiar shapes of the furniture in the room. There were candles in the living room, she thought. She would finish dressing by candlelight and then run up to the refuge of Bibi's apartment, where there would be welcome and light and the comfort of Bibi's and Teresa's company. She started to walk toward the living room, moving slowly, her tentative hand trailing along the wall. There'd been many other times when she had walked through the darkened living room on her way to the kitchen, but there'd always been enough light streaming in through the wide windows facing the park to light her way.

She glanced at the windows. They were as black as if someone had painted them over, or as if the entire building had been lifted out of the brightly lit city into some bleak, vast area of space where no light ever shone and the stars themselves had become opaque. She experienced a quick feeling of vertigo, and then, still moving slowly, walked toward the windows.

The whole city was dark.

There must have been a power blackout, she realized. The streetlights had been extinguished, and the darkness was so total she couldn't even see the outline of the distant building on the other side of the park. The only lights came from the cars in the street below, and if it hadn't been for the sound of their horns, she would have thought they looked like fireflies searching the summer night.

She thought immediately of Nick. She wondered if he was trapped in an elevator suspended between floors, or in a subway tunnel where he might be confined for hours until someone came to release the passengers and lead them in a narrow file to the nearest station. There'd been two other major blackouts in the city, she knew, times when a number of people had been trapped like animals in a cage. She felt the horror of their claustrophobia as if it were her own. Let Nick be all right, she prayed, and knew that wherever he was, he'd be thinking about her.

She turned back toward the room. There were some candles above the mantelpiece and some more on the table. But no matches. Where had she put the matches? She felt along the desk top and the top of the coffee table without success. She wished they had a flashlight. Her father, wise in the ways of the country, had always insisted on having a flashlight in each room. Never mind. She would light the candles from the gas burners in the kitchen, assuming the gas was still on, of course.

She had taken the candles off the mantelpiece and was heading toward the kitchen when she thought she heard something in the room. She stopped, listening. Silence. Her nerves were overwrought and she was allowing them to play tricks with her. It would never do.

She lit the candles at the kitchen range and walked back into the living room, walking slowly and carefully so that they wouldn't blow out. She had always thought candlelight was romantic, but now it had a curiously opposite effect, two wan circles of light surrounded by thick shadows that seemed more sinister than total darkness had been.

She put one of the candleholders down on the coffee table and started to walk toward the bedroom with the other one in her hand. Her shadow moved, immense and ominous, along the wall beside her.

And then she heard it again. It was a soft, slithering sound, as light as an indrawn breath or the soft noise of a moth hitting a windowpane. But it was unmistakably real.

There was someone with her in the apartment.

30

There are few children who haven't played hide-and-seek at one time or another, tiptoeing ever so quietly to a secret hiding place—an upstairs closet, the cubicle beneath the staircase, the refuge behind the long living-room curtains—and then waited patiently, with bated breath and heart pounding wildly in response to that subterranean flow of fear and excitement that erupts in a small shriek when the probing fingers of the seeker reach out to touch a shoulder.

The waiting, Paula remembered, had been the most awful thing of all. She held up the candle with an unsteady hand and the massed shadows in the room shifted against the moving light.

"Hello?" she called out.

Silence.

"Is anybody here?"

There was still no answer, but all her senses were stretched to their outermost boundaries and she could *feel* another presence with her in the room. The front door, she thought. She'd run out into the hallway and pound on her neighbors' door to ask for help. Silent on her bare feet, she started moving toward the door, ready to make a dash for it at the last minute.

Gently, she told herself. Gently. She mustn't tip her hand and let the intruder know what she planned to do. She was within five feet of the door when she saw the shadow moving against it.

Her own shadow? No. Whoever it was had his or her arms spread wide, barring her way.

They stood motionless, facing each other, and then Paula expelled her pent-up breath in a low moan. She whirled around so quickly that the candle in her hand flickered and

215

almost went out. What if it *had* gone out? The thought of total darkness was unbearable, and the other candle burning on the low coffee table didn't shed much light. And yet she didn't have much freedom of movement while standing there with that candle in her hand, and—even more frightening—she realized she made a perfect target. She placed the candle on the desk and leaned against the desk top, trying to still the trembling of her legs.

"Who is it?" she repeated.

She was answered by a soft, slurred giggle that sent goose bumps down her skin. She clutched her terry robe more closely around her, as though the soft material might afford some protection against that low, infinitely evil sound. It seemed to have come from the other end of the room. Either there were two people after her, or her pursuer had an uncanny ability of moving swiftly from one place to another without the noise of revealing footsteps. In either case she was helpless in this deadly game of cat and mouse, playing out of her league.

The telephone. The telephone was right there beside her hand, and help would be as close as the phone if she could see well enough to dial. Bibi's number? No. That would take too long. She picked up the receiver and dialed 911, the emergency number. It was busy. There would be many frantic calls to the emergency switchboard during the blackout. She was still holding the receiver in her hand when she heard a slight click and the telephone went dead. The line had been cut.

She could scream, of course, but if she did, no one would hear her, not in this building planned so many decades ago for total privacy and silence. If only she could win a little time. Nick would come looking for her soon, or else Teresa and Bibi would start to wonder what was taking her so long and come down.

She placed the silenced receiver on the desk and started to walk toward the bathroom. The door was sturdy enough to withstand any assault, she knew, and if only the lock held until Nick came, she might still be all right. She walked quietly, her hand pressed to her mouth to repress the gasping breath that would be bound to give her whereabouts away.

"Come in," a voice called to her from behind the bathroom door.

She whirled around and fled back to the living room. Her lungs felt as if they were going to explode, and she was breathing in great gasps that sounded like sobs to her own ears.

More light. She had to have more light! She had to see.

Half stumbling and falling she reached the fireplace and lifted her hand to find the other candles on the mantelpiece. And then she looked in the mirror and she froze.

Her own face was looking back at her, wide-eyed with panic. But there was another form taking shape just a few feet behind her, a tall slender shape with a straight fall of pale hair and a face as white and bloodless as her own. She had seen that same face peering over her shoulder at Bibi Marcovaldi's party. She had seen it in the pictures in Nick's album. She had glimpsed it over and over again in her dreams.

She turned around slowly.

"Stephanie," she said.

The face in front of her wavered and then steadied, as a picture on a television screen acquires clarity and depth when the antenna is adjusted. It smiled, and that small amused smile was infinitely ominous.

"Here I am," she said. "You must have known I would catch up with you sooner or later. You're not surprised, are you?"

Paula was not surprised. She had gone along with Nick's decision to hire a detective, and having done so, had tried to convince herself that he would discover a logical solution to it all. She had hoped that he would find the insane killer who, motivated by jealousy or hatred, had cunningly plotted their destruction.

She had been deluding herself, she realized now. Way deep in her subconscious she had known that it was Stephanie all along, and why not? She herself had evoked her out of her own curiosity, which had grown into an obsession; she had given her life and breath as surely as if she had used the living matter of her own mind to recreate her. What had Bibi said? "Time is a stream flowing among curved banks." It is I who damaged the structure of those banks, thought Paula with that sweeping clarity of mind that one often acquires when looking in the face of death. It is I who am responsible for the flow of the past and the present blending together. Where are we now? she wondered. Had she stepped backward into Stephanie's time or had Stephanie moved forward into hers?

"Listen," said Paula. "Please listen to me. I know what you believe, but I haven't taken Nick away from you."

"Haven't you indeed? Then what are you doing here, what have you been doing here all along?" said Stephanie. There was something wrong with the sound of her voice, as though it were a tape recording that was beginning to wear thin.

How did you tell someone that she was dead?

She would have to play for time, thought Paula desperately. Someone would come along soon; Nick would come home in a short while and Stephanie would vanish like a dream. She seemed to lose her power when Nick was around, perhaps because he had put her so firmly and totally out of his mind. But supposing Nick *was* trapped in an elevator or a subway? She couldn't afford to think about that possibility. She would have to play a deadly game with Stephanie, because there was no longer anything else that she could do.

"Stephanie," she said. "There's a copy of the *Times* on the coffee table. Would you look at the date?"

"What for, my dear?" Stephanie said, and this time Paula heard the unmistakable whisper of insanity in that insistent voice. She backed away slowly and stepped behind a chair, as though to place a shield between herself and the evil and madness spreading throughout the room.

She said, "Look at the *Times,* Stephanie."

"Very well," said Stephanie. "I don't mind playing your silly game for a while. It's a game I'm going to win, you know."

She walked over to the table and picked up the paper with one hand, keeping the other hand hidden behind her. She held the paper to the flickering light of the candle and stared at it.

And then she threw her head back and screamed out loud.

Her scream reverberated throughout the room, and when it stopped, Paula could still hear its echo piercing her eardrums. Stephanie threw the newspaper down and raised her other hand, and as she raised it, Paula saw the dull glimmer of a knife.

"So that's the game," Stephanie whispered, advancing toward her. "You're still trying to drive me insane, you and Nick. You want me to believe two years have passed without my knowledge. Oh, you're willing to go to any lengths to have me put away, aren't you? Back in that hideous nursing home that's worse than any prison."

"No, Stephanie, no. No one wanted to . . . no one wants to hurt you."

"But now it's my turn."

"Please listen to me, Stephanie."

"Go ahead, little girl. Let me hear you plead. Beg me not to hurt you. Try to convince me that there is an innocent reason for you being here in my apartment. My home. I want to hear you beg. You won't get away from me this time, not like you did in the subway."

She was moving toward Paula with the leisurely grace of a cat well assured of its prey.

"So it was you on the subway platform?" said Paula, backing away while staring at that long blade aimed toward her face.

"Of course it was me. Who did you think it was? And it almost worked, didn't it, until that man pulled you back. I was glad he did. You don't believe that, do you, but I really was glad. I couldn't see your face, you see, and I so much wanted to see the horror on your face. The way I see it now."

She jumped forward with the swiftness of a practiced fencer, and her knife flashed through the air in a deadly arch. Paula fell to her knees and rolled away, but not before the point of the knife had pierced her shoulder. She felt a sharp sting and touched herself instinctively. Her hand came away wet, sticky with blood.

She stumbled over to the other corner of the room. Why didn't someone come? Bibi must be getting worried about her by now; she would probably try to call and realize that something was very wrong when she couldn't get through. She would probably come down to see what was happening. But how could she come down when the elevator wasn't working? Her arthritis had become almost crippling and she would never make it down the stairs by herself, not unless Teresa helped her with each step. Would they be sufficiently worried to come down?

Please come, she prayed. Please, please come.

She looked around for escape the way a trapped animal does, and for a fleeting second her gaze rested on the wide-open windows. Now that her eyes were adjusted to the dark she could see the width of the park and the tall buildings at its other end. When she looked up, she saw a number of pale stars glimmering through the thick layers of heat and smog. Would this be the last time that she saw the stars? The open windows were like an invitation. Cindy. Cindy had jumped out of the window rather than face the horror inside the room.

"You killed Cindy," she whispered.

"She killed herself," Stephanie told her in that uneven, worn-out voice in which insanity murmured like the buzz of bees. She was standing still now, looking in wonderment at the stained point of the knife as she might examine a trophy she had deserved and won.

She said, "But I wanted to kill her. I want to kill all of you and I will yet. Oh, how I hate you all, plotting behind my back and planning to destroy me. Yes, all of you. Even Buddy—Buddy, who was my friend. We had some good laughs together, he and I, but when I knocked on his door the last few nights, he wouldn't let me in. I warned him I would kill him if he broke off with me, so it's all his fault. Isn't it? He has only himself to blame for what happened. It's his own fault that I followed him and stabbed him out in the street," she said with the grave logic of madness.

She stood there for a minute, seemingly at a loss, confused by her own thoughts. But then she shook her head as if to clear it and turned back to where Paula stood half hidden at the other end of the room.

"It's time," Stephanie said.

Her words were like a sigh, like the breath of a winter wind among dead branches, like the haunting sound of a piano tinkling across the air on a hot summer day.

She moved forward, the knife held out in front of her, and Paula stepped back and walked around the chair. They circled the room in a silence in which the only sound was

Paula's ragged, painful breathing as she tried to draw extra air into her lungs.

The door, thought Paula. If only she could reach the door and make her escape. She started to make a run for it, but in her haste she didn't see the footstool in her way, and the next thing she knew she was falling; she could feel herself falling and she had just managed to pull herself up on her hands and knees when Stephanie's hand wound herself in her hair and pulled her head back with a sharp wrench.

"I told you the game was over," Stephanie said softly.

Still grasping Paula's hair, she pulled her head steadily back until they could look into each other's eyes. Stephanie's were ablaze with a passion that combined not only hatred and insanity but something else as well: an all-pervading malice that had been repressed for far too long and that, finally set loose, seemed triumphant in its newly found freedom to wreak havoc at its own pace and in its own way.

She held the point of the knife an inch from Paula's upturned face.

"You won't be so pretty when he finds you," she whispered. "Will he cry, I wonder? I hope he cries. I hate him even more than I hate you, but I can't reach him, for some reason. When I talk to him, he pretends not to hear me, he acts as though I weren't in the room."

She lowered the knife until it touched Paula's cheek, and then, with a deliberately restrained movement, sliced downward through the skin.

"There," she said. "And now for the other side, and then your eyes, your mouth . . . he won't even recognize you when he finds you, will he?"

Paula felt the warmth of her own blood streaming down her face and heard that shrill, terrible giggle echoing above her. She wrenched against the restraining fingers grasping her hair and managed to break loose. She no longer felt either pain or fear. She felt nothing at all except for that deeply ingrained, primal, and instinctive determination to survive.

She was fleeing into the darkness, stumbling against the furniture looming in her way, gasping, righting herself, and running as Stephanie's knife came down again and again. She could feel the cold steel penetrating her flesh, but there was still no pain, only that sharp desire to live that was stronger

221

than any sensation she had ever known, a desperation that kept her on her feet even as her vital blood welled out. She stumbled against another piece of furniture and rolled away as she sensed the knife stabbing toward her back. The desk. She had fallen against the desk. She was no longer thinking clearly, but some instinctive urge had replaced her conscious process of thought, and she opened the drawer and searched around with fingers that were almost too numb to close around Bibi Marcovaldi's small and deadly gun.

She pointed the gun with both her hands.

"Don't!" she called out in warning, prompted by the same human instinct that was urging her to achieve her own survival, but Stephanie's berserk shape didn't falter for one instant as she swooped down for the kill, and Paula's finger pressed the trigger and the gun exploded in her hands once, and once again before she dropped it.

Stephanie, caught in her final leap, seemed almost suspended in midair, the downward-pointing knife held tightly in her hand. I tried to fight back, thought Paula, waiting in resignation for that last stab that would rob her of her life, and then, as if in slow motion, she saw a huge purple flower blossom in Stephanie's pale throat, saw a similar flower burst forth out of the hate-filled face hanging above hers. Stephanie's body seemed to waver and shimmer in the air before it collapsed, but Paula didn't see it, because by that time she had fallen across the desk.

She was falling into a trance that was very similar to sleep. Wake up, something told her, but she was walking in a tranquil field where she didn't want to be disturbed, a vast green field strewn with wild poppies—or was it roses? She didn't know which, and it didn't really matter because when she leaned down to touch one of the delicate petals it melted in her hand, blood red. She was walking in a field of blood and there was blood streaming from her face and her shoulders and arms as she walked beneath a red oppressive sky that seemed to lean against her, crushing her to the ground. It took her a long time to become aware of the loud pounding at the door.

31

There were people milling around her in the room and she was lying on the couch where someone had deposited her, firmly but gently, after she'd let them in. Everyone seemed to be carrying flashlights and the pleasant-looking couple from down the hallway had brought an oil lamp, which was very sensible of them and proved to be the type of people who were most probably prepared for all sorts of contingencies.

Someone had tried to phone the hospital to call for an ambulance, and when they realized the line was dead, left to make their call from another apartment. Someone said the police should be called right away, and someone else said that it was a terrible thing when you couldn't be safe in your own home and that New York was getting impossible and it was such a pity that there was absolutely no place else to go.

"Be still," Teresa told Paula as she held up the flashlight to inspect her wounds.

Teresa, ever practical, had placed two blankets beneath her so that her blood wouldn't stain the couch, and now was checking her over with a calm, stolid competence that hinted at vast experience in such matters. Her face was set in a harsh, implacable expression that would have convinced the most obtuse of criminals that Teresa would make a very bad enemy indeed. But when she spoke to Paula, her voice was as gentle as though she were speaking to a child.

"Does it hurt?" she said. "Is it very bad?"

"Not really," said Paula.

The pain was bad and it seemed to be getting worse as it spread from the open lips of her wounds to the other parts of her body, but it was remote at the same time, so that she seemed able to view its increasing progress almost objectively. She was very weak. When Teresa's flashlight moved up

223

toward her face to explore the gash on her cheek, she closed her eyes and turned her head away.

"Hold still," Teresa ordered. "I'm going to tie something around your arm. It will hurt a little, but it will make the bleeding stop."

Paula heard a ripping sound and felt the tourniquets bite down into her flesh, heard Bibi's and Teresa's staccato exchange as they discussed her condition. It didn't matter that they were speaking in Italian and that she couldn't understand a word they were saying, because it was all out of her hands now and there was nothing else that she could do.

"The police are on their way," she heard someone say. "But the ambulance will be delayed by at least an hour. Traffic is snarled and all their ambulances are out."

"Did you tell them it was an emergency? She's bleeding badly."

"They said they'd be here as soon as they could."

Bibi Marcovaldi's cool, commanding tones rose above the hubbub in the room.

"Get Ed Bartlow," she said. "Down on the second floor. If he's not home, try Marcia Everett and tell her to bring her medical kit up here. Teresa says none of the wounds are critical, and she's had more than her share of experience in these things. But the sooner we have that facial cut stitched up, the better."

She turned back to Paula and pushed her damp hair off her forehead with cool fingers. "Don't worry, my child, don't worry," she murmured. "There won't be a scar."

Did it really matter whether or not there was a scar? They would put her in prison, of course; they would take her and put her away some place where the precious years of her life would sift away like grains of sand through a timer. By the time she came out, everything would be different, because even if Nick waited for her she would have changed, become one of those sad, hopeless-eyed women one sees roaming the street when daylight turns to dusk.

How long would her term be? One year? Two years? Five? They would know that it had been self-defense, of course, but she had used a gun for which she had no license and the police would not take kindly to that. Hadn't they just arrested that storekeeper who'd killed two men during the course of an attempted robbery?

She was very weak. Her thoughts felt muddled and she felt herself slipping in and out of consciousness, so that the figures clustered around her seemed like one-dimensional shapes sporadically glimpsed in a badly patched film. She had started slipping back into the surrounding fog when she heard the sound of unfamiliar voices.

She opened her eyes. Two uniformed policemen had walked into the room. She couldn't see them clearly, but she could see their badges gleaming in the candlelight.

"What happened here?" one of them asked.

"The woman who lives here was attacked. She's badly wounded."

"Was she molested sexually?"

"I don't believe so, but it's possible. She wasn't fully dressed. . . ."

"I'm sure she wasn't," someone else interrupted. "She's hurt and close to shock, but she would have told us if she had been. We heard the sound of shots and came running."

"It's just like two years ago," said the woman who'd been speaking earlier. There was a strong undertone of excitement in her voice. "It's just the way it was two years ago. It was an evening much like this one, a hot summer evening, you know, and we were sitting there reading when suddenly we heard the sound of shots. The woman who was living here at that time wasn't as lucky, of course. She was dead when we broke the door down. She had a knife in her hand, I remember, and—"

One of the policemen interrupted her breathless recitation.

"Let's stick with tonight," he said sharply. "Does anyone know what happened? Who did this? Was there more than one man? Did anyone here see anything?"

"No," said the man who'd gone to make the phone calls. "He, or they, must have gotten away before we got here. Mrs. Girard was quite alone when she unlocked the door."

"When she unlocked the door? You mean she locked it after her attackers fled?"

A small silence fell across the room, as if they had all suddenly realized how absurd that sounded. It seemed, indeed, like one of the more preposterous examples of locking the stable door after the horse had been stolen.

Paula listened to the sound of their voices rising and falling around her like the waves of an ocean from which she'd never make her way back to land. What were they all talking about? Was it so dark they couldn't see Stephanie's body where it lay against the desk? That dead, still body that the bullets had penetrated to burst forth into those dreadful blossoms?

"We must talk to Mrs.— What's the name again?"

"Mrs. Girard."

"We must talk to Mrs. Girard. The sooner we get an identification in these cases, the better. As soon as she's well enough we'll want her to come over to look at the mug books."

She heard them walking toward her, heard Teresa's low mutter, heard Bibi protest that she was much too weak to answer any questions. But what was the point of postponing it? She would rather get it over and done with before Nick got back. It would be hard enough on him as it was. She could at least spare him this.

They were all clustered around her, watching her like participants in a theater.

"Who was it, Mrs. Girard?" said the second policeman, the one who hadn't spoken until now. If he was taken aback by her appearance, he didn't show it.

"Stephanie," she said. "It was Stephanie."

"Stephanie? Who's Stephanie?"

"My God, can't you see her? There," she said, and pointed toward the desk.

She saw the look of total incomprehension on his face, heard a muffled gasp from someone in the room. She managed to pull herself up until she was half sitting, half leaning against the couch.

"There," she repeated, still pointing.

He shone his flashlight in the direction of the desk and they all turned to look. But there was nothing to be seen. Nothing at all. Not even the merest trace of blood staining the carpet. Stephanie's body had vanished as if she had never been.

Moving with deliberate slowness, he let the light probe the

shadows of the room until it rested squarely on the desk. The gun was still there, where she had dropped it. He started to walk toward it while the second policeman took a pencil and slid it through the trigger guard. He picked up the gun and sniffed it.

"It's been fired recently," he said, and laid it back down.

They both walked toward her.

"Did you fire the gun, Mrs. Girard?" one of them asked her.

She heard the words, but they held no meaning for her, as if she had strayed into a foreign land whose language she had never heard before. All her powers of thought were concentrated on the enormity of one single fact. Stephanie's body had vanished as if she had never been. It lay in the grave where she had been buried over two years ago, after being shot by a person or persons unknown. Unknown no longer, thought Paula. But how can one kill someone who's already dead? And how can they leap out of the past armed with a knife? It was impossible, it had to be impossible. A trickle of blood was seeping down her wounded cheek down to the corner of her lips. She wiped it with her hand. The blood was real.

"Did you fire the gun, Mrs. Girard?"

This time she understood the meaning of her words, but her lips felt numb and she was unable to answer. She stared at him, and as she tried to nod her head, she saw Nick push past him to kneel at her side. His face was as drawn and filled with pain as though her wounds were his own.

"Did you fire the gun, Mrs. Girard?"

"Yes," she whispered, and then she felt herself sliding into a vortex where everything was mercifully blank.

Epilogue

The man behind the desk is watching her with his flat, lidless eyes. His face has never changed expression, not once, as though it had been carved in that narrow, foxlike mold sometime at puberty and had become set and hardened through his lifetime. He might be forty, fifty, sixty-five. He would probably look much the same if he reached a hundred.

"An interesting story, Mrs. Girard," he says, emphasizing the word *story* in such a way that it's obvious he thinks it's just that, something she's invented, a story, a lie.

"An interesting story. But we're here to deal with facts, Mrs. Girard. And the one, the most pertinent fact is that you admit you killed Stephanie Girard, your husband's first wife. Is that correct? You did kill her."

"I did," Paula admits.

"You shot her with the gun we found in your apartment? The gun registered in the name of Countess Marcovaldi?"

"I told you that. Yes."

"Quite so. Our ballistic tests prove that she was, in fact, shot with that gun. And your blood type matches the blood on the knife Stephanie Girard used to protect herself. That, too, is an uncontrovertible fact. As for the rest of it—I suggest you changed the series of events to suit your convenience."

He pauses to contemplate the extent of her villainy and deceit. He seems in no hurry to continue. He's learned the tyranny of silence and is fully aware of the myriad anxieties that waiting can induce in those he's questioning as they sit, trapped and still, in the comfortable chair facing his desk. The technique is effective. Paula wishes she had followed Nick's advice and insisted on the presence of a lawyer. She

228

wishes Nick were here. As it is, the odds are uneven. Three against one.

"She's trying to cop an insanity plea," one of the other two men in the room suggests.

The man behind the desk ignores the comment. This is his show and he's going to run it according to his rules. Paula wishes she had caught his name. Lieutenant something or other, he had said, and his clear clipped voice had slurred the introduction. It places her at a disadvantage not to know his name.

"I suggest that this is what actually happened," he says. "You met Nick Girard sometime after you moved into town three years ago. You fell in love with him. Or perhaps you fell in love with his position and money. It doesn't matter. You decided you would marry him, but there was a problem. He was already married. Married to a woman who wouldn't give him a divorce, a woman whom he wouldn't divorce because of her health. So there was only one thing left for you to do. You waited until Nick Girard was out of town, and then you went up to their apartment. And you killed her."

She can't believe what he's saying. "My God, no!" she cries out.

He ignores her protest as he'd ignored his assistant's comment.

"She would have opened the door and let you in without hesitation," he continues. "Why not? You were a young woman close to her own age, well dressed, seemingly harmless. There were no lights in the apartment, we understand, and she might even have been relieved to have your company while waiting for the electrician. Did you tell her you'd been seeing her husband? She knew he was seeing someone else, of course. We know that from her diary. The first part of her diary, that is—the part you didn't forge. A clever forgery, incidentally, even our handwriting experts have been fooled. You're to be congratulated. But let us go back to the night of the murder."

He taps his fingers on the desk and looks at them with the critical appraisal a pianist might accord to the dexterity of his hands.

"Yes," he says, "let us go back to the night of the murder. You pulled out your gun and shot Stephanie Girard, who managed to wound you with her knife before she died. After she was dead you left the apartment and locked the door with a key you had taken from Nick Girard—or a key he'd given you. And then, after the proper amount of time had elapsed, you got him to marry you."

"Is that all?" she says evenly.

"Not quite. There was only one person who knew you'd been seeing Nick Girard, who knew that you'd met him before the death of his wife. Cindy Michaels, your roommate. As time went by, you realized she was a potential threat to you. Perhaps she suspected what had happened. Perhaps you quarreled. At any rate, you decided that she, too, must go. And so she died. It must have been easy. You called her over to the window on some pretext and then a slight push—and she was a threat no longer."

"Stop it!" Paula cries out.

Her anger gives her an authority she never had before. She hates him. She hates his calm, calculating voice; she hates his inquisitor's mind; she hates the ugly, hateful suspicions that stain and corrode everything she loves.

"I loved Cindy," she tells him. "She was my friend. The closest friend I had. I wouldn't have hurt her for the world. And I didn't meet Nick until months after Stephanie's death."

"But you do admit that you shot her."

"Yes. Last week."

"After she'd been dead for two years? Come, Mrs. Girard. You don't really expect us to believe that. I suggest that the little scene you staged last week was the result of a guilty conscience. Your guilt grew on you until you could no longer live with it. And so you forged a number of entries in the diary and then stabbed yourself over and over again, seeking your own punishment. You stabbed yourself, Mrs. Girard."

He falls into one of his practiced silences, but Paula is no longer intimidated by his brainwashing techniques. He has a narrow and inflexible mind. How many people are in prison, she wonders, because he was incapable of believing anything outside of his own experience?

"I don't care whether or not you believe me," she says wearily.

He senses she's not responding according to plan, and the

realization makes him angry, though he's too self-controlled to allow a hint of that anger to show in his manner or his face.

"It is true," he concedes, "that we have no proof that you met Mr. Girard before his first wife died. And we've talked to at least a dozen people who knew you and your husband. You must have been lucky or cautious or both. The fact remains, however, that you shot Stephanie Girard and that we have the gun you used to shoot her with. The gun you borrowed from Countess Marcovaldi. We have a clear-cut case."

But if he does, why is she here being questioned? Why is there no hint of triumph or satisfaction in his voice? Quite suddenly she knows why.

"I couldn't have borrowed Bibi's gun two years ago," she tells him, "because I didn't know her then. And I was with her the afternoon Cindy died. Ask her. She'll tell you."

"We did ask her," he admits, "and she told us just that. She categorically states that the gun didn't leave her possession until two weeks ago. She must be lying, of course. I could break her, make her tell the truth. But it appears that she has powerful friends. I've been told to lay off."

"And so . . ."

"And so you're free to go."

He sits back in his chair with the disenchantment and bitterness of the dedicated hunter who has his prey almost within reach as it slips away. Paula stands up and looks at him, undecided. If it weren't for Bibi Marcovaldi and her connections, she'd be facing a trial, but Bibi has stated that she didn't lend the gun to Paula until two weeks ago, and no district attorney in his right mind would question Bibi's word without tangible proof.

"You're free to go," the lieutenant tells her. "Scot-free."

They all watch her as she heads toward the door. Scot-free? Not really. Not ever. It was true that she had acted in self-defense, but she *had* pulled that trigger, and she would live with that fact for the rest of her life. And what if, sometime, somewhere, it were to happen all over again? What if sometime she took a step and found that once again she had turned the corner into a world outside temporal boundaries? If it had happened once, it could happen again. It might well happen again, she thinks with dread. Please, God, don't let it happen again, she prays as she walks out into the hallway where Nick is waiting for her. Please.

Casually, as though nothing had happened and never would, they link hands together and walk out into the sunshine and the traffic.

More Bestsellers from SIGNET

* Price slightly higher in Canada
† Not available in Canada

Buy them at your local
bookstore or use coupon
on next page for ordering.